SKINNED

ALSO BY ROBIN WASSERMAN

Hacking Harvard

The Seven Deadly Sins series

SKINNED

ROBIN WASSERMAN

Simon Pulse

NEW YORK   LONDON   TORONTO   SYDNEY

For Norton Wise,
under whose warm and watchful eye
this story first began, even if neither of us
realized it at the time

SIMON PULSE
An imprint of Simon & Schuster Children's Publishing Division
1230 Avenue of the Americas, New York, NY 10020
First Simon Pulse paperback edition August 2009
Copyright © 2008 by Robin Wasserman
All rights reserved, including the right of reproduction in whole or in part in any form.
SIMON PULSE and colophon are registered trademarks of Simon & Schuster, Inc.
Also available in a Simon Pulse hardcover edition.
For information about special discounts for bulk purchases, please contact Simon & Schuster
Special Sales at 1-866-506-1949 or business@simonandschuster.com.
The Simon & Schuster Speakers Bureau can bring authors to your live event. For more
information or to book an event contact the Simon & Schuster Speakers Bureau
at 1-866-248-3049 or visit our website at www.simonspeakers.com.
Designed by Mike Rosamilia
The text of this book was set in Adobe Caslon.
Manufactured in the United States of America
2 4 6 8 10 9 7 5 3 1
The Library of Congress has cataloged the hardcover edition as follows:
Wasserman, Robin.
Skinned / Robin Wasserman. — 1st Simon Pulse ed.
p. cm.
Summary: To save her from dying in a horrible accident, Lia's wealthy
parents transplant her brain into a mechanical body.
ISBN 978-1-4169-3634-3 (hc)
[1. Science fiction.] I. Title.
PZ7.W25865Sk 2008
[Fic]—dc22
2008015306
ISBN 978-1-4169-7449-9 (pbk)
ISBN 978-1-4169-9635-4 (eBook)

If you had never seen anything but mounds of lead, pieces of marble, stones, and pebbles, and you were presented with a beautiful windup watch and little automata that spoke, sang, played the flute, ate, and drank, such as those which dextrous artists now know how to make, what would you think of them, how would you judge them, before you examined the springs that made them move? Would you not be led to believe that they had a soul like your own . . . ?

—Anonymous, 1744
Translated from the French by Gaby Wood

THE FIRST DAY

"As last days go, mine sucked."

Lia Kahn is dead.

I am Lia Kahn.

Therefore—because this is a logic problem even a dim-witted child could solve—I am dead.

Except here's the thing: I'm not.

"Don't panic."

It was my father's voice.

It was—and it wasn't. It sounded wrong. Muffled and tinny, but somehow, at the same time, too clear and too precise.

There was no pain.

But I knew—before I knew anything else—I knew there should have been.

Something pried open my eyes. The world was a kaleidoscope, shapes and colors spinning without pattern, without sense until, without warning, my eyes closed again, and there was nothing. No pain, no sensation, no sense of whether I was lying down or standing up. It wasn't that I couldn't move my legs. It wasn't even that I couldn't *feel* my legs. It was that, with my eyes closed, I couldn't have said whether I had legs or not.

Or arms.

Or anything.

I think, therefore I am, I thought with a wave of giddiness. I would have giggled, but I couldn't feel my mouth.

I panicked.

Paralyzed.

There had been a car, I remembered that. And a noise, like a scream but not quite; not animal and not human.

And fire. Something on fire. The smell of something burning. I remembered that.

I didn't want to remember that.

I couldn't move. I couldn't speak. I couldn't open my own eyes.

They don't know I'm awake in here. In my mind I heard the pounding heartbeat that I could no longer feel, felt imaginary lungs constricting in terror, tasted the salt of invisible tears. *They can't.*

To my father; to my mother, who I imagined huddled outside the room, crying, unable to come inside; to the doctors, who my father would surely have had shipped in from all over the world; to Zoie, who should have been in the car, who should have been the one—

To all of them I would appear unconscious. Unaware.

I could imagine time slipping by, the doctor's voice rising over my mother's sobs. Still no response. *Still no movement, no sound, no flicker of her eyes. Still no sign of life.*

My eyes were opened again, for longer this time. The colors swam together, resolving into blurry shapes, a world underwater. At the upper fringe of my vision I caught something bulbous and fleshy, fingers prying my lids apart. And hovering over me, a dim, fuzzy figure, speaking with my father's voice.

"I don't know if you can hear me yet." His tone was steady, his words stiff. "But I assure you everything will be all right. Try to be patient."

My father pulled his hand away from my face, and my eyelids met again, shutting me behind a screen of black. He stayed. I knew, because I could hear his breathing—just not my own.

As last days go, mine sucked.

The last day I would have chosen—the last day I deserved—would have involved more chocolate. Significantly more. Dark. Milk. White. Bittersweet. Olive infused. Caramel filled. Truffle. Ganache. There would have been cheese, too, the soft, runny kind that stinks up a room as it dribbles down your throat. I would have lay in bed all day, eating the food I can no longer eat, listening to the music I no longer care to hear, *feeling*. The scratchy cotton of the sheets. The pillowcase, at first cool to the touch, warmth slowly blooming against my cheek. Stale air hissing out of the vent, sweeping my bangs across my forehead. And Walker—because if I had known, I would have made him come over, I would have said screw my parents, forget my sister, just be here, with me, today—I would have felt the downy hair on his arms and the scratchy bristles sprouting on his chin, which, despite my instructions, he was still too lazy to shave more than once a week. I would have felt his fingertips on my skin, a ticklish graze so light that, for all that it promised and refused to deliver, it almost hurt. I would have tasted peppermint on his lips and known it meant he'd elected gum over toothpaste that morning. I would have made him dig his stubby nails into my skin, not only because I didn't want him to let go, but because along with one last real pleasure, I would have wanted one last pain.

This can't be happening.
     Not to me.
     I lay there. I tried to be patient, as my father had asked. I waited to wake up.

Yeah, I know: total cliché. *This must be a dream.* You tell yourself that, and maybe you even pinch yourself, even though you know it's cheesy, that the mere act proves it's *not* a dream. In a dream you never question reality. In a dream people vanish, buildings appear, scenes shift, you fly. You fall. It all makes perfect sense. You only reject weirdness when you're awake.

So I waited to wake up.

Big shock: I didn't.

Stage one, denial. Check.

I learned the five stages of grief when my grandfather died. Not that I passed through them. Not that I grieved, not really, not for some guy I'd only met twice, who my father seemed to loathe and my mother, the dead man's only daughter, claimed to barely remember. She cried anyway, and my father put up with it—for a few days, at least. We all did. He brought her flowers. I didn't roll my eyes, not even when she knocked over her glass at dinner for the third time in a row, with that same annoying aren't-I-clumsy giggle. And Zo pumped the network and dug up the five stages of grief.

Denial. Anger. Bargaining. Depression. Acceptance.

Since I was dead—or worse than dead, buried alive in a body that might as well be a coffin except it denied me the pleasure of suffocation—I figured I should be allowed to grieve.

No, not grieve. That wasn't the right word.

Rage.

I hated everyone, everything. The car for crashing. My body for burning, for breaking. Zo for sending me in her place. For living, breathing, partying somewhere beyond the darkness, in a body that worked. I hated Walker for forgetting me, like I knew he would, for the girls he would date and the girls he would screw and the girl he would curl up with in his bed, his arms closing around her, his lips whispering promises about how she was the only one. I hated the doctors who marched in and out, prying my eyes open, blinding me with their pen-size lights, squinting, staring, waiting for some kind of reaction I couldn't give them, all while I was screaming in my head *I'm awake I'm alive Hear me Help me* and then the lids would shut me into the black again.

My father stayed by my side, the only one to speak to me, an unending monotonic litany: *Be patient, Lia. Try to wake up, Lia. Try to move, Lia. It will be okay, Lia. Work at it, Lia. You'll be okay*. I wanted to believe him, because I had always believed him. I wanted to believe that he would fix this like he'd fixed everything else. I wanted to believe him, but I couldn't, so I hated him most of all.

Next came bargaining. There was no one to plead with, but I pleaded anyway. First, to wake up—to open my eyes, sit up, swing my legs out of bed, walk away, and forget the whole thing. But that obviously wasn't happening. So I compromised: Just let me open my eyes, let me be able to speak, let me be able to move and feel. Let this not be permanent. Let me get better.

And then, later, still no change, still no hope: Let me open my eyes. Let me speak. Let me escape.

That was before the pain.

Like the doctors, it didn't bother to sneak up on me. It exploded, a starburst of light in the black. I lived in the pain. It was my whole being, it was timeless, it was forever—and then it was gone.

That was the beginning.

Intense pleasure, a spreading warmth building to an almost intolerable fire. Biting cold. Searing heat. Misery. A bubbling happiness that wanted only to laugh. Fear—no, terror. Sensations sweeping over me from out of nowhere, disappearing just as fast as they came, with no reason, no pattern, no warning. And—never staying away too long before returning for a visit—the pain.

I never slept. I could feel the time pass, could tell from the things the doctors muttered to one another that days were slipping by, but I never lost consciousness. I lost control when the waves came, I lost reason and lost myself in the bottomless sensations, but I never got swept away, much as I wanted to. And in the moments in between, when the dark waters were still and I was myself again, I went back to bargaining.

Let me sleep.

Let me die.

"I'll do it—but you owe me," I had told Zo. Before.

She'd ignored me, twisting her hair into a loose bun and clipping it just above her neck. Her hair was blond, like mine, except mine was shiny and full and bounced around my shoulders when I laughed, and hers was tangled and limp and, no matter what she did, looked like it hadn't been washed. I always told her she was just as pretty as me, but we both knew the truth.

"Try again. *You* owe *me*," she finally said, pulling on a faded brown sweatshirt that made her look like a potato. I didn't mention it. Our parents had selected for girls, selected for blond hair and blue eyes, paid the extra credit to ensure decently low body-mass indexes and decently high IQs, but there was no easily screened-out gene for sloth—no amount of cash that would have guaranteed a Zo who didn't piss all over every genetic advantage she'd received. "Or do you want me to tell Dad where you *really* were this weekend? I'm sure he'd love to know that when you said 'cramming for exams' you really meant 'cramming your face into Walker's'—"

"I said I'd do it, *Zoie*." She hated the name. I snatched the key card out of her hand. "So, do I get to know where you'll be while I'm changing diapers and wiping snot on your behalf?"

"No."

Neither of us had to work. Given the size of our parents' credit account, neither of us would *ever* have to work. Except for the fact that our father was a big believer in productivity.

Arbeit macht frei, he used to tell us when we were kids. It's German, like my great-great-great-grandparents. *Work will set you free.*

I was twelve the day I repeated that to one of my teachers. She slapped me. And then she told me where the slogan came from. The Nazis preached it to their prisoners. Right before working them to death.

"Ancient history," my father said when I gave him the bad

news. "Statute of limitations on grudges expires after a hundred years." He had the teacher fired.

I wasn't required to get a job because I was an athlete. *A winner*, my father said every time I brought home another track trophy. *A worker*. He never came to the meets, but the first-place trophies lined a bookshelf in his office. The second-place ones stayed in my room. Everything else went in the trash.

Zo didn't play a sport. She didn't, as far as I could tell, do anything but hang around parking lots with her loser friends and get zoned on dozers, some new kind that puffed out these foul clouds of smoke when you sucked, so you could feel like a retro from the bad old days before the nicotine ban. "Explain to me why it's cool to look like Grandma," I asked her once.

"I don't do things because they're cool," Zo snapped back. "That's you."

Just for the record, I didn't do things because they were cool.

Things were cool because I did them.

So every day, I ran ten miles at the track while Zo worked her dad-ordained shift at the day-care center, wiping drippy noses and changing shitty diapers, except on the days she suckered me into doing it for her.

"Fine," I told Zo. "But I swear to you, this is the last time."

It was.

The coordinates were already programmed into the car. Our

father would check that night to make sure it had gone where it was supposed to, but he'd have no way of knowing which sister had gone along for the ride. TotLand, I keyed in, then flung myself into the backseat. Walker couldn't wait to be eighteen so he could drive manually, but I didn't get the point. Better to curl up and let the seat mold itself to my body, listen to a mag, link in with Walker to remind him about that night's party, cruise the network to make sure none of my friends had stuck up pics of something I shouldn't have missed (an impossibility since, by general agreement, if I'd missed it, it was worth missing).

But that day I unplugged. No chats, no links, no vids, no music, no nothing. Silence. I closed my eyes.

There was this feeling that I only got when I was running, a couple miles in, after the tidal wave of exhaustion swept past and the world narrowed to the slap of my feet on the pavement and the air whistling through my lungs and the buzzing in my ears—not a feeling, actually, but an absence of feeling, an absence of self. Like I didn't exist anymore. At least not as Lia Kahn; that I was nothing but a blur of arms and legs, grunts, pounding blood, tearing muscle, wind, all body, no mind. Lying there that day with my eyes closed should have been nothing like that, but somehow it was. Somehow *I* was: Empty. Free of worry, free of thought. Lost in the black behind my lids.

Like a part of me knew it was going to happen.

Like when everything flipped upside down and the scream of metal on metal exploded the silence and the world churned around me, ground over sky over ground over sky, and then, with a thunderous crack and a crunching of glass and steel, a twisted roof crushing me into a gutted floor, *ground*, I wasn't surprised.

I tell people I don't remember what happened after that. I tell them I hit my head and it all went dark. They believe me. They *want* to believe me.

They don't want to hear how I lay trapped, skin gnashed by metal teeth; legs numb, *absent*, like the universe ended at my waist; arms torn from sockets, twisted, white hot with pain. They don't want to hear how one eye was blinded behind a film of blood but the other saw clearly: black smoke, a slice of blue through a shattered window, freckled skin spattered with red, the white gleam of bone. An orange flicker.

They don't want to hear what it felt like when I started to burn.

I wish I could say my life had flashed before my eyes while I was trapped in that bed. It might have made things more interesting. I tried to force it. I thought if I could remember everything that had ever happened to me, moment by moment, then maybe it would be almost like being alive again. I could at least kill some hours, maybe even days, reliving Lia Kahn's greatest hits. But it was useless. I would start with the earliest moment I could remember—say, screaming at the pinprick pain of my first morning med-check, convinced by toddler rationality that the tiny silver point would suck out all my blood, while my mother smoothed back my hair and begged me to stop crying, promising me a cookie, a lollipop, a puppy, anything to shut me up before my father arrived. I would remember the tears wet on my face, my father's disgust clear on his—and then I would think about how the daily med-checks and DNA-personalized medicine were supposed to make us all healthy and safe and live nearly forever, and how *nearly* wasn't close enough when your car's nav system crapped out and rammed you into a truck or a tree and flipped you over and chewed you up. I would remember my mother's hand across my forehead, and wonder why I never heard her voice in my room.

Days passed.

I made lists. People I knew. People I hated. Words starting with the letter *Q*. I tried to make a list of all the ViMs I'd ever owned, from the pink My First Virtual Machine with its over-size buttons and baby-proofed screen to my current favorite, a neon blue nanoViM that you could adhere to your shirt, your wrist, even, if you felt like flashing vids as you sashayed down the hall, your ass. Not that I'd tried that . . . more than once. But things got hazy midway through the list— There'd been too many ViMs to remember them all, since if you had enough credit, which I did, you could wire almost anything to function as a virtual computer that would link into the network.

I sang songs to myself. I practiced the lines I'd been forced to memorize for English class, because, according to my clueless teacher, "the theater may be dead, but Shakespeare is immortal."

"To die,—to sleep;—
No more; and by a sleep to say we end
The heart-ache, and the thousand natural shocks
That flesh is heir to, 'tis a consummation
Devoutly to be wish't."

Whatever that meant. Walker had done a passage from *Romeo and Juliet* with Bliss Tanzen playing Juliet, and I wondered if Bliss would be the one—or if you counted her D-cups, the three—to replace me.

I listened to the doctors, wishing they would betray some detail of their personal lives or at least say *something* other than "delta waves down," "alpha frequency boosted," "rhythm confirmed as normal variant," or any of the other phrases that floated back and forth between them. I tried to move my arms and legs; I tried to *feel* them. I could tell, when they opened my eyes, that I was lying on my back. It meant there must be a bed beneath me, some kind of sheets. So I tried to imagine my fingers resting on scratchy cotton. But the more time passed, the harder it was to even imagine I had fingers. For all I knew, I didn't.

I stopped trying.

I stopped thinking. I drifted through the days in a gray mist, awake but not awake, unmoving but uncaring.

So when it finally happened, it wasn't because of me. I wasn't trying. I didn't even know what I was doing. It just . . . *happened*. Eyes closed, eyes closed, eyes closed—

Eyes open.

There was a shout, maybe a doctor, maybe my father, I couldn't tell, because I was staring at a gray ceiling, but I'd done it, I'd opened my eyes, somehow, and they stayed open.

Something else moved. An arm.

My arm. And, for a moment, I forgot everything in the pure blast of relief: *my* arm. Intact. I couldn't feel it, wasn't trying to move it, but I *saw* it. Saw it jerk upward, across my field of vision, then back down to the bed again, hard, with a thump. Then the other arm. Up. Down. *Thump.* And my legs—They must have been my legs. I couldn't feel them, couldn't see them, but I could hear them against the mattress, a drumbeat of *thump, thump, thump.* My neck arched backward and the ceiling spun away, and I was flying and then a thud, loud, like a body crashing against a floor. *Crack, crack, crack* as my head slapped the tile, slapped it again, again, all noise and no pain, and then feet pounded toward me and all I wanted was the motionlessness of the dark again, but now I couldn't close my eyes, and two hands, pudgy and white and uncalloused, grabbed my face and held it still, and then for the first time since I'd woken up, everything stopped.

To sleep: perchance to dream.

EYES WIDE OPEN

"Some kind of total freak?"

There were no dreams.

I opened my eyes.

I opened my eyes. It was a triumph. If I could have smiled, I would have.

But I couldn't.

I closed my eyes, just because I could. Then opened them again. Close. Open. Close. Open. It wasn't much.

But it was something.

"Lia, can you hear me?" It was a new voice, one I didn't recognize. The face appeared. Small mouth, big nose, squinty brown eyes with a deep crease between them. His parents must not have cared enough to spend the credit on good looks, I decided. Either that or his gene pool was so crowded with ugly, this was the best he could get. "Lia, I want you to listen to what I'm saying and try to respond if you understand me."

Respond how? I wondered. For a doctor, he didn't seem to have much grasp of the situation.

"Our instruments are indicating that you've gained control of some key facial muscles, Lia. You should be able to blink. Can you blink now, if you understand me? Just once, nice and slow?"

I closed my eyes. Counted to three. Opened them again.

All I'd done was blink, but the doctor beamed like I'd won a championship race. Which should have seemed completely lame. Except I felt like I had.

And that felt pretty good, right up until the point when I started wondering why I could blink, but still couldn't speak or move. I wondered how long that would last.

I wondered if I could figure out the blink code for "Kill me."

"You were in an accident," he said with a little hesitation in his voice, like he was telling me something I didn't know. Like he was worried I would freak out. How much freaking out did he expect from a living corpse?

"I'm sure you have questions. I think we've got a way to help you with that. But first we need to establish a cognitive baseline. Is that okay? Blink once for yes, twice for no."

No. *Not* okay. Okay would have been him telling me exactly what was wrong with me and how he was planning to fix it. And when. But that answer wasn't an option. I was stuck in a binary world: Yes or no. I blinked once.

It was something.

"Are you in pain right now?"

Two blinks. No.

"Have you been conscious at any point before now?"

One blink.

"Have you been in pain?"

One blink. I kept my eyes closed for a long time, hoping he'd get the point. His expression didn't change.

"Are you able to move any part of your body?"

Two blinks.

I suddenly wondered if I was crying. I probably should have been crying.

"I'm going to apply some pressure now, and I want you to blink when you feel something, okay? This might hurt a little."

I stared at the ceiling. I waited.

No blink.

No blink.

This can't be happening to me.

The doctor frowned. "Interesting."

Interesting? Forget asking him to kill me. I wanted *him* to die.

His face disappeared from view, replaced by a large white paper, filled with row after row of block letters in alphabetical order.

"We're going to try this the old-fashioned way, Lia. I'm going to point at the letters one by one, and you blink when I get to the one you want. Make sense?"

One blink.

"Do you know your name?" This from the idiot who'd been calling me Lia from the moment he walked in the room.

His stubby finger skimmed along the letters. I blinked when it got to *L*. He started again at the beginning, and I blinked at *I*. Again, *A*.

"Good, very good. And your last name?"

Letter by letter we finally got there. It was just so freaking slow.

There was more pointless trivia: my parents' names, the year, my birthday, the president's name, and all of it painfully spelled out, letter by letter, blink by blink. I'd waited so long to make contact, but pretty soon I just wanted him to go away. It was too hard. I didn't let myself think about what would happen if this was it, all I would ever have. A white sheet, black letters, his stubby finger. Blink, blink.

"Now that you've reached this level, we should be able to move on to the next stage. It's just going to take a little longer to implement. Is there anything you want to ask in the meantime?"

One blink.

The letters reappeared and his finger crawled along.

W. Blink.

H. Blink.

A. Blink.

T. Blink.

WRONG WITH ME.

Blink.

I could tell from his expression it was the wrong question.

"As I said, Lia, you've been in an accident. Your body sustained quite a bit of damage. But I assure you that we've been able to repair it. The lack of motive ability and sensation is quite normal under the circumstances, as your neural network adjusts to its new . . . circumstances. The pain and other sensations you may have experienced while you've been with us are a positive sign, an indication that your brain is exploring its new pathways, relearning how to process sensory information. It's going to take some time and some hard work, Lia, and there may be some . . . complications to work through, but we *will* get you walking and talking again."

He said more after that, but I wasn't listening. I didn't hear anything after "walking and talking again." They were going to fix me. Whatever complications there were, however long it took, I would get my life back.

"Is there anything else you want to ask?"

Two blinks. After the second one, I kept my eyes closed until he went away.

The bed was mechanical. It whirred quietly, and slowly the ceiling tipped away until I was sitting up. For the first time, I could see the room. It wasn't much, but it was at least a different view, a better one than the ceiling, whose flat, unblemished gray plaster was even less interesting than the black behind my eyes. It didn't look like any hospital room I'd ever seen. There was no machinery, no medical equipment, no sink, and no bathroom. I couldn't smell that telltale hospital mélange of disinfectant and puke. But then, I realized, I couldn't smell much of anything. There was a dresser that looked like my dresser, although I could tell it wasn't. A desk that looked like my desk. Speakers and a vidscreen, lit up with randomly flickering images of friends and family. No mirror.

Someone had gone to a fair amount of effort to make the place feel like home.

Someone was expecting me to stay for a while.

A horde crowded around me. Doctors, I assumed, although none of them wore white coats. At the foot of the bed, clutching each other, my mother and father. Although, to be accurate, only my mother was doing much clutching, along with plenty of weeping and trembling. My father stood ramrod straight, arms at his sides, eyes aimed at my forehead; an old trick he'd taught me. Most people would assume he was looking me in the eye. Most people didn't pay much attention.

My mother pressed her head to his shoulder, squeezed him tight around the waist, and used her other hand to pat my foot, gingerly, like she was afraid of hurting me. Apparently no one had told her that I couldn't feel her touch, or anything else. More likely she was in selective memory mode, tossing out any piece of information that didn't suit her.

"We've hooked up a neural output line from the language center of your brain, Lia," the squinty-eyed doctor said. Now that I had a better view, I could see that he was also short. For his sake—and mine—I hoped his parents had spent all their credit on IQ points. Because clearly, they'd spared little for anything else. "If you speak the words clearly in your mind, the computer will speak for you." Then it was like the whole room paused, waiting.

Hello.

Silence.

"It might take a little practice to get the words out," he said. "I wish I could tell you exactly how to do it, but it's like moving an arm or raising an eyebrow. You just have to find a way to turn thought into action."

If I could speak, I might have pointed out that I *couldn't* move my arm or raise my eyebrow. And then thanked him for rubbing it in.

Hello.

Hello.

Can anyone hear me?

Is this piece of shit equipment ever going to work or are you all just going to keep standing there and staring at me like I'm

`"some kind of total freak?"`

My mother let loose a whimpery squeal and buried her face in my father's chest. He didn't push her away.

"Very good, Lia." The doctor nodded. "Excellent."

21

The voice was female, an electronic alto, with that artificially soothing tone you hear in broken elevators, assuring you that "assistance is on the way." It trickled out of a speaker somewhere behind my head.

Hello, I thought, testing it. The word popped out instantly.

"Hello," my father said, like I'd been talking to him. Which maybe I had. His eyes stayed on my forehead.

"You're going to be okay, honey," my mother whispered. She squeezed the foot-shaped lump at the end of the bed. "I promise. We'll fix this."

"Can someone tell me what's happening?" the speaker said.

I said.

"How bad was I hurt? How long have I been here? What happens next? Why can't I—" I stopped. "I'll be able to move again, right? Walk and everything? You said I could. When?"

I didn't ask why Zo wasn't there.

"It's been several weeks since the accident," my father said. "Almost four." His voice was nearly as steady as the computer's.

One month trapped in a bed, in the dark. I'd missed three tests, a track meet, who knew how many parties, nights with Walker, hours and hours of my favorite vidlifes. A month of my life.

"Of course, you've only been conscious for the last week

or so," the doctor said. "And as I explained before, your brain needed this recuperation period to adjust to its new circumstances. Involuntary motion indicated the first stage had been achieved. We actually expected you to reach this point a bit sooner, but, of course, these things vary, and nothing can be rushed, not in cases like this. Given the severity of your injuries, you've really been quite lucky, you know."

Right. Lucky. I felt like I'd won the lottery.

Or been struck by lightning.

"Voluntary control over the eyelids, that's stage two. You'll gradually achieve control over the rest of your body. In fact, you may already be started down that path. We've immobilized the rest of you for the moment, after your . . . episode. For your own safety. But when you're ready, your rehabilitation therapists will work with you, isolating individual areas. Sensation should return as well, if all goes smoothly."

He didn't say what would happen if things didn't go smoothly, or how big the *if* was. I didn't ask.

"How bad?"

The doctor frowned. "I'm sorry?"

"You said severe. How severe?" I hated that this man, a stranger, knew my body better than I did.

"When we brought you in after the accident . . . Incidentally, although you didn't ask, I assume you'll want to know what happened? A chip malfunction on a shipping truck, I believe. It slipped through the sat-nav system, and coincidentally, your car's backup-detection system malfunctioned, reading the road as clear. It was a colossally unlikely confluence of events." He said this clinically, casually, as if noting a statistical aberrance he hoped to study in his spare time. "When we brought you in after the accident, your injuries were severe. Burns covering—"

"Please, stop!" That was my mother. Of course. "She doesn't need to hear this. Not now. She's not strong enough." Meaning "*I'm* not strong enough."

"She asked," my father said. "She should know."

The doctor hesitated, as if waiting for them to reach a unanimous decision. He'd spent the last month with my parents and still thought the Kahn family was a democracy?

My father nodded. "Continue."

The doctor, smarter than he looked, obeyed. "Third-degree burns covering seventy percent of your body. That was the most immediate threat. Skin grafts are simple, of course, but in many cases infection proves fatal before we have the chance to do anything. Crush injuries to the legs and pelvis. Spinal cord abrasion. Collapsed lung. Damage to the aortic valve necessitated immediate bypass and may have required an eventual transplant. Internal bleeding. And, as far as secondary injuries, we were forced to amputate—"

"Please," the computer voice cut in. It was so calm.

My father raised his eyes, waiting. Believing I was strong enough.

Keep going, I forced myself to think. The words were in the air before I could take them back.

"Amputate the left leg, just below the thigh. Several hours were spent trying to salvage the left arm, but it wasn't possible."

There were two feet beneath the blanket. Two legs. I could see them. Maybe I couldn't feel them or move them, but I *knew* they were there.

Prosthetics, I realized, retreating to a part of my brain the computer couldn't hear. *They can do a lot with prosthetics.* They made fake limbs that moved, that even, in some way, felt. That looked almost normal. Almost.

The doctor had said I would walk. He just didn't say how. He didn't say on what.

This can't be happening to me.

How could it be happening—how could it *keep* happening— and still seem so unreal?

But then how could it be real? How could I, Lia Kahn, be a one-armed, one-legged, burned, scarred, punctured *lump*?

`"I need to see."`

"See what, Lia?" my mother whispered. What did she think?

`"See. I need to see what I look like. I need a mirror."` In my head I was shouting. The voice was not.

"That's not advisable at this point," the doctor said. "I only told you about your injuries so you would realize how lucky you are to be making a full recovery. So you would understand that certain decisions were made for your own good. Some sacrifices were needed to save your life."

Some "sacrifices," like an arm and a leg?

`"I need to see."`

The doctor frowned. "We really should wait until the final, cosmetic procedures have been completed. It's ill-advised at this stage to—"

"Let her see," said a man who hadn't spoken yet. He stood closest to my parents, his gray suit flashing, very subtly, in time with his heartbeat. The style had been in and then very definitely out a couple years ago, but it worked for him. Although with his face—chiseled cheekbones, long-lashed brown eyes, dimpled chin, nearly-but-not-quite feminine lips—anything would have worked. "She'll have to find out eventually. Why not now?"

I was sorry I couldn't smile at him.

Then I reminded myself that the smile would have been bound by blistered lips, pulled back to reveal cracked teeth, or dark empty gaps, along bloody gums. As for the blond hair I would have liked to flick over my shoulder, just quickly enough that the scent of lavender wafted out to greet him? It was probably gone. I'd smelled it burning. My eyes were both still there, that was obvious. At least one of my ears. But my mouth didn't work, my nose didn't work— Who knew whether they were intact or just sunken caverns of flesh? The pretty doctor didn't see pretty Lia Kahn, I reminded myself. He saw the lump.

He found a mirror.

It was small, about the size of a hand stretched flat, with the fingers pressed together. Framed with black plastic that maybe was supposed to be shiny but wasn't, not anymore. He paused, tipped his head toward my father. "Do you want to . . . ?"

My father shook his head.

So it was the pretty doctor, the kind of guy Walker would be someday if he remembered to shave and stopped flunking gen-tech, who approached, mirror in hand. He kept it angled safely away. "You ready?"

As if it mattered. I closed my eyes.

The computer said yes.

They'll fix it, I promised myself. *No matter how much it costs, no matter how long it takes.* If my mother could keep her skin looking like she was twenty-two, if Bliss Tanzen could show up with a new nose to match every new season's shopping spoils, a few scars were nothing. Maybe I'd even keep a couple. Becca Mai had a delicate white fault line running down her cheekbone that she claimed came from a close encounter with jagged glass on some illicit venture into the city. Everyone knew Becca Mai was too prep to sneak out of the house and too petrified to sneak into the city, and Bliss had spotted one of those home tattoo kits on Becca's shop-log, just before it mysteriously got edited out. But guys still loved her sexy little shiver as they traced their fingers down the scar. Becca gave good shiver.

I could do better.

"Lia, if you want to see, you're going to have to open your eyes." The doctor's voice didn't quite match up to his pretty face. I liked voices lower, a little husky. Of course, Walker was nearly a tenor. Carved cheekbones, a tight six-pack, and a girl can get used to just about anything.

Anything, I told myself. And then, deep breath.

Eyes wide open.

I didn't know computers could scream.

NOTHING

"I was a ghost in the machine."

*T*he lips, I thought. *Focus on the lips.*

Because they were normal. Pale pink, washed out. Curved into a half pout. A glimpse of white teeth barely visible, straight and whole. It was a mouth, a normal mouth.

Just not my mouth.

The nose, too. It was a nose. Narrow, nearly sharp but not unpleasantly so, no bumps or hooks, delicate nostrils, a gentle slope up the face toward the—

No, not the eyes.

Don't look at the eyes.

No scars. No burns. It wasn't the Halloween fright mask I'd imagined. It was . . . perfect. The skin was unmarked, stretched taut and smooth across the face. A stranger's face.

And the eyes. The eyes that weren't my eyes. Pale, watery blue, unspeckled iris; black, motionless pupil; and at the center, a pinprick circle of amber. Unblinking. Dead.

But when I closed one eye, the eye in the mirror closed, too.

Brown lashes brushed against a too-smooth cheek. I opened the eye, and the mirror eye opened. It was dead. It was mine.

Which meant that what lay above it was mine, too. Blondish brows with a high, perfectly plucked arch, like they'd been penciled in. A wrinkle-free forehead. And above that?

The machine.

Scalp flayed back. A mess of circuitry, like when Zo was five and cracked open my new ViM because I wouldn't let her use it. Wires spooling out of my head. Wires feeding into my head. Silvery filament crisscrossing a waxy, flesh-colored base.

It wasn't until the computer fell silent that I realized I was still screaming. But now the screams were just inside my head.

What else was inside my head?

"Try to calm down," said the first doctor, the ugly one. The mirror was gone, but I couldn't stop seeing the face. "I'll turn the speaker back on, but you have to stay calm, for your own good. Let us explain. Can you do that?"

As if I had any choice.

One blink.

I forced the screams back inside myself.

"This is why I didn't want you to see at this stage," the doctor said irritably. "Cranial exposure is only necessary until we confirm neurological stability. Once the skullcap is attached and the hair—"

"What did you do to me?"

Dr. Handsome shot the uglier guy a look that made me realize who was really in charge. And he was the one who finally answered. "We saved your life."

"What did you do?"

No one spoke.

My mother lifted her head from my father's shoulder. She looked me in the eye. Not the forehead, the eye. She wasn't crying anymore. "You know about BioMax," she said. "You remember."

I knew just about as much as I cared. Which was very little. BioMax, some biotech subsidiary of my father's corporation, hyped on the vids the year before with some freaky new tech that—

"No."

I knew.

"We had to," my mother pleaded. "We didn't have any other choice."

"No."

"Honey, you heard the doctors, you were going to *die*. This was the only way."

"No."

"Lia." My father balled up his fists, shoved them into his pockets. *"Yes."*

"We held off for as long as we could," the pretty doctor said. I felt like he was leering at me, like I was some mechanical puzzle he was desperate to take apart, then try to put back together. Except he'd already done so. "Dr. Dreyson"—he jerked his head toward his troll-like partner—"had you on the table for seventeen hours before we made the decision."

"Before you gave up."

"We would never give up on you," my mother said.

My father frowned. "That's why you're still here."

But I wasn't.

I was a ghost in the machine.

A mech-head.

A Frankenstein.

A skinner.

"The download process was a complete success," Dr. Handsome said. "Your brain came through the accident completely intact, and we were able to make a full transfer. The body is, I'm afraid, not the customized unit you might have selected under less critical circumstances, but we did our best to choose a model that would emulate your baseline specs, height, weight, coloring."

He was talking like I was a new car.

Everyone knew about the download freaks, or at least, we knew they were out there, computer brains stuffed into home-made bodies, walking around looking like real, live people. Sort of. The first few were all over the vids for a while, until they got boring and people moved on to something else just as irrelevant, like betting on how long it would be before the president went AWOL from rehab again.

"You turned me into a skinner."

Dr. Troll wrinkled his big nose. "We prefer not to use that word."

But that's what they were called, because that's what they did.

Skinners. Computers—*machines*—that hijacked human identities, clothing themselves in human skin. Except the flesh was just as artificial as what lay beneath. A skinner was nothing more than a computer that wore a human mask, hiding wiring and circuitry underneath a costume of synthetic flesh. A mechanical brain, duped into thinking it was real.

Or, in this case: a mechanical brain duped into thinking it was Lia Kahn.

"You *are* Lia," the repulsively handsome one said. "All your memories, all your experiences, everything you are was simply transferred to a more durable casing. Just like copying a file. Nothing more mysterious than that."

"Put me back."

"Lia . . ." My mother pressed her eyes closed with her left hand, massaging the lids.

"Once we train the neural network to accommodate itself to its new physical surroundings, you should be able to pick things up right where you left off." Dr. Handsome was unstoppable. "You'll see we've done remarkable things with sensation, motion . . . Of course there are things to get used to, but many of our clients have found life postdownload nearly indistinguishable from their experiences before the procedure. And quality of life will certainly be far superior to anything you would have experienced with your degree of injuries—"

"Put me back the way I was. I don't care about the injuries. I don't care. Put me back."

One leg, one arm, no skin, I didn't care. As long as I was human. As long as I was *me*.

"It's not possible."

"Anything's possible if you want it enough."

Another of my father's favorite slogans.

The doctor's voice was cold. "There's nothing to put back. There's no body to go back to. The body of Lia Kahn is dead. Be grateful you didn't die with it."

And when I wouldn't believe him, he offered to prove it. Wires were detached. Machines wheeled away. Two men— not doctors; the doctors never touched me—grabbed my sides. They hoisted me into a sitting position. My head lolled forward on my neck, and I saw my hands for the first time. They hung limp in my lap, fingers half curled, nails round and smooth; useless. Somebody else's hands, resting on somebody else's legs. The flesh was unnaturally smooth, just like the skin on the face. There were no creases and whorls, no subtle shifts of color or thready blue veins beneath the surface. I wondered if there were fingerprints.

One of the men grabbed me under the armpits and hoisted

me off the bed. He looked like the type of guy who would have bad breath, and for a moment his mouth was close enough to mine that I could have smelled it, if I could have smelled anything. I was wearing a sleeveless paper-thin blue gown, loose around the armholes. His hands pressed bare skin, or whatever it was. He could probably see down the front of it if he'd wanted to. I didn't care. It wasn't my body under there. It was a thing. A thing I couldn't feel and couldn't move, a thing I was trapped inside. It wasn't me.

He didn't peek. Instead he dumped me into a high-backed wheelchair and fastened a belt around my waist. Then another around my forehead, pressing my head against the seat and fixing my eyes straight ahead. Through it all, he never looked at my face.

The pretty doctor, who got less attractive every time he spoke, told me to call him Ben. He wasn't actually a doctor, he said. Which made sense. Doctors took care of people, right? Sick people, injured people. *People*. I wasn't one of those, not anymore. Thanks to *Ben*. My mechanic.

Call-me-Ben wheeled me down a long corridor. I couldn't feel the body, couldn't feel the seat. It felt like I was floating through the hall, just a set of eyes, just a mind, just a ghost. My parents stayed behind. My mother said she couldn't see it again. *It*, she said. My father didn't say anything, but he stayed with her.

"We've kept it in cold storage for you," Ben said from behind me. "Most clients request a viewing."

It.

We wheeled into a narrow room, its white tiled walls lined by silver plates. Ben pressed his palm to one, and it slid out of the wall, revealing a long, metal panel bearing a sheet-covered lump. A body-shaped lump.

"You sure?" Ben asked, guiding the wheelchair into position. "This can be difficult."

I couldn't stand to hear the computer speak for me, not here. Not now.

I blinked once.

He began with the feet. Foot.

The flesh was red and ruined, gouged. Mottled with deep, black scabs. There were thick streaks of pearl white, as if the skin had calcified. Or maybe the flesh had been flayed and I was looking at bone. The knee was bent at the wrong angle; the other leg was gone, ending just below the thigh, swirls of dried blood and charred flesh winding around one another, like the rings of a severed tree stump.

The sheet drew farther back.

I wish I could say I didn't recognize it, that it was some monstrous mound of skin and bones, broken and unidentifiable.

It was. But it was also me.

I recognized the hips jutting out below my waist, always a little bonier than I would have liked. The dark freckles along my collarbone, still visible on a patch of skin the fire had spared. My crooked ring finger, on the arm that remained intact, a family quirk my parents had chosen not to screen out, the genetic calling card of the Kahns.

My face.

The burns were worse there. Pockets of pus bubbled beneath the skin. One side had caved in, like my face had been modeled from clay, then crushed by an iron fist. The left eye sagged into a deep hollow. My lips were gone.

There was a gray surgical cap stretched over my head.

"The brain?"

I felt as dead inside as the voice sounded.

Call-me-Ben sighed. "You don't want to know the technical details."

"Try me."

He did.

He told me how the brain—my brain—was removed.

Frozen.

Sliced into razor-thin sections.

Scanned.

Functionally mapped onto a three-dimensional model, axons and dendrites replaced by the vector space of a quantum computer, woven through with artificial nerves, conduits that would carry impulses back and forth from an artificial body, simulating all the pains and pleasures of life. In theory.

He told me how the frozen leftovers were discarded. Because that's what you do with medical waste.

Now I understood: *Skinner* was the wrong word after all. I wasn't the thief. I hadn't stolen an identity; *I* hadn't stolen anything. They were the ones who stole from me. They flayed back my skin, reached inside and dug up whatever secret, essential quality made me who I was.

Then they ripped it out.

They ripped it out—ripped *me* out—and left me exposed, a naked brain, a mind without a body. Because this *thing* they'd stuck me in, it wasn't a body—a sculpted face, dead eyes, and synthetic flesh couldn't make it anything but a hollow shell. Maybe I hadn't lost the essential thing that made me Lia Kahn, but I'd lost everything else, everything that made me human.

I wasn't a skinner.

I was the one who'd been skinned.

When we were kids, Zo and I used to fight. Not argue. *Fight.* Hair-pulling, skin-pinching, wrist-burning, arm-twisting, squealing, spitting, punching, shrieking *fight*. And once—it wasn't our worst fight or our last one—after she kneed me in the stomach, I punched her in the face. Her nose spurted blood all over both of us. She threw up. I passed out. It's the one thing we'd always had in common: Fear of blood. Fear of doctors. Fear of hospitals. Fear of anything that stinks of sick.

But here I was, inches from a dead body. *My* dead body. Inches from flesh that looked like raw meat, a crumpled face, an empty skull cavity. Listening to a stranger describe, in detail, all the ways he'd torn me to pieces. And I didn't feel sick. I didn't feel anything.

I don't just mean on the outside, like the chair under my ass or my ass or the straps digging into my waist and forehead or call-me-Ben's hand on my shoulder, the same hand he'd used to pull back the body's sheet. It was that, but it wasn't *just* that. I couldn't feel anything on the inside, either. I wasn't nauseated; I wasn't dizzy. My stomach wasn't clenched; there was no hollowness at the base of my throat, warning me I was about to explode into tears. I wasn't breathing quickly. I wasn't breathing at all. I wasn't trembling, although even if I had been, I wouldn't have known.

My brain—or whatever was up there—told me I was horrified. And furious. And terrified. And disgusted. I *knew* I was all of those things. But I couldn't feel it. They were just words. Adjectives pertaining to emotional affect that modified nouns pertaining to organic life-forms.

I no longer qualified.

MOUTH CLOSED

"You don't need a tongue to sound like a sheep."

I don't want to talk about it." Translation: "I don't want to think about it."

It didn't matter how much crap they spewed about adjustment pains and emotional connection and statistically probable results of repression, there was no way in hell some random middle-aged loser was milking me for intimate details of my daily life in hell, aka rehab. No matter how many times she asked.

"It's okay if you don't feel ready." Sascha leaned back in her chair, her head almost touching the window. "You may never *feel* ready. Sometimes we need to just take a risk, have faith in our own strength."

She had a corner office on the thirteenth floor, which meant a 180-degree view of the woods surrounding the BioMax building. I'd only seen one other floor: the ninth. That was where they stored the bodies until it was time to destroy them. Mine wasn't there anymore. I knew, because I'd asked

Sascha. They burn the bodies. They don't bury them— You only bury people who are dead. The bodies are just medical waste. I told Sascha, no, I didn't want the ashes. She said it was a positive sign.

"I don't need faith," I said. "I know my own strength. I do fifty push-ups every morning. Sit-ups, too. It's in your report." It was easier to talk than to sit there for an hour in silence, although I'd tried that, too. I'd probably try it again. One thing about my new life, or whatever I was supposed to call it: I had plenty of time.

She frowned, then templed her fingers and rested her chin on her fingertips. "I think you know I'm not talking about that kind of strength."

I shrugged.

"It's natural to be concerned about how your family will react to the new you," she said.

"They've seen the new me."

"It's been a month, Lia. You've made remarkable progress since then. Don't you want to show off a little?"

"Show off what? That I learned how to take a few steps without falling on my face? That I figured out how to make actual *words* with this thing in my throat?" I gave her one of the smiles I'd been working on, knowing—from the hours I'd spent practicing in the mirror—that it looked more like a grimace. "Yay, me. I'm finally better off than a two-year-old."

Sascha hated sarcasm. Probably because she didn't get it.

After all, if she'd had an acceptable IQ, she would have been on some other floor, building new people like me, rather than stuck on lucky thirteen, upping my self-esteem. Her parents had obviously opted to dump more EQ than IQ in their chromosomal shopping cart. Not that she was much good when it came to emotions. At least, not emotions like mine. "You can't undervalue yourself like that," she said. "I know how hard you've worked to get to where you are."

She knew nothing.

The benefit of artificial skin constructed from self-cleaning polymer: No one has to sponge the dirt off my naked body while I'm lying in bed like a frozen lump of metal and plastic.

No, not like that.

I am that.

The benefit of an artificial body with no lungs, no stomach, no bladder, and a wi-fi energy converter where the heart should be: No machine has to breathe for me while my brain tries to remember how to pump in the air. No one has to spoon food into my frozen mouth. No one has to thread in a bunch of tubes to suck the waste out of my body; no one has to wipe my ass.

No one has to do much of anything. Except for me.

"I can't."

"You can." Asa is terminally perky. Even when my spasming leg kicks him in the groin.

An accident, I swear.

"You're just not trying hard enough."

I hate him.

He puts the ball between the hands lying uselessly in my lap. I can finally hold up my own head, and I do, so I don't have to see them—mechanical digits covered with layers of fake skin, threaded with fake nerves.

I can feel them now, sometimes.

"Feel" them, at least. Know when someone is squeezing them. Know, even with my eyes closed, when Asa dips them in boiling water, when he presses them to ice. I know, the way I know my name, as a fact. This is cold. This is hot. *I know, but that doesn't mean I feel. It's not the same.*

Nothing is.

"Try to throw the ball to me," Asa chirps. He's all blond hair and brawny muscles, like a twelve-year-old's av, the virtual face you choose for yourself before you realize that pretty and perfect is perfectly boring. "You can do it. I know you can."

Move, *I tell my arms.* Just do it.

It would be easier if they hurt. If there was pain to push through, to guide me back to where I started. If I knew that the more it hurt, the closer I was getting. But there hasn't been any pain since that first day with call-me-Ben. The brain was exploring its new environment, they say. All that is behind me now.

I don't tell them that I miss it.

Move! *I think, and I know I am angry, at myself and at Asa. I am angry all the time now. But the voice in my head sounds nearly as calm as the computer I still use to talk, and will use until I can make more than grunts and groans with the artificial larynx. That may take the most time of all, they warn me. But most people master it eventually. Most.*

The arms jerk away from the body, and the ball dribbles out of the hands, then drops, rolling under the bed.

"Good!" Asa exclaims, looking like he wants to applaud.

And then the session is over, and Asa hoists me out of the chair, like I'm a giant baby, his thick arm cradling my knees, another digging into my armpit. I forget to hold up my head, and it flops backward against his shoulder. This is life now.

From the bed, to the chair, to the bed again.

They turn me off at night—I'm supposed to call it "sleep," but why bother?—and turn me on in the morning. Soon, they tell me, I will learn how to do it myself. Just like I will learn to monitor my status, to will the system diagnostics to scroll across my eyes. I will learn how to upload my memories for safekeeping. I will learn to speak. But that's all later. Now, life is lived for me. Asa monitors me, Asa dresses me, Asa turns me off and on, and off again. It's how I know one day has passed. And another. I play catch with Asa and I stare at the ceiling and I wait and I try not to wonder whether I would rather be dead or whether I already am.

I hated to picture myself like that. Helpless. I tried to forget, but Sascha kept forcing me to remember. Like I was supposed to be proud or something. Like I was supposed to be happy. Even when I tuned her out, which was often, I couldn't escape the memories. The frustration. The *humiliation*. As long as I was stuck in this place, part of me was still stuck back at the beginning, a patient—a *victim*.

I guess remembering those early days in rehab was better than remembering what came before: the crash, the fire, the long hours frozen in the dark.

Better, but not by much.

"Are you worried that if you see them, you might find that you've changed?" Sascha asked. "That your family might think you're different now?"

"I *am* different now." I wondered how much they paid her to force me to state the obvious.

I could tell from her smile that I'd said the right thing, which meant I'd said the wrong thing, because it meant she thought we were about to make *progress*. Sascha was big on progress.

I, on the other hand, was big on reality. A concept with which Sascha didn't seem to be acquainted.

"I'm not talking about physical differences, Lia. I'm talking about *you*." She leaned forward, tapping me on the chest where my heart would have been. "About what's going on in here, and"—she tapped the thick blond weave that covered the titanium plates—"up here. You've been through a serious trauma. That would be enough to change anyone."

"I guess."

"But I'm thinking it might be more than that."

Big surprise.

"Many clients in your position worry about what the download process *means* for them. Whether they lost something of themselves in the procedure or if they'll ever be the person they were before. They worry a lot about who they are now. Do these concerns sound familiar?"

Sooner or later, wherever our conversations began—if you wanted to call them conversations rather than verbal dodgeball games where Sascha pelted and I ducked and weaved until, inevitably, she managed to slam me square in the face—we ended up in the same place.

"I know who I am," I said. Again. "Lia Kahn."

"Yes." She smiled. I could see the beads of white frothy saliva forming in the corners of her mouth. I didn't have any saliva. The tongue was self-lubricating. "*Yes*. You *are* Lia Kahn. But surely some of the things you've been seeing and hearing on the vids about . . . people like you . . . They don't trouble you at all?"

I was still practicing my emotional responses: when to raise the eyebrows and how far. What to do with the nose when the mouth was stretched into a smile. When to bare teeth, when to press lips together, how often to pretend to blink. It was all a lot of trouble, so most of the time, I just left my face as it was, blank and impassive. Sometimes that came in handy.

"I've never seen any vids about 'people like me,'" I lied. They didn't go for concrete nouns here, nouns like "skinner" or "mech-head." Or "machine." "I don't know what you're talking about."

Sascha looked torn. Should she cram my head full of new-found terror that the world would reject me, or let me wander into the big, scary out-there, like a naive lamb prancing to the slaughter?

Lesser of two evils, apparently: "Lia, you should be aware that you're going to encounter some people who don't yet understand the download process. You're going to have to help them make peace with what's happened to you. But I assure you that with time, those who know and love you will accept it."

But that was a lie. I knew what I was; I knew what the people who loved me could handle. They couldn't handle this.

You'd think I would at least get some superpowers as part of the deal. Legs that could run a hundred miles an hour. Arms that could lift a fridge. Supersight, superhearing, super something. But no. I get skin that washes itself and is impervious to paper cuts. Legs that have barely learned how to walk. A tongue that lies in my mouth like a dying fish flopping and thrusting and scraping against heavily fortified porcelain teeth, mangling every burst of sound I manage to choke out of the voice box.

No lungs, just an intake hose feeding into the larynx, so

*I can shoot air through when necessary, make the artificial
cartilage vibrate at the right frequency, funnel the sound waves
up the throat, into the mouth. That was the first step.* "A big
one!" *Asa says, clapping as I grunt and groan. I can do all the
animal noises now. Monkey hoots. Cow moos. Dolphin squeals.
And, as of this morning, sheep.* "Baa! Baa!"

"Your first word," *Asa cheers.* "Almost."

I still hate him.

*You don't need a tongue to sound like a sheep. But if you
want to sound human, that's another story.*

*I wonder if Asa goes home at night and imitates me for his
girlfriend; someone like him must have a girlfriend. Does he tell
her how he's spent all day with his hands on my body, prodding
and pulling and stretching? Does he tell her how he dressed me
until I learned to dress myself or about the day he opened the
door without knocking and discovered me checking to make
sure the body was—fully—anatomically correct? Is she jealous,
I wonder, of the girl with the perfectly symmetrical synthetic
breasts, the living doll that Asa molds into whomever he wants
her to be? Or does she think of him as a handyman, spending his
days tuning up a machine that just happens to look like a person
and grunt like a chimpanzee?*

"Good night, Lia," *he says as he goes wherever it is he goes
when he leaves the thirteenth floor and rejoins his life.*

"Unnnh," *I* "say" *in response. I am not allowed to use the
voice synthesizer, not while I'm speech training, not—Asa says,*

and his boss, call-me-Ben, agrees—unless I want to be one of those clients who has to use it indefinitely, speaking with closed lips and a computerized monotone for the rest of my so-called life. "Omph. Aaaaap."

"You too, Lia. See ya."

"Baaa, baaa."

Bye, bye.

I have fingers again, fingers that can barely feel but can mostly type. Which means it's time to link in to the network. I will not speak, not with the computer voice and not with the animal groans, but I will type, I will face them, I will.

I tell myself that every night.

Tonight I do it.

There is a six-week dead hole in my zone. I have never been off the network for that long, not since I was three and got my first account, my first ViM, and my first avatar, a purple bear with an elephant snout and a lion's tail. I dressed him in a top hat and called him Bear Bear, which, at the time, I thought was clever.

It occurs to me now that if Bear Bear existed in the real world, he'd probably sound a lot like me.

Every day, since I was three, life on the network shadowed life off the network, and sometimes it was the opposite. Sometimes it was the network that seemed more real. Every text, every pic, every vid got posted in my zone, every fight and every make up was reflected in the zone. My first boyfriend

*gave me my first kiss in the zone, his av a red-haired ninja,
mine a black-winged pixie with purple hair and knife-spiked
heels. The zone was how I knew who I was, how I knew that
I was, except now there's a gap, starting with the accident and
stretching on as if, for all those weeks, Lia Kahn ceased to exist.*

*There are flowers waiting for me, flowers from everyone—
not just Cass and Terra and even Bliss, but from all the
randoms who wish they counted enough to get a niche in my
zone, the ones whose names I don't know and won't remember,
all of them leaving messages and pink-frosted cupcakes and
pixilated teddies that remind me of Bear Bear. My zone is a
shrine.*

*Walker's messages are behind the priv-wall, where no one
can see them but me. There are only two, both voice-talk, and I
play them four times, eyes closed, listening to his warbling tenor,
wishing I had more of him than my least-favorite part.*

"Please don't die," *the first one says. He sent it the
night of the accident, when I was still alive, when, according
to call-me-Ben, I was hemorrhaging and suffocating and
seizing, all at the same time.*

*The next one came weeks later, when I was lying in the bed,
eyes closed, listening to footsteps and waiting to die.*

"The turtle is hungry," *it says.* "The turtle is starving."

*Code. Left over from our first few months, when Zo
wouldn't go away. She was always snooping in my room and
hacking my zone, all big ears and a bigger mouth, so Walker and*

I talked in riddles and nonsense until eventually she left and we stopped talking altogether.

"The turtle is hungry."

Meant "I love you."

I want to see him. I want to touch him. I want to at least voice him back. But what would I say?

Ahhh ovvvvv ooooooo.

We speak in different codes now.

I stay in stealth mode. They are all linked in and to one another, Cass to Terra to Walker to Zo, all in priv-mode, and I wonder if they are talking about me, but I can't find out without showing myself, and I can't do that, not today.

There are 7,346 new pub-pics and texts, and there will be more behind their priv-walls, and I know I should catch up, but I can't do that, either.

There's no point.

I try my favorite vidlife, technically a realistic one because there are no vampires or superheroes, but there's nothing particularly realistic about the number of people Aileen manages to screw—and screw over—each night. Since the last time I watched, Aileen has already forgotten about Case, and is screwing some new guy and, secretly, the new guy's sister, who's engaged to Aileen's former best friend's cousin, and I can't keep up with all the new names and bodies, and I don't understand how so much can happen in six weeks.

I used to feel sorry for the woman who lives as Aileen, and

*for Case and for all of them. I used to think it was pathetic,
arranging your life around someone else's script, letting some
random text the words you were forced to speak. So they got
rich on it, so they got famous, so I watched all night sometimes
because I didn't want to miss anything, so what? It wasn't their
life they were living, it wasn't anyone's.*

But now I don't know.

*If someone gave me a script, if someone whispered in my
ear and told me how to act, what to say, what to do, if I could
be their puppet and they could pull the strings, that would be
easier. That would, maybe, be okay. But I have no script and
no off-screen directions, and I sit frozen, watching the screen,
waiting to know what to do.*

Whatever else has changed, at least my av is still the same.

*There was a time when I changed it every day—new
eyes, new hair, bunny whiskers one day, cat ears the next—but
that was before. That was kid stuff. Now my av is me, the
virtual Lia, the better Lia, the Lia that would exist in a world
without limits. Purple hair so dark it looks black, until you see
it shimmer in the light. Violet eyes; wide, long lashes pooling
across half the head, like in the animevids. Pouty blue lips. The
morning of the accident, I gave her a pink boa and spray-on
mini, like the one I'd just seen a pop-up for but knew I probably
wouldn't have enough credit to buy, because that's another of
my father's favorite lines: "We're not rich. I'm rich." The credit
is mine to ask for; his, depending on his mood, to deny. Now*

I wonder whether I am the virtual Lia, while my av is real.
There is nothing left of what I used to be.
    But she is exactly the same.

I didn't get in touch with Walker, not that night or any of the nights that followed. Even after I got my voice back—*a* voice, at least, although it would never sound like *mine*—I couldn't do it. I didn't know what I would say. I didn't want to know what he would.

"I still think it might be good for you to meet with one of our other clients," Sascha said. "She's your age."

That meant nothing. All the skinners were my age. The procedure wouldn't work on adults—something about how their neural pathways weren't malleable, couldn't adjust to an artificial environment—and it hadn't been approved for anyone younger than sixteen. If I'd had the accident a year earlier, I'd be dead right now. All dead, instead of . . . whatever this was.

"So what?"

"So I think you two have a lot in common," Sascha said. "It might help to share your experiences, get her perspective on things. Plus she's eager to meet you."

"All we have in common is *this*." I looked down at the body. My body. "And you keep telling me that *this* doesn't mean anything."

"You don't want to meet her."

Sascha's brilliant intuitive powers never ceased to amaze. "No."

"Maybe we should talk about why."

"Maybe not."

Sascha crossed her arms. I wondered if I'd finally managed to break through the professional placidness, if Sascha was about to prove she had an actual personality, one that could get irritated when a bitchy "client" pressed hard enough.

Not a chance.

"Let's try something new," she said with an I-have-a-secret-plan smile. "Why don't you tell me what *you* want to talk about."

"Anything?"

"Anything. As long as it's something."

I *didn't* want to talk. That was the point. Now that I had my voice back, I had nothing to say.

"Running," I said. It was the first thing that popped into my head. Maybe because I thought about it all the time. How it would feel to run in the new body. Whether I would be slower or faster, whether I would find a new rhythm. What it would mean to run without getting out of breath; whether I could run forever. They told me the body would simulate exhaustion before it had reached its limits, a gauge to prevent total system failure, but no one knew exactly what those limits would be.

"You're a runner?" Sascha asked, faux clueless. It was her default mode; at least when she wasn't acting the all-knowing wisdom dispenser. She knew I was a runner, because she had a file that told her everything I was. Everything she thought mattered, anyway.

Was a runner.

I nodded.

"Do you miss it?"

I shrugged.

"You run on an indoor track or . . ."

"Outside," I said immediately.

Sascha leaned forward, as she always did when she thought she was about to crack my code. "That's unusual," she said. "Someone your age, spending so much time outside."

"It's required." But that wasn't true, not really. Yes, we were all forced to spend a few hours a week outdoors, but for most people, that was the end of it. Five whiny hours shivering in the grayish cold, then back inside. It was one way I'd always been different. The only way.

"What do you like about it?" Sascha asked. "Running."

"I don't know." I paused. She waited. "It felt good. You know. Especially a long run. You get an adrenaline high. Or whatever."

"Have you tried it? Since the procedure?"

I shook my head. There was supposedly a track somewhere in the building, but I hadn't bothered to find it.

"Why not?"

I looked down. The hands were sitting in my lap. I

stretched one of them out along my thigh. It felt good to be able to move again. After almost a month of rehab, I didn't even need to think about it most of the time; the hands clenched themselves into fists when I wanted them to, the fingers closed around balls and hairbrushes and tapped at keyboards just like real fingers. They registered the fabric on my legs—standard issue, hideously ugly BioMax thermo-sweats. Not that I needed thermo-regulation now, not when I had it built in, but that's what they had, so that's what I wore, because it was easier than buying all new clothes, and my old clothes no longer fit.

"What would be the point?" I said finally.

"The point would be to feel good."

In my head I laughed. The mouth spit out something harsh and scratchy. Laughing was tricky.

"You disagree?" Sascha asked.

"I guess it depends on your definition of 'feel.'"

"You're processing emotional and physical sensation differently now; that's natural," Sascha said, oozing understanding. Not that she could ever actually understand. "But your programming is designed to emulate the neurotransmitters that stimulate emotional response. Your emotions *are* the same, even if they don't feel that way."

"I feel the same, even if I feel different? Is that supposed to make sense?"

My father would kill me if he ever knew I was talking to

an authority figure like this, even a figure with such question-able authority as Sascha.

"When I get angry, my stomach clenches," Sascha said. "I feel sick. When I'm upset, my hands tremble. Sometimes I cry. What happens when you're upset?"

I said nothing.

Which was pretty accurate.

"Without a somatic response, it's natural that the emotions will seem weaker to you," she said. "More distant. But the stronger the emotion, the more 'real' it may feel, partly because you'll be too consumed with the powerful emotion—or sensation—to analyze all the things you're *not* feeling. And as your mind relaxes into old patterns and finds new ones, as it *will*—"

"I'll be my old self again. Right."

"Lia, haven't you been able to find *any* advantages to your new body?"

That had been my "homework" from the other day: design a pop-up for the download process, complete with catchy slo-gan, and a list of fabulous advantages available to every down-load recipient. Sascha thought it would tap into my creativity skills.

It turned out I didn't have any.

"I can link in whenever I want," I muttered. But that wasn't new. For my sixteenth birthday, I'd finally gotten a net-lens, which meant that once I got used to jamming a finger in my eye, I could link with a blink, just like the pop-ups said. Could superimpose my zone and my av over blah reality, type on a holographic keyboard that only I could see. But the pop-ups didn't mention how it made you nauseated and made your head burn. Now I had a built-in net-lens, and migraines weren't an issue.

Hooray for me.

"Good," Sascha said, nodding. "Anything else?"

"I guess no more getting sick." Not that anyone got sick much these days, anyway. Not if you could afford the med-tech, and if you couldn't, well, you had bigger problems than the flu. "And if I get hurt, it won't, you know. Hurt. Much." There would be pain, they'd told me that. Of all the sensations, the neurochemistry of pain was the easiest to mimic, the best understood—and the most necessary. *Pain alerts the brain that something is wrong,* call-me-Ben had said. *An alarm you can't ignore.* So there would be pain, they had promised, and I knew it was possible, because I'd felt it when I was still trapped in the bed, when it seemed to crawl out from inside my head. But out of the bed, back in the world, pain was just as distant as everything else.

"You're beautiful," Sascha said. "That's something."

I was beautiful before.

"And then there's the big thing," Sascha prompted. "A lot of people would envy you for that. If the government allowed it, a lot of people might even download voluntarily."

"Doubtful."

"To never age . . ." Sascha looked dreamy, and her hand flickered to the corner of her left eye, where the skin was pulled taut. "Some might call that lucky. Miraculous, even." She couldn't be more than seventy, I decided, since after that even the best doctors left behind a few stretch marks—and no younger than thirty, because you can always tell when someone's had their first lift-tuck, and she definitely had. First, second, and probably eighth, I guessed. No one so lame could be any younger than that.

Call-me-Ben was the one who'd taught me how to back up my memories each night, preserving that day's neural adjustments and accretions in digital storage—"just in case." He'd had the same dreamy look as Sascha. They all did, when the subject came up.

"The body ages," I countered. "They say it'll only last fifty years."

"The *body*," Sascha said. "But now you know bodies can be replaced."

The body would last fifty years. But brain scans could be backed up and stored securely, and bodies could be replaced. And replaced again.

I had died more than a month ago; I could live forever. Exactly like this.

Lucky me.

VISITING DAY

"Kahns don't lie."

They were late. Only by ten minutes, but that was weird enough. Kahn family policy: never be late. It meant an immediate disadvantage, a forfeit of the moral high ground. Still, at 10:10 a.m., I was alone in the "social lounge," which, if the building-block architecture, hard-backed benches, and spartan white walls were any indication, was clearly intended to preclude any socializing whatsoever. I didn't want them to come. Any of them. I hadn't invited them, hadn't agreed to see them . . . hadn't been given a choice.

10:13 a.m. : Waiting, my back to the door, staring at the wall-length window without seeing anything but my reflection, ghosted into the glass.

10:17 a.m. : Three more ghosts assembled behind me, milky and translucent on the spotted pane. Three, not four.

Not that I'd expected Walker to show up, to pester my parents until he got an invitation to come along, to perch nervously in the backseat, his long legs curled up nearly to his chest, his back turned to Zo as he stared out the window, watching the miles roll by, suffering the Kahn family as a means to an end—to me. If he'd wanted to visit, he wouldn't have any need to tag along with them.

If he'd wanted to visit, he already would have.

"Lia," my father said from the doorway.

"Honey," my mother said, in the tight, shivery voice she used when she was trying not to cry.

Zo said nothing.

I turned around.

They stood stiff and packed together, like a family portrait. One where everyone in the family hated one another but hated the photographer more. The huddle broke as they moved from the doorway, my mother and father a glued unit veering toward me, Zo's vector angling off to a bench far enough from mine that, if she kept her head in the right position, would keep me out of her sight line altogether.

My mother held out her arms as if to hug me, then dropped them as she got within reach. They rose again a moment later; I stepped backward just in time. My father shook my hand. We sat.

My mother tried to smile. "You look good, Lee Lee."

"This brain hates that nickname just as much as the last one."

She flinched. "Sorry. Lia. You look . . . so much better. Than before."

"That's me. Clean, shiny, and in perfect working order." I raised my arms over my head, clasped them together like a champ. "You'd think I was fresh off the assembly line." I told myself I was just trying to help them relax. My mother wiped her hand across her nose, quick, like no one would notice the violation of snot-dripping protocol.

"Lia—" My father hesitated. I waited for him to snap. The unspoken rule was, we could—and should—mock our mother for her every flaky, flighty word until he deemed (and you could never tell when the decision would come down) that we had gone too far. "The doctors tell us you're nearly ready to come home. We're looking forward to it."

That was it. His tone was civil. The one he used for strangers.

You did this, I thought, willing him to look at me. Not over me, not through me. And he did, but only in stolen glances that flashed to my face, then, before I could catch him, darted back to the floor, the ceiling, the window. *Whatever I am now, you chose it for me.*

"Zo, don't you have something for your sister?" my mother asked.

Zo shifted her weight, then rolled her eyes. "Whatever." She dug through her bag and pulled out a long, thin rod, tossing it in my direction. "Catch." I knocked it away before it could hit me in the face, but the body's fingers weren't fast enough to curl around it. The stick clattered to the floor.

"Zo!" my mother snapped.

"What? I *said* 'catch.'"

I picked up the stick, turning it over and over in my hands. It was a track baton.

"We won the meet last week," Zo muttered. "Coach wanted me to give it to you. I don't know why."

"We?"

My father smiled for the first time. At Zo. "Your sister's finally discovered a work ethic." He beamed. "She joined the track team. Already third in her division, and moving up every week, right?"

Zo ducked her head; the better to skip the fakely modest smile.

"You hate running," I reminded her.

She shrugged. "Things change."

"Tell us about your life here," my mother said. "How do you spend your days? You're not working too hard, are you?"

I shook my head.

"And you're getting enough to—" She cut herself off, and her face turned white before she could finish her default question: *You're getting enough to eat?*

"Ample power supply around here," I said, tapping my chest and noting the way her smile tightened around the corners. "My energy converter and I are just soaking it in."

I wish I could say I wasn't trying to be mean.

She didn't ask any more questions. Instead she talked.

Aunt Clair was helping design a new virtual-museum zone with a focus on early twenty-first-century digital photography. Great-uncle Jordan had come through his latest all-body lift-tuck without a scratch, literally, since the procedure had worn away that nasty scar he'd gotten skateboarding in the exquisitely lame Anti-Grav Games, which, it turned out, were actually full-grav, anti-knee-pad. Our twin cousins, Mox and Dix, were outsourcing themselves to Chindia—Mox had snagged an internship at some Beijing engineering firm and Dix would do biotech research for a gen-corp in Bombay. Last I'd seen them, Dix had "accidentally" broken Zo's wrist in a full-contact iceball fight, and Mox had tried to make out with me. *Second* cousins, he argued, so it was okay. Bon voyage, boys.

Then there was our parents' best friend, Kyung Lee, who was having trouble with his corp-town, the workers who lived there rioting for better med-tech, something about a biotoxin that had slipped through the sensors. Kyung was afraid if things didn't calm down soon, he might have to ship them all back to a city and hire a whole new crop, although the threat of that, according to my mother, should be enough to settle anyone.

As the half-hour mark passed, I tuned out. After another twenty minutes my father stood up, giving his pants a surreptitious brush, like he wanted to shed himself of the rehab dirt lest it soil the seat of his car. A new car, according to my mother. After all, I'd ruined the last one.

"This has been a lot of excitement for you today, Lia," he said politely. "You must be tired."

I didn't get tired anymore. I only shut down at night because it was on the schedule, and I only followed the schedule because I didn't have anything better to do.

I nodded. They filed toward the doorway, and I followed, half-wishing I could leave with them and half-wishing they would go and never come back. This time my mother forced herself to hug me, and I let her, although I kept my arms at my sides. It was strange to have her so close without breathing in the familiar scent of rosemary. But then, it was probably strange for her, with our chests pressed together and her arms around my shoulders, that I wasn't breathing at all. I thought about faking it for a few seconds, just to make things easier for her. But I didn't.

"We're so proud of you," she whispered, as if I had done anything other than what I was told—turn off, turn on, survive. I felt something brush my cheek as she pulled away, but I couldn't tell what. Maybe a stray hair. Maybe a tear. Maybe I was just wanting to feel something so badly that I'd imagined it.

My father squeezed my shoulder. The new body was taller than mine, I realized. He and I were the same height. He didn't say he was proud of me.

Another family policy: Kahns don't lie.

Zo was last, and I stopped her before she could slip out the door. Her hair was looking better than usual. Not so greasy.

And cut shorter, so that it bounced around her shoulders, the way mine used to when it was real.

"Zo, people at school . . ." I kept my voice low, so our parents wouldn't hear. "Are people asking about me? Or, you know. Talking about me?"

She gave me a funny half smile. "Aren't they always?"

"No, I mean . . ." I didn't know what I meant. "Have you seen, I mean, have you talked to any of my friends? You know, Terra or Cass or . . ."

"Walker knows I'm here, if that's what you're asking." Zo leaned against the doorway and kept scratching at the bridge of her nose, which, unless she'd developed a rash, seemed mostly like a convenient way to stare at her hand rather than at me.

"Did he—" But if he'd sent along a message, she would have said so already. And if he hadn't, I didn't want to ask. Besides, he would never reach for me that way, through Zo. "Is he doing okay?"

"I know it's hard to believe, but the world is managing to revolve on its axis even without your daily presence," Zo snapped.

"Rotate."

"What?"

"The world *rotates* on its axis," I corrected her, because it was all I could think of to say.

"Right. It *revolves* around you. How could I forget?"

I grabbed her arm. She yanked it away, like I'd burned her. Her face twisted, just for a second, and then the apathetic funk was back so quickly, I almost thought I'd imagined the change. "Why are you acting like such a bitch?" I asked.

"Who says I'm acting?"

I hadn't necessarily expected her to burst into tears and sweep me into her arms when she first saw me, just like I hadn't expected her to tell me how much she loved me and missed me or to gush about how scary it had been when she thought I was going to die. I guess, knowing Zo, I hadn't even expected her to be particularly nice. But we were sisters.

And she was the reason I had been in the car.

I'd expected . . . something.

"Come on, Zo. This isn't you."

She gave me a weird look. "How would you know?"

"I'm your sister," I pointed out, aiming for nasty but landing uncomfortably close to needy.

She shrugged. "So I'm told."

After she left, I sat down again on one of the uncomfortable benches and stared out the window, imagining them piling into the car, one big happy Lia-free family, driving away, driving home. Then I went back to my room, climbed into bed, and shut myself down.

I'd set my handy internal alarm to wake me nine hours later. But the brain was programmed to wake in the event of a loud noise. A survival strategy. The footsteps weren't loud, but in the midnight quiet of floor thirteen they were loud enough.

"Sleeping Beauty arises." A girl stood in the doorway, silhouetted by the hallway fluorescents, a cutout shadow with billowing black hair, slender arms, and just the right amount of curves. "I guess I don't get to wake you with a kiss." She stroked her fingers across the wall and the room came to light. I sat up in bed.

It wasn't a girl. It was a skinner.

I knew it must be the one Sascha had told me about, the one I was supposed to be so eager to bond with. I was mostly eager for her to get out and leave me to the dark. She didn't.

"You're her," I said. "Quinn. The other one."

She crossed the room and, uninvited, sat down on the edge of the bed. "And here I thought I was the one and *you* were the other one." She held out her hand.

I didn't shake.

Instead I stared—I couldn't help it. I'd never seen another mech-head, unless you counted the vids. Or the mirror. So this was what my parents saw when they looked at me. Something not quite machine and not quite human, something that was definitely a *thing*, even if it could lift its hand and tip its head and smile. It was better at smiling than I was, I noticed. If you focused on the mouth and looked away from the dead eyes, it almost looked real.

"You're Lia," Quinn said, dropping her hand after realizing

I wasn't going to take it. "And yes, it is nice to meet me. Thanks for saying so."

I didn't speak, figuring I could wait her out until she got bored and left. But the silence stretched out; I got bored first.

"Quinn what?" I asked.

"Lia who?" she said. "Or Lia when? Lia why? If you want to play a game, you have to fill me in on the rules. But fair warning: I play to win."

So did I. At least, when I was in the mood. Which I wasn't.

"What's your last name?" I asked.

"Doesn't matter."

"I didn't ask if it mattered, I just asked what it was."

"It *was* something," she said. "But now it's irrelevant."

I didn't get her, and suspected that was the idea, like she thought I'd be so intrigued by her ridiculous air of mystery that I wouldn't kick her out. I wondered if Sascha had put her up to it. If so, they were both seriously overestimating my level of curiosity. "What do you want?" I knew I sounded like a sulky kid. I didn't care.

"Heard your parents finally showed. Figured I would see how it went."

They'd driven two hours for a fifty-minute visit, then gotten the hell out.

"Great," I said sourly. "Heartfelt family reunion. You know how it is."

She raised her eyebrows. It was a nice trick, one I resolved to master myself. "Not really. My family's not an issue."

"Too perfect for 'readjustment pains'?" I used Sascha's favorite phrase for anything and everything that could possibly go wrong.

"Too dead."

"Oh."

I refused to feel guilty. Not when she'd so blatantly manipulated the conversation to reach this point. "Sorry." I lay back down again and turned over on my side, my back to her; universal code for "go away."

"Don't you want the details?" Quinn asked, sounding disappointed. "The whole poor little orphan saga, from tragic start to triumphant finish?"

If I'd still had lungs, I would have sighed. Or faked a yawn. "Look, if Sascha sent you in here to give me the whole 'you should be grateful for what you have' guilt trip, I'm not interested. Yeah, it sucks that your parents are dead, but that doesn't make mine any easier to deal with."

Silence.

I couldn't believe I'd just said that.

"I'm sorry." I twisted in bed, risking a glance at her face.

She raised just one eyebrow this time, which was even more impressive. "Yeah. You are." She turned away, revealing a broad swath of artificial flesh exposed by her backless shirt. I didn't know how she could stand it. Even at night I tried to cover up as much as possible. The more of me I could hide under the clothes, the less there was for others—for me—to see. Beneath the clothes I could imagine myself normal. Quinn, on the other hand, left very little to the imagination. She stalked out of the room, but paused in the doorway, tapping her fingers against the wall console. Lights off, lights on. Lights off. "You coming?"

I was.

"What are you doing?" I whispered as we waited at the elevators. "It's not like they'll work for us."

"Why not?"

"Because . . ." Wasn't it obvious? "We're not supposed to leave here. The elevators are probably programmed."

"Have you actually tried?" Quinn sounded bored, like she already knew the answer.

"No, but—"

"I have." The elevator door opened, and as I hesitated, she asked again. "You coming?"

It had never occurred to me that I would be allowed to leave floor thirteen. Of course, it had never occurred to me to want to.

"The other floors are biorestricted," Quinn said, nodding toward the skimmer that would collect and analyze our DNA samples. If, that is, we'd had any to give. "But the ground floor's all ours."

"Where are we going?" It felt strange to be talking to

someone new after all this time. I had no reason to trust her. But I did.

It's because she's like me, I thought. *She knows.*

But I pushed the thought away. It was like I'd told Sascha. Quinn and I had nothing in common but circuitry and some layers of flesh-colored polymer.

"Field trip." She smiled, and, again, it killed me how much better her expressions were than mine, how much more natural. In the dark it had been easy to mistake her for someone real. No one would make that mistake about me. "Don't get too excited."

The grassy stretch bounding the woods was larger than it had looked from the lounge window. The grass was beaded with dew, cold drops that seeped through the thin BioMax pajamas, but that didn't bother me. Just like the brutal wind raking across us didn't matter.

"Can you imagine actually seeing the stars?" Quinn asked. She'd selected a dark swath of grass sandwiched between the floodlit puddles of light, then stripped off her clothes and let herself fall backward, naked against the brush. I kept my clothes on my body and my feet on the ground.

At least at first.

"Get down here," Quinn had commanded.

"Look, Quinn, it's okay if you . . . but I don't—"

She laughed. "You think I brought you out here for *that*?" She stretched her arms out to her sides and down again, stick wings flapping through the grass. "Shirts or skins, I don't care. Just lie down."

I wasn't about to take orders from *her*.

But I lay down.

"You used to be able to see them. Stars and planets and a moon," she said now, pointing at the reddish sky.

The back of my neck was already smeared with dew. But she'd been right. It felt good to lie there in the grass, in the dark. The sky felt closer.

"You can still see the moon." The telltale white haze was hanging low, making the clouds shimmer.

"Not like that," Quinn said. "A bright white circle cut out of pure black. And stars like diamonds, everywhere."

"I know. I've seen."

"Not on the vids," she said. "That doesn't count."

"It's the same thing."

"If you say so."

We were quiet for a minute. I stared up, trying to imagine it, a clear sky, a million stars. Most of the vids I'd seen came from just before the war turned the atmosphere into a planet-size atomic dust ball. The dust was mostly gone—along with the people who'd built the nukes and the nut jobs who'd launched them and the thousands who'd gone up in smoke in the first attacks and the millions who'd been dead by the end of that year or the next. Along with the place called Mecca and the place called Jerusalem and all the other forgotten places that exist now only as meaningless syllables in the Pledge of Forgiveness. The dust was gone, but the stars had never come back. Pollution, cloud cover, ambient light, whatever chemicals they'd used to cleanse the air and patch up the ozone, the law of unintended consequences come to murky life. Someone would fix it some-day, I figured. But until then? No stars. My parents talked about them sometimes, late at night, usually when they were dropped on downers, which made them goopy about the past. But I didn't get the big deal. Who cared if the sky glowed reddish purple all night long? It was pretty, and wasn't that the point?

"Why are we here, Quinn?"

She clawed her fingers into the ground and dug up two clumps of grass, letting the dirt sift through her fingers. "So we don't miss any of it."

"What?"

"*This.* Feeling. Seeing. Being. Everything. The dew. The cold. That sound, the wind in the grass. You hear that? It's so . . . real."

I didn't know I'd had the hope until the hope died. So she wasn't the same as me, after all; she *didn't* understand. She didn't get that *none* of it was real, not anymore, that the dew felt wrong, the cold felt wrong, the sounds sounded wrong, everything was wrong, everything was distant, everything was fake. Or maybe it was the opposite—everything was real except for me.

I'd been right the first time. Quinn and I had nothing in common. "Whatever you say."

"It feels good, doesn't it?" she asked.

"What does?" Nothing did.

"The grass." She laughed. "Doesn't it tickle?"

"Yeah. I guess." No.

"It's like us, you know."

"What, the grass?" I said. "Why, because people around here are always walking on it?"

"Because it looks natural and all, but inside, it's got a secret. It's better. Manmade, right? New and improved."

Just because the grass—like the trees, like the birds, like pretty much everything—had been genetically modified to survive the increasingly crappy climate, smoggy sky, and arid earth, didn't make it like us. It was still alive. "The grass still looks like grass," I told her. "Seen a mirror lately? There's no secret. We look like . . . exactly what we are."

"You got a boyfriend?"

"What?" Under other circumstances I would have wondered what she was on. But I knew all too well she wasn't on anything. If there were such a thing as a drug for skinners, I'd be on permanent mental vacation.

"Or girlfriend, whatever."

"Boyfriend," I admitted. "Walker."

"You two slamming?"

"*What?*"

"You. Walker. Slamming. Poking. Fucking. You need a definition? When a boy and a girl really love each other—"

"I know what it means. I just don't think it's any of your business."

"I'm only asking because . . . Well, have you? Since, you know?"

The thought repulsed me. The idea of Walker's hands touching the skin, the look on his face when he peered into the dead eyes, the feeling—the nonfeeling—of his lips on the pale pink flesh-textured sacs that rimmed my false teeth. The thick, clumsy thing that functioned as a tongue. Would I even know what to do, or would it be like learning to walk again? Or worse, I thought, remembering the grunting and squealing. Like learning to talk. And that was just kissing. Anything else . . . I couldn't think about it. "Have *you*?" I countered.

She shook her head. "But look at my choices. Like I'm going to slam Asa?"

"You *trying* to make me vomit?"

"Good luck with that, considering the whole no-stomach thing." She laughed. "Obviously options are limited. And I've been waiting a long time."

"How long have you been here?"

"Longer than you. Four months, maybe? But that's not what I'm talking about." She didn't offer to explain.

This girl was completely creeping me out. But not in an entirely bad way.

"So you haven't, uh, had any visitors?" I asked finally. "No guys or . . . whatever?"

"No guys. No whatevers."

"Sorry."

"Why?" Quinn sat up, crossing her legs and resting her elbows on her knees. "According to you, it's not like I'm missing out on much family fun time."

"Yeah, but . . ."

"Go ahead," she said.

"What?"

"Ask. You know you want to." Quinn brushed her hands through her long, black hair, smiling. "I love this," she said, dropping the inky curtain across her face, and then giving her head a violent shake, whipping the hair back over her shoulders. "They got it exactly right."

She was crazy, I decided. It was as if she *liked* living like this.

"Go ahead, ask," she said again. "I really don't care."

"And I really don't want to know," I lied. "But fine. Why no visitors?"

"Dead parents, remember?"

If she wanted to act like it was no big deal, so would I. "Yeah. You said. Poor little orphan. But there's got to be someone."

She lay back down in the grass, turning her face away from me. "Doctors. Staff. No one important. Not that it matters now."

"Why not?"

"Because everything's different now. Once I'm out of here? It's a new life. Anything I want. *Anything*."

"How did they die?" I asked quietly.

"I thought you didn't want to hear the tragic saga?"

"Maybe I changed my mind. Unless it's too hard for you to talk about." But I didn't say it the way Sascha would have, all fake sensitive and understanding. I said it like a challenge, and that's the way she took it.

"Okay, but I'm just warning you, it's quite tragic. You're going to feel pretty sorry for me."

"Don't count on it."

"It was a car accident," she said.

I flinched. And even in the darkness she must have seen.

"Yeah, weird, isn't it? Who gets in car crashes anymore? But here we are. Statistically improbable freaks."

"Were you in the car? When it . . ."

"I was three. We were—" She paused, then barked out a laugh. "This is the first time I've ever had to actually tell someone, you know? I didn't know it would be so . . ."

"You never told *anyone*?" That was too much, too soon. Especially from a girl who wouldn't even tell me her last name.

"It's not like you're special or anything. I just don't . . . I don't meet a lot of new people. Or I didn't. Before."

"You don't have to—"

"I was three," she said quickly. "We were going to visit someone, I don't even know who. I just remember they got me all dressed up, and it was exciting. I mean, they must have taken me off the grounds before, at least a couple times, but I guess I was too young to remember. I remember this, though. I remember being in the car seat, and listening to some song, and playing some stupid vidgame for babies— You remember, the one with the dinosaurs?"

I nodded.

"I was winning. And then—I don't know. I don't remember. Next thing, I wake up, and I'm in a hospital. They're dead. And I'm . . ." She threaded her fingers through her hair, then let her arms fall across her face. "It was a bad accident."

"You were hurt."

She didn't say anything.

"Bad?" I guessed.

"Worse."

"Worse than what?"

"Than whatever you're picturing. Worse." Her voice hardened. "Let's just say that prosthetics and organ transplants and all that? Fine. Great, if you're an adult. But when you break a three year old, it's not so easy to put her together again."

Enough, I thought. *I get it.* But I didn't say anything. And she didn't stop.

"Picture a room. Lots of machines. A bed. People to shovel in the food, shovel out the shit, shoot up the painkillers. People to clean. People to do anything and everything. And in the bed, well . . . a thing that eats and shits and gets high and gets cleaned and the rest of the time just pretty much lays there."

But I didn't want to picture it. "How long did it take?"

"To what?"

"To recover."

"Who said I recovered?"

"I just assumed. . . ."

"Sorry to disappoint, but that was it. That room. That bed."

"But what about school? What about friends, or . . ." Or a life.

"I saw it all on the vids. Same thing, right? That's what you said."

That's what I had said.

"I had it all," she said. "Stuff to read. People to talk to. Vids to watch. The whole network at my fingertips. Well, not fingertips. There weren't any of those. But I got by. Massive amounts of credit will do that for you. And then as soon as I turned sixteen . . ."

"What?"

She stood up. "This," she said, sweeping her arms out and spinning around. "This body that actually *works*. This life. Anything I want."

"You did this to yourself?" I asked, incredulous. "On purpose?"

"Did you hear anything I said?"

"I did, I get it, I just can't imagine anyone actually choosing . . . *this*."

"You obviously don't get it. Or you would see this was

better than anything I could have had. And from what I hear, anything *you* could have had, after what happened."

I should have known. The inevitable you-should-be-grateful guilt-trip bullshit. Like she knew anything about me.

"You let them *kill* you," I said. "You walked in here—"

"Walked." She snorted. "Yeah, right."

"—and asked them to kill you. To chop up your brain, make a copy, and stick it into some machine."

"Damn right. Quinn Sharpe is dead. I would have killed her myself, if I could. You're walking around here all day sulking—yeah, I've been watching; you've been too busy whining to notice—when you should be celebrating. You should be fucking ecstatic."

"Look, I get it, I do. It makes sense, why you'd want to do it. And I get why this would seem better for you than before. But it's different for me. What I was, what I lost— It's different."

Quinn shook her head. "The only difference is that you don't get it, not yet. It doesn't matter how you got here. What matters is that we're here, now. The past is over. The people we were? Dead. Like you would be. Like you *should* be. Dead. You want the rest of your life to be a funeral? Or you want to actually *live*?"

That was my cue. I was supposed to jump to my feet and clasp her hands, spin in circles, somersault through the grass, dance in the moonlight, drink in the fact that I could swing my arms and pump my legs, that I was alive, in motion, in control.

I was supposed to embrace the possibilities and the future, to wake up to a new life. It would be the turning point, some kind of spiritual rehabilitation, an end to the sulking and the self-pitying, a beginning of everything.

I lay still.

"You'll figure it out." She shrugged. "I'm heading back up. You coming?"

"Later."

Shooting me a wicked grin, Quinn sprinted back toward the building, her hair streaming behind her and shimmering under the fluorescent lights, her clothes abandoned in a pile by my head. She ran flat-out, full-speed, running like she didn't know how, arms flailing, feet stomping, rhythm erratic, running like little kids run, without pacing or strategy, running like nothing mattered but the next step. Running just to run. I wanted to join her, to race her, to beat her, and in that moment I knew the legs could do it. I knew I could do it.

I lay still.

I'm not like her, I told myself. Quinn's life had sucked. Mine hadn't. Quinn needed a new start. I didn't. Quinn, if she wanted—*because* she wanted—was a different person now.

I wasn't.

No wonder my father had treated me like a stranger that afternoon. I was acting like one. I was sulking in my room, I was snapping at people who were only trying to help. I was shutting myself off, shutting myself down; I was spewing self-pity. I was lying around, standing still, wasting time wondering what I was going to do and who I was going to be, when the answer was obvious. I was the same person I had always been. I was Lia Kahn. And I was going to do what Lia Kahn always did. Get by. Get through. Work. Win.

I wasn't a skinner. I wasn't a mech-head. I was Lia Kahn. And it was about time I started acting like it.

One week later they sent me home.

FAITH

"God made man. Who made you?"

S omeone must have tipped them off, because when we got
home, they were waiting.

Getting into the car was hard enough. When it lurched
into motion I curled myself into a corner, shut my eyes, and
tried to pretend I was back in my room on the thirteenth floor,
standing still. I wasn't afraid of going home. Lia Kahn had
nothing to fear from her own house. It was just the ride—the
pavement speeding underneath the tires, the sat-nav whirring
along, veering us around a corner, a tree, a truck . . .

I linked in, picked a new noise-metal song that I knew I
would hate, turned the volume up too high, and waited for the
ride to end.

Except that when the car stopped, we still weren't home.
The music faded out, and a new voice shrieked inside my head.
"An abomination! We shall all be punished for her sins!"

I cut the link. Opened my eyes. A sallow face stared
through the window, mouth open in a silent howl. When he

saw me watching he extended his index finger, and his lips shifted, formed an unmistakable word. "You."

My father, behind the wheel even though he wasn't actually using it, pounded a fist against the dash. The horn blared. My mother stroked his arm, more a symbolic attempt to calm him down than anything that actually had a prayer of working. "Biggest mistake they ever made," he muttered. "Programming these things not to run people down."

"Honey . . ." That was symbolic attempt number two. Except in my mother's mind, these things actually worked; in the fantasy world she inhabited, her influence soothed the savage beast.

"I should plow right through you!" he shouted at the windshield. "You want something to protest? I'll give you something to really protest!"

They crowded around the car, pressing in tight, although not too tight. The legally required foot of space remained between us and them at all times. They planted themselves in front of the car, behind it, all around it, blocking us in, so we had no choice but to sit there, twenty yards from the entrance to our property, waiting for security to arrive and, in the meantime, reading their signs.

"I'm sorry, Lee Lee," my mother said, twisting around in her seat and reaching for me. I pulled away. "I don't know how they found out you were coming home today."

Their signs were hoisted over their shoulders, streaming in

red-letter LED across their chests, pulsing on their foreheads. Jamming the network so we couldn't call in reinforcements.

GOD MADE MAN. WHO MADE YOU?

FRANKENSTEIN ALWAYS BURNS

BREATH, NOT BATTERIES

"It's fine," I said. "I don't care."

My father cursed quietly, then loudly.

"Just close your eyes," my mother suggested. "Ignore them."

"I am," I said, eyes open.

My favorite sign depicted a giant extended middle finger, with a neon caption:

SKIN THIS!

It didn't even make sense. But it got the point across.

My father fumed. "Goddamned Faithers."

"Apparently we're the damned ones," I pointed out. "Or I am."

"Don't you listen to them." My mother flicked her hand across her console and my window darkened, blotting out the signs. But it wasn't the signs I'd been watching, it was the faces. I'd never seen a Faither, not up close. Before the accident, I hadn't even seen much of them on the network. But after . . . Somehow my name had ended up on a Faither hit list. Until I fixed my blockers, they'd flooded my zone with all the same crap about how I was a godless perversion, I was Satan's work, I didn't deserve to exist. But I hadn't expected them to come after me in person.

Religion went out of style right after the Middle East

went out in a blaze of nuclear glory. Not that some people, maybe lots of people, didn't keep privately believing in some invisible old man who gave them promotions when they were good and syphilis when they were bad. If you had the credit, you could even snag enough drugs for a one-on-one chat. You sometimes heard rumors about people—especially in the cities, where it's not like there was much else to do—actually gathering together for their God fix, but as far as most people were willing to admit in public, God was dead. The Faith party was for all those leftover believers who—even after the nukes and the Long Winter and the Water Wars of the western drought and the quake that ate California and the wave that drowned DC—refused to give up the ghost. They were for life, for morality, for order, for gratitude, and, until recently, not against much of anything. Except reason, my father was always quick to point out. Then BioMax unrolled its download process, and the Faithers found their cause.

Now they'd found me.

My window was still blocked, but I could see them through the front windshield, silent now, all of them pointing.

"That's it, we'll go manual," my father said, gunning the engine. "I'm going through them."

My mother shook her head. "It won't let you."

"You have a better idea?"

She didn't.

"Come on, Ana, we're listening."

She sighed.

He put his hands on the wheel, switched to manual. "I'll find a way."

"Wait." I leaned forward, touching his shoulder without thinking. He didn't flinch. I glanced out the windshield, and he followed my eyes, saw the man at the center of the crowd, the one with close-cropped blond hair and black-brown eyes, who had his hands in the air. It was a signal, and his followers—for it was obvious who was leading and who was following—fell back, clearing a path for the car. The man bowed low, but kept his face raised toward the car, his eyes fixed on me. He swept his arm out, his meaning clear. *You may go. For now.* And then it was our turn to follow.

It was Thursday, and Thursday meant Kahn family dinner. Even if one-fourth of the family no longer ate. They probably would have let me out of it, just this once let me sneak off to the room I hadn't seen in nearly three months, close the door, start my new-life-same-as-the-old-life on my own, but that would have meant asking, and I didn't. The food arrived before we did, and Zo, who usually showed up to family dinner an hour or two late, if at all, waited at the table, playing the good girl. "I got steak," she said instead of "hello" or "welcome home" or "I missed you." "And chocolate soufflé. All your favorites."

And so we sat in our usual spots, and I watched them eat all my favorites.

"But what happens if you *do*?" Zo asked, stuffing the meat into her mouth. She didn't even like steak. "Does it screw up the wiring? Or would it just sit there and, you know, rot? Like you're walking around with chewed-up bits of moldy bread and rotten meat inside you?"

"Zoie!" My mother's fork clattered to her plate.

"She's just curious," my father said. "It's only natural."

"It's *rude*. And it's not appropriate at the dinner table. Not while we're eating."

"We're not *all* eating," Zo pointed out.

I did not ask to be excused.

"There'd be nowhere for the food to go," I said. "There's a grating over the vocal cavity. Air goes out when I talk. Nothing goes in. Want to see?" I opened my mouth wide.

Zo shirked away. "Ew, *gross*. Dad!"

"Not at the table, please," he said mildly.

To *me*, not to Zo.

"We thought you might want to take tomorrow off, dear," my mother said. "Maybe do some shopping, spruce up your wardrobe?" Unspoken: Because my old clothes, custom-tailored for my old measurements, wouldn't fit my new body. Another factoid she'd neglected to mention: I hadn't shopped with my mother since I was nine years old. Now, for Cass, Terra, and me, it was a tradition—or, as Cass called it, a fetish—first the full-body scan, then the designer zones, ignoring the pop-ups for crap we would never wear, sending our virtual selves on fashion model struts down virtual runways, knowing that whatever we selected would, automatically and immediately, become the new cool, the new *it*, and savoring the responsibility.

"I'm just doing a reorder," I said. Same look, new size. It's what you did after an all-body lift-tuck or a binge vacation, when you didn't want anyone to notice your new stats. It was ill-advised—no, that was too mild; it was potentially disastrous—to do a reorder with an all-new body. New hair, new face, new coloring. Fashion logic demanded a new look, especially for a fashion leader. But I preferred the old one. The masses would deal.

"Express it," my father said. "So you're ready for Monday."

"Monday?"

"School. You've missed enough."

"I thought . . ." I didn't know what I had thought. I had, in fact, tried not to think. I still hadn't peeked out from behind the priv-wall on my zone. As far as anyone knew, I was still missing in action. Although obviously, they'd seen me on the vids. They knew what I'd become. "Sascha, the counselor, said maybe I should take things slow."

"Things?"

"Readjustment . . . things. Like, school. I figured, maybe I could link in for a while, and then—"

"You know how your father feels about that," my mother said.

I knew.

School was the "crucible of socialization." School was where we would be molded and learn to mold others. Meet—and impress and influence and conquer—our future colleagues. We were, after all, preparing to take our place behind the reins of society. There'd be time enough for linked ed when we finished high school and started specialization. And when we did we'd beat out all the asocial losers who'd spent their formative years staring at a ViM. So he'd said when I was six, desperate to escape day one and all the days that followed; so he'd said when Zo got caught cutting, when Zo got caught dosing, when Zo got caught scamming a biotech lab for one of her zoned-out friends and almost got kicked out for good. I didn't want to make him say it again.

Zo stared down at my empty plate. "If she's too scared to go to school, I don't think you should make her."

Thanks a lot, Zo.

"I'm not scared."

Zo rolled her eyes. "Yeah, right."

"I'm *not*."

"Then you're an idiot."

"Zoie!" That was our mother again, trying, always trying, to keep the peace.

"What? I'm just saying, if it were me, I'd be afraid people would think I was, you know."

Say it.

"You've been gone for a long time," Zo said, like a warning.

I looked at my father. "Long enough. So, fine. Monday."

I was ready.

Or I would be.

No one was linked in, no one but Becca Mai, who didn't count, not even in an emergency, which this wasn't, not yet. Of course no one was there. It was Thursday night, and Thursday night meant Cass's house—not her parents' neo-mod manor of glass and steel, but the guesthouse they'd built by the lake, even though they had no guests and never would.

I voiced Walker, who never went anywhere without a flexi-ViM wrapped around his wrist, set to vibrate with incoming texts and to heat up when I voiced. But he wasn't there, and I pussed out. I couldn't let him hear the new voice for the first time in a message. So instead I texted:

I'm home.

I flicked on the mood player, but no music played.

Right. Because the selection was keyed to biometrics, body temp, heart rate, and all the other signs of life I didn't have anymore. So I skimmed through the playlist, chose at random, a soulsong from one of those interchangeable weepers we'd all worshipped a couple years before, when they'd first engineered the musical algorithm that would make you cry.

It didn't.

But it was more than a lack of tear ducts. Or tears. It just wasn't music for me, not anymore, not in the same way. I'd tried it a few times back in rehab, putting on a favorite track, something guaranteed to sweep me out of myself, and it had just been rhythmic noise. Song after song, and I heard every note, I tracked the melodies, I mouthed the lyrics—but it didn't mean anything. It was noise. It was vibrating air, hitting the artificial eardrum with a certain frequency, a certain wavelength, resolving into patterns. Meaningless patterns.

It wasn't a download thing, Sascha said. It was a *me* thing. Plenty of mech-heads still got music. I just wasn't one of them. "There are some things about the brain even we don't understand," Sascha had admitted. "Your postprocedure brain is functionally identical to the organic model, but many clients encounter minor—and I can't emphasize that enough, *minor*—differences in the way they process experiences. Finding themselves indifferent to things they used to love. Loving things they used to hate. We don't know why."

"How can you not know?" I'd asked. "You built the . . . brain. Computer. Whatever you want to call it. You should know how it works."

"The download procedure *copies* the brain into a computer," Sascha had said. "But each brain is composed of billions of cognitive processes. We can model the complete structure without understanding each of its individual parts. Which is why, for example, we don't have the capacity to create new brains from scratch. Only nature can do that. For now."

"So all you know how to do is make copies," I'd said. "Except you can't even get that right. Not exactly." When we were talking about my brain, the things I loved and hated, when we were talking about *me*, "close enough" didn't really get the job done.

"It can be disconcerting at first, but you'll learn to embrace the exciting possibilities. One client even emerged from the procedure with a newfound artistic passion. He's already so successful that he's linked on the *president's* zone!" Saying it like that was some kind of achievement. Like the president wasn't too doped up to notice who stuck what on her zone; judging from the vids, she'd barely even noticed being re-elected.

I didn't have any new passions, certainly none that would make me famous. And I'd thought maybe the music thing was just temporary, that once I got off the thirteenth floor and back to the real world, things would return to normal.

I shut down the music. What was the point?

Susskind, our psychotic cat, sashayed into the room and leaped up onto the bed. And maybe he had the right idea. Except that going to bed would mean facing all the other things that hadn't gone back to normal. All the prebed rituals that had been made obsolete.

I had my own bathroom, tiled in purple and blue. My own shower, where I washed off the grime every night and washed on the UV block every morning, now no longer necessary. My own toilet with a med-chip that analyzed every deposit for bio-irregularities—no longer required. My own sink, where I would have hydroscrubbed my teeth if they weren't already made of some gleaming white alloy impervious to microbes. Not like they came into contact with any, what with the whole no-food thing. My own medicine cabinet, with all the behavior modifiers I could ever need, uppers for perk, downers for sleep, Xers for parties, stims for work, and blissers for play, but no b-mod could help me now. On the face of the cabinet, my own mirror. I stayed away from mirrors.

Psycho Susskind crawled into my lap.

"Great." I rested my hand on his back, letting it rise and fall with each breath. "Of course you like me now." Sussie was afraid of people, even the people who housed and fed him; maybe—judging from his standard pattern of hissing and clawing—especially us. Or make that, them. Because apparently Sussie and I were now best friends.

I didn't dump him off my lap.

"I smell good to you now, Sussie?" I whispered, scratching him behind his ears. He purred. "Like your other best friend?" That would be the dishwasher, which Sussie worshipped like he was a Faither and the dishwasher had a white beard and fistful of lightning bolts.

It's not like I had no way to fill the time. Showers and music weren't generally the bulk of my standard evening activities. There was always a game going on the network. Or I could tweak my av, update my zone, chat with the net-friends who'd never seen my flesh-and-blood body and so wouldn't notice it was gone. I could even hit the local stalker sites and read all about myself, wealthy scion of the Kahn dynasty stuffed into a mech-head and body. What will she do next, now that she's home, where will she go, who will she see, what will she wear?

Instead I pumped the network for information on emotion, for why people feel what they feel and how. But I couldn't make myself read through the results, facts and theories and long, dense explanations that had nothing to do with me.

Walker still hadn't texted back.

I cut the link.

My tracksuit didn't fit me any better than the rest of my clothes. The pants and sleeves were too short and too baggy, the thermo-lining, cued to body temp, was superfluous, and the biostats read zero across the board. But they would do, as would the shoes I got from BioMax, which didn't cushion my feet like the sneakers that no longer fit, but still registered body weight and regulated shock absorption, which was all I needed. Zo was out somewhere; my parents were in bed. There was no one to notice I was gone.

It was a cold night, but that didn't matter, not to me. There was a path behind the house that wove through the woods, a path I'd run every morning for the last several years, layered in thermo-gear, panting and sweating and cursing and loving it. The gravel sounded the same as always, crunching beneath my soles.

I need this, I said silently, to someone, maybe to myself or maybe to the body that locked me in and denied everything I asked of it. *Please. Let this work.*

It didn't.

I ran for an hour. Legs pumping. Feet pounding. Arms swinging. Face turned up to the wind. The body worked perfectly. I didn't sweat. I didn't cramp up. I didn't wheeze, gulping in desperate mouthfuls of oxygen, because I didn't breathe at all. I pushed faster, pushed harder, until something in my head told me I was tired, that it was time to slow down, time to stop, but my muscles didn't ache, my chest didn't tighten, my feet didn't drag, I didn't *feel* ready to stop. I just knew I was, and so I did.

There was no rush, no natural upper coasting me through the last couple miles. There was never that sense of letting go and losing myself in my body, of *existing* in my body, arms, legs, muscles, tendons, pulsing and pumping in sync, the world narrowing to a pinprick tunnel of ground skimming beneath my feet. None of the pure pleasure of absence, of leaving Lia Kahn behind and existing in the moment—all body, no mind.

The body still felt like someone else's; the mind was still all I had left.

I walked the rest of the way back to the house, navigating the path in darkness. The heavy clouds hid even the pale glow of the moon, and so I didn't see the shadows melt into a figure, a man, not until he was close enough to touch.

Fingers wrapped around my arm. Thick, strong fingers. A hand, twisting, and my arm followed the unspoken command, my body tugged after it. He pinned me against a tree, his forearm shoved against my throat.

Lucky I didn't need to breathe.

His face so close to mine that our noses nearly touched, I recognized him. It was the face I'd seen through the car window that morning, the hollow face howling at me through the glass.

I should run away, I thought, *I should scream.* But the ideas seemed distant, almost silly.

"It is He that hath made us, and not we ourselves," the man hissed. "We are His people, and the sheep of his pasture." His breath caressed my face. I wondered what it smelled like.

I wondered if his boss knew he was still here, lurking. I wondered who his boss was. The man with the too-pale skin and the too-dark eyes? Or did he report directly to the big boss, the eye in the sky? I wondered what he would do to me if I asked.

"Thou shall not make unto thee any graven image, or any likeness of any thing that is in heaven above, or that is in the earth beneath, or that is in the water under the earth."

I was linked in. I could have sent for help. But I didn't particularly want any. His arm bore down harder against my throat.

"That's you," he spat out. "A graven image. A *machine.* Programmed to think you're a real person. Pathetic."

Enough. "Yeah, *I'm* pathetic," I snapped back. "You're hiding behind a tree, trespassing on private property, and about five minutes away from being picked up by the cops and probably shipped off to a city, and *I'm* pathetic."

"*Tzedek, tzedek tirdof,*" he whispered, grinning like the nonsense words harbored some secret power. I shuddered.

"Righteousness, righteousness shall you pursue." He reached up his other hand and stroked my cheek. "God says be righteous to your fellow man. But he doesn't say *anything* about what to do with things like you." The fingers traced the curve of my ear. I jerked my head away, but he grabbed a chunk of hair and tugged, hard. "Guess I'm on my own, figuring out what to do. Got any ideas?"

He laughed, and that's when the fear came, fast and hard, like a needle of terror jabbed into my skull. "Anything," that was the word that echoed. He could do anything. I grabbed his hand, the hand that was crawling down my neck, along my spine, grabbed his fingers and bent them back until I heard the joints crunch and the arm at my throat reared back, struck me across the face, snapped my head back into the tree but my leg had already swung into motion, had connected with his groin. He doubled over and I ran, and I could hear him behind me, cursing and grunting, crashing through the brush, closing in as I pushed faster and pulled away and I could almost imagine a beating heart and heaving lungs, because the panic was so real. But he fell behind, and I made it through the electronic gate in plenty of time, locking him out, locking me in. The fear faded almost immediately, and as it leaked out of me, I had one last, terrifying thought.

I should go back.

To slip through the gate again, to face the man, to *fight* the man—or not to fight, to let him do whatever he wanted, to choose to meet him and his consequences, to turn back, because behind me, where the man glowered from the treeline, was something real. Something human.

The stronger the emotion, Sascha had promised, the more real it would seem.

I'd felt it. I was hooked.

Back in my room, safe and alone. The man, whoever he was, long gone. And with him, the fear.

I stripped off the sweat-free tracksuit. Uploaded the day's neural changes, ensuring—with nothing more than a few keystrokes and an encrypted transmission to the server—that if anything happened to this body, a Lia Kahn with fully up-to-date memories would remain in storage, ready and waiting to be dumped into a new one. Would it be me or a copy of me? And if it was a copy, did that make *me* a copy too, of some other, realer Lia? Was she dead? Was the man right that I was just a machine duped into believing I was human? And if I had been duped, then how could I be a machine? How could any thoughtless, soulless, consciousness-free thing believe in a lie, believe in anything, *want* to believe?

And did I consider those questions while I was dealing with my brand-new bedtime ritual? Did I follow the primrose path of logical deduction all the way to its logical endpoint, to the essential question?

I did not.

I dumped the tracksuit; I uploaded; I pulled on pajamas; I twisted the blond hair back into a loose, low ponytail; I dumped psycho Susskind into the hall. I did it all mechanically. Mechanically, as in without thought, as in through force of habit, as in instinctively, automatically, involuntarily. Mechanically, as in like-a-machine.

And I did not think about that, either.

Instead of turning out the lights and climbing into bed, I mechanically—always mechanically—entered the purple-and-blue tiled bathroom for the first time. The stranger's face watched me from the mirror, impassive. Blank.

I pulled up the network query I'd made earlier, the one I hadn't had the nerve to read. The words scrolled across my left eye, glowing letters superimposed on my reflected face.

I froze the parade of definitions and expanded the one that seemed to matter. The guy's name was William James, and he was way too old to be right. Two hundred years ago, no one knew anything; it's why they all died young and wrinkled with bad hair. Two hundred years ago, they thought light could go as fast as it wanted, they thought the atom was indivisible and possibly imaginary, they thought "computers" were servant girls who added numbers for their bosses when they weren't busy doing the laundry. They knew nothing. But I read it anyway.

> *If we fancy some strong emotion, and then try to abstract from our consciousness of it all the feelings of its characteristic bodily symptoms, we find we have nothing left behind, no "mind stuff" out of which the emotion can be constituted, and that a cold and neutral state of intellectual perception is all that remains.*

The face didn't move; the eyes didn't blink. *Cold and neutral*, I thought. It wasn't true. I had felt anger; I had felt fear. But fear of what? The man couldn't have hurt me, not really. At least, he couldn't hurt me forever. Whatever he did to the body, I would remain. I couldn't die. What was to fear in the face of that?

> *What kind of emotion of fear would be left if the feeling neither of quickened heartbeats nor of shallow breathing, neither of trembling lips nor of shallow weakened limbs, neither of gooseflesh nor of visceral stirrings, were present . . . ?*

Even now, in my pajamas, in my bathroom, I felt. The tile beneath my feet. The sink against my palms. I felt absence: the silence that should have been punctuated by steady breathing, in and out. Fingers against my chest, I felt the stillness beneath them. I felt loss.

In like manner of grief: what would it be without its tears, its sobs, its suffocation of the heart, its pang in the breast bone? A feelingless cognition that certain circumstances are deplorable, and nothing more.

Nothing more.

THE BODY

"Aren't you going to kiss her good-bye?"

Their whispers slithered through the crack beneath my bedroom door, and I fought the temptation to press myself against it, to find out what Zo and Walker, who had for years shared a mutual, if mostly unspoken, oath of eternal dislike, could possibly need to discuss. Not that the topic was in doubt.

The topic was me.

The whispers stopped. I struck my best casual pose, legs dangling off the side of the bed, elbows digging into the mattress, ankles crossed, head tipped back to the ceiling as if the track of solar panels had proven so engrossing as to make me forget what was about to happen. The door opened, and I held my position, letting Walker see me before I saw him.

Giving him time to erase his reaction before I could see it on his face.

Not enough time. When I sat up, he was still in the doorway, one hand in his pocket, the other gripping the frame, holding himself steady.

"Hey," I said.

He didn't move. "Your voice . . ."

"Weird, right? I hear myself talk and I'm like, wait, who said that?" I forced a laugh, but stopped as soon as I saw him wince. I'd forgotten that I wasn't very good at the laughing thing yet. Especially when I was faking it.

"It's nice," he said, like he was trying to convince himself. "I like it."

I hated it. Someone else's voice, husky and atonal, coming out of the mouth.

My mouth, I reminded myself. *My* voice. But I could only believe that when I was alone. With Walker finally standing there, watching me, I was forced to admit it: The voice belonged to the *thing*, to the body, not to me.

"It's been a while," I said, even though I'd promised myself I wasn't going to bring it up. He hadn't voiced me back on Thursday night or on Friday. And then Saturday came, and he was here. That should have been enough.

Walker shrugged. He rubbed his chin, which was shadowed with brown scruff. Without me around to remind him to shave, he'd grown a beard. "I was going to text you, but . . ."

"Yeah. But." I stood up. He was still in the doorway. If he wouldn't come to me, I would go to him. *It can be difficult at the beginning,* Sascha had said. *But the people who know you, the people who love you, they'll see beneath the surface. They'll get that it's really* you *under there. You just have to give them some time.*

No one knew me better than Walker. But when I curled the hand around his wrist, he jerked away. "Sorry, I—"

I stepped back. "No, it's fine." It wasn't. "I shouldn't have." He shouldn't have.

"No, really. I just . . ." Walker finally stepped into the room, edging around me as he passed, careful not to touch the body. He sat in my desk chair, back straight, feet flat on the floor. Arms crossed, hugging his chest.

I dropped back down on the bed and waited.

"I'm very glad you're all right," he said finally, like he was passing along a message from his mother to some old lady who'd broken her hip. Like he'd been rehearsing.

I risked a smile. I'd been rehearsing too. "I missed you."

"You, too." He stared down at the floor. His hair was longer than I'd ever seen it, almost to his shoulders, like one of Zo's retros. I wanted to smooth it back. I wanted to stand behind him and bury my face in it, resting my cheek against the back of his head, wrapping my arms around his shoulders, letting him grip my hands in his. But I stayed where I was. "It's, uh, it's pretty," he said. "I mean—*you're* pretty. Now. Like this."

"You don't have to lie."

He shifted in the seat. "No— It's just, I guess, I just thought you'd look a little more like . . . I mean, on the vids, and you looked . . . But now . . . I thought you'd look more . . ."

"Like me?" But as soon as I said it, I knew that wasn't what he'd meant. I *didn't* look like me, not anymore, not with the hair that was the wrong color and texture and wasn't even hair, just a synthetic weave that was grafted on and would never grow. The nose was too small, the eyes too wide, the fingers the wrong thickness, the wrong length, the teeth too straight and too bright, the mouth bigger, the ears smaller, the body taller and too symmetrical, too well proportioned, too perfect. But it wasn't that. I knew what he'd wanted to say; I knew him too well.

I thought you'd look more . . . human.

And I saw the body again like I'd seen it for the first time, like *he* was seeing it. The skin, smooth and waxy, an even peachy tone stretched out over the frame without sag or blemish. The way it moved, with awkward jerks, always too slow or too fast. The stranger's face with dead eyes, pale blue irises encircling the false pupils, and in the center of the black, pinpricks of light, flashing and dimming as the lens sucked up images. The eyes that didn't blink unless I remembered to blink them. The chest that neither rose nor fell unless I pretended to breathe. The body that wasn't a body.

His girlfriend, the machine.

"It's just weird," he admitted. "I'm sorry, I know I shouldn't—"

"It's okay," I said quickly. "It *is* weird. It's weird for me too."

"I mean, I know it's you, I get that, but you sound different, and you look different, and . . ."

"It's because it was an emergency. They had to give me a generic model. My dad picked it out. He says it's the one that looked the most like me. Not that it looks like me, I know, but it was the best he could do." *Too much detail*, I told myself. *Stop talking*. But I couldn't. Once I stopped, he would have to start again. Or he wouldn't. And then we'd just sit there, and he would try not to stare at me, and I would try not to look away. "Some people get these custom faces designed to look just like them, the way they were—or like anything they want, I guess. It's totally crazy what they can do. The voice, too. You just make a recording and they match it. I mean, it's not exactly the same, I know, but it's . . . closer. Easier. But you've got to place the order in advance. You've got to give them time, and if there's an accident or something, well . . ." I tried another smile. "There's nothing I can do about it now. The artificial nerves and receptors are already fused to the neural pathways or whatever, and they say structural changes would screw with the graft, but next time, I'll do it in advance, so I'll be able to order whatever I want. Then I'll look more like . . ."

"Lia," he said.

I am Lia.

But I said it in my head, where there was no one to hear.

"I'll look more like *me*," I said out loud. Calmly. "Next time."

"Wait, what do you mean, next time?"

"When the, uh, body wears out or—" I closed my eyes

for a moment, trying to block out the echo of the crash, the scream of metal that refused to die—"if something happens to it, they'll download the, uh . . ." *Data? Program? Brain? Soul?* There was no right word. There was only *me*, looking out through some *thing's* dead eyes. "They'll do it again. When they need to."

"So you just get a new body when the old one runs out?" he asked. "And they keep doing it . . . forever?"

"That's the plan." As the words came out of the mouth, I finally saw it, what it meant. I saw the day he found the first tuft of hair stuck in the shower drain or woke up to a gray strand on his pillow. His first wrinkle in the bathroom mirror. The day he blew out his knee in his last football game. The day his potbelly bulged as he stopped playing and kept eating. Any of the days, all of the days, starting with tomorrow, when he'd be one day older than today; and then the next, two days older, and the next and the next, as he grew, as he aged, as he declined . . . as I stayed the same. Shunted from one unchanging husk of metal and plastic to the next.

I got there a moment before he did, but only a moment, and then he got there too. I saw it on his face.

"Forever." Walker grimaced. "You'll be like . . . this. Forever." He stood up.

Don't leave, I thought. *Not yet.* But I wasn't about to say it out loud. Even if he couldn't see it, I was still Lia Kahn. I didn't beg.

"So, what's it like?" he asked, crossing the room. To the bed—to me. He sat down on the edge, leaving a space between us. "Can you, like, feel stuff?"

"Yeah. Of course." If it counted as feeling, the way the whole world seemed hidden behind a scrim. Fire was warm. Ice was cool. Everything was mild. Nothing was right.

I held out a hand, palm up. "Do you want to . . . ? You can see what it feels like. To touch it. If you want."

He lifted his arm, extended a finger, hesitated over my exposed wrist, trembling.

He touched it. Me.

Shuddered. Snatched his hand away.

Then touched me again. Palm to palm. He curled his fingers around the hand. Around my hand.

"You can really feel that?" he asked.

"Yes."

"So what's it feel like?"

"Like it always does." A lie. Artificial nerves, artificial conduits, artificial receptors, registering the fact of a touch. Reporting back to a central processor the fact of a hand, five fingers, flesh bearing down. Measuring the temperature, the pressure per square inch, the duration, and all of it translated, somehow, into something resembling a sensation. "It feels good." I paused. "What does it feel like to you?"

"You mean . . . ?"

"The skin."

"It's . . ." He scrunched his eyebrows together. "Not the same as before. But not . . . weird. It feels like skin." He let go.

I brushed the back of my hand across his cheek. This time he didn't move away. "You need to shave."

"I like it like this," he said, giving me a half smile. It was the same thing he always said.

"You're the only one." That was the standard response. We'd had the fight that wasn't a fight so often it was like we were following a script, one that always ended the same way. And if I acted like everything was the same, maybe . . .

"It looks good," he argued, the half smile widening into a full grin.

"It doesn't *feel* good. So unless you want to scratch half my face off when—" I stopped.

Nothing was the same.

The coarse bristles sprinkling his face wouldn't hurt when he kissed me.

If he kissed me.

"Lia, when you were gone all that time, I . . ."

"What?"

A pause.

"Nothing. I'm just . . . I'm glad you didn't, you know. Die."

It was what he had to say, and I gave him the answer I had to give. "Me too." For the first time, sitting there with him, I could almost believe it was true.

Another pause, longer this time.

"When you were in that place . . . I should have come to visit."

"You were busy," I said.

"I should have come."

"Yeah."

Not that I would have let him see me like that, spasmodic limbs jerking without warning, muscles clenching and unclenching at random, the mouth spitting out those strangled animal noises, the tinny speaker speaking for me until I could control the tongue, moderate the airflow, train the mechanism to impersonate human speech. If he'd seen me like that, he would never have been able to see me any other way. He would never see that I was Lia.

"I should go," he said. "You must be . . . Do you get tired?"

I shook the head. "I sleep, but it's not . . . I don't dream or anything. I just . . ." There was no other way to say it. "Shut down."

"Oh."

"I'm sorry," I said suddenly.

"What?" He scrunched his eyebrows together again. "Why?"

"I don't know." There were no mechanical tear ducts embedded in the dead eyes. No saltwater deposits hidden behind the unblinking lids. Add it to the list of things I wouldn't do again: cry. "I just am. I'm sorry that I'm . . . like this."

I admit it. I wanted him to wrap his arms around me. I

wanted him to tell me that *he* wasn't sorry. That I was beautiful. That the hair felt like real hair and the skin felt like real skin and the body felt like a real body and he wasn't weirded out by the thought of touching it. That he saw me.

He stood up. I didn't. "You going back to school soon?"

"Monday."

"So I guess I'll see you there." He backed toward the door. When he opened it, Zo was on the other side. Like she'd been there the whole time, waiting, as she'd done when Walker and I had first gotten together, and she'd been a kid, annoying, always around, hovering outside with her ear pressed to the door, giggling every time we were about to kiss.

"Guess so."

He hesitated, like he was waiting for my permission to leave. The old Walker had waited for my permission to do everything.

"Aren't you going to kiss her good-bye?" Zo asked, sounding so sweet, so helpful, so hopelessly ignorant, and then she smiled, and the smile was none of those things.

Walker didn't move. Not until she gave him a gentle push, digging her fists into the shallow concavity beneath his rib cage. He lurched across the room, and I felt frozen again, like I had that first day, locked inside the body.

Blink, I reminded myself. But when I shut the lids, I didn't open them again.

He didn't taste like anything. Nothing did anymore. His

lips feathered across mine. I registered the touch, and then it was gone.

"Bye, Lia."

I kept my eyes shut as his footsteps crossed the room. The door closed.

Bye.

SOBERED UP

"Survival of the fittest. And we were the fittest."

It began Monday at six a.m., when the bed whispered me awake—or would have if an inner alert hadn't already forced my eyes open and my brain back to full-scale conscious dread. It began as I picked through a stack of clothes in disgust, rejecting favorites—the mood dress useless, its temperature-activated swooshes and swirls requiring fluctuations in body temperature which themselves required an actual body; the sonicsilk with its harmonic rippling just another reminder of the music I'd lost; the LBD, a linked-in black dress whose net-knit flared neon with every voice or text, too sensational; the soundproofed hoodie functional and cozy but not sensational enough, blah and gray, like I planned to fade into the background, scenery instead of the star—and finally being forced to resort to jeans and an old print-shirt that snatched random phrases from the network and scrolled them across the fabric. The look had been very hot, and then quickly very not, but it had settled into a neutral acceptability, and it was the best I could do.

It began—my official return to school and an officially normal life—with breakfast, another meal I could no longer eat. Or maybe with the sound of the car door slamming shut, Zo and me tucked inside, or with the hills giving way to a long, flat stretch of familiar green, the castle of brick and stone rising above the horizon.

In that old, normal life, it began after every break—whether two days or two months—with a squeal in stereo, Cass and Terra catching sight of me, fashionably late, pulling into the lot. It began with a rocket-launched embrace, arms locked, shoulders encircled, styles critiqued, stories spilled, all, it seemed, released in a single, shared breath. This time I had no stories, at least none I was willing to share. This time nothing was normal. But as the car pulled into the lot, I saw them bounce off the steps in front of the school. I opened the door and heard the squeal.

It begins now.

The first thing that registered were their clothes. Loose, ill-fitting, dull-colors, Cass in a T-shirt with a printed, unchanging slogan, Terra in jeans that sagged on her ass and a black shirt too loose and too worn, without any visible tech, like something you'd find in a city, or from one of those thrift zones Zo was always haunting for new retro rags.

The second thing: *"Zo Zo!"*

That was Cass's squeal, Cass's wide grin—and then she saw me, and both of them faded away.

She'd cut her black hair short and spiky, cropping it with a dusting of pink. "Lia?" Cass narrowed her eyes as if squinting would squeeze my features back to their familiar shape—or maybe block them out altogether. "Is that . . . you?"

"It's me." I didn't dare try a smile. "In the flesh."

No one laughed. Terra looked sick. She hip-bumped Zo.

"Zo Zo, why didn't you tell us that your sister was coming back today?" she asked with a determined perk. "We would have . . . done something special. To celebrate."

Terra's hair was the same, but she was actually—it didn't seem possible—wearing *lipstick*. And some kind of purple glitter above her eyes. Which didn't make sense, because no one wore makeup anymore, except the wrinkled poor who couldn't afford gen-tech or lift-tucks, and trashy retro slummers who thought it was cool to pretend they fit in to the first group. Oh, and seniles, who didn't count, since they didn't even know what year it was and so couldn't be expected to remember that makeup had gone out with TVs and artificial preservatives. Why spend all that credit on the perfect face if any random could match the effect with a black marker and some pinkish paint? Zo was wearing lipstick too, of course, but that was nothing new.

"I asked, uh, *Zo Zo*"—I shot Zo a look. She ignored it—"not to say anything." A lie. Like I could ever have imagined Zo talking to *my* friends. "Don't blame her."

"Doesn't matter now," Cass chirped. "You're back!"

"Tell us everything," Terra said. *"Everything."*

"Zo Zo wouldn't spill," Cass said, thwapping Zo's shoulder. "No matter how many times we asked. And, of course, *someone* has been totally zoned out forever."

"Yeah . . ." I didn't want to explain how I'd been lurking on the network in stealth mode, peeking over everyone's shoulders, or why I hadn't texted anyone back. Especially not with Zo—excuse me, *Zo Zo*—standing right there, listening to every word. "Sorry about that. I had a lot to, you know, deal with. For a while."

"We can imagine," Cass said.

"No, we can't." Terra sounded pissed. "Because we don't know anything."

"But we want to." Cass touched my shoulder. "We do."

Zo flicked a finger across her inner wrist, and the small screen she'd temp-adhered flashed twice. "Time, ladies."

"Oh!" Cass blushed. "Right. We're late. So, info dump later? Lunch?"

"Uh, sure— Wait, no, it's Monday." When it came to ruling the pack, lunch was key, but that was Tuesday through Friday. Mondays belonged to Walker. That had always been the deal, from the beginning.

"You and *Walker*?" Terra asked. "You mean he didn't—"

"Walker will deal," Cass cut in.

He didn't what? I thought. But didn't ask.

"It'll be fine," Cass said. "Trust me. Lunch."

"Lunch," I agreed. Walker could wait. "But where are you going?"

"Too complicated." Cass giggled as Terra tugged her away. "Later. Lunch."

"Right. Later. Lunch." I grabbed Zo before she could follow them. "So?"

She shook me off. "So what?"

"So since when do you steal my best friends?"

She smirked. "Maybe they stole me."

"And where are you all going?"

"They're *your* best friends. Shouldn't you already know?"

"You know I haven't talked to them in months," I said.

"Exactly."

"Zo!"

"I'm late." She spun away, pausing only to shoot back the last word. "And at school it's Zoie. Or Zo Zo."

I was used to people watching me. I just wasn't used to them gawking, then twisting away as soon as I caught them at it. The hallways were the worst. Conversation died as soon as I got close—sometimes tapering off, like a seeping wound that finally, as the heart stops pumping, runs out of blood, and sometimes cut off in its prime, a gunshot victim dropped by eight grams of lead. I knew the conversations that reached a violent, abrupt end were the ones about me, the machine roaming the halls claiming to be Lia Kahn. The other ones—

the stumbling, mumbling trailings off into awkward silence—
were just the result of nobody knowing what to say. That was
at least better than the randoms who came up to me all day
knowing *exactly* what to say, and this—no matter which words
they used to disguise it—boiled down to "smile for the camera"
as they aimed their ViMs at my face, zooming in for a close-
up, pumping me for details they could post on their zone or a
local stalker site and turn us both into fame whores.

I didn't smile.

In class, even the teachers stared, not like they had much
else to do beyond babysit us while we got our real education
from the network. Which meant I watched my ViM screen
while the rest of them watched me. The only relief came in
biotech, usually the worst of all possible evils, but hidden
behind the thick plastic face mask, hunched over my splicing
kit, I could almost pass for normal.

Walker didn't respond to my text about lunch, and when
I showed up in the cafeteria, he wasn't there. So I sat with the
usual suspects—plus Zo—at the usual table in the front of
the room, where everyone could look as much as they wanted.
Surrounded by my friends, it was almost possible to pretend
they were staring for the old reasons, wondering what we had
that they didn't, where they'd gone wrong between *then*—
the half-remembered, better-forgotten days of all-men-are-
created-equal playdates and birthday parties when no one
cared how loud you were, how rude you were, how ugly you

were, how stupid you were, how lame you were, because we were all too young and so too dumb to notice—and *now*, when how you looked and how you talked mattered as much as it should.

The Helmsley School was built three hundred years ago, for people who were almost as rich as we were, and the cafeteria, with its wood panels, floor-to-ceiling windows, and scalloped ceiling, was a suitably regal match for the exterior, all stone columns and brick arches. Thanks to the population crash and the upswing in linked ed, only half the tables were filled, but any group larger than three is enough for an us/them divide. After all, that was—as we'd learned in kindergarten—the key to civilization and the survival of the species. Finite supply plus infinite demand equaled conflict, battle, nature red in tooth and claw; bloody struggle for turf, status, sex equaled survival of the fittest. And we were the fittest.

Staying at the top meant defying expectations and reversing the norm, because there was nothing exclusive about acting like everyone else. Which meant that if the rest of the school was gaping at my new face and freakish body, my friends, not to mention the people I counted as friends by virtue of social proximity, would ignore the obvious, forgo the questions, and act as if they ate with a skinner every day—as, from now on, they would. Except for the fact that the skinner wasn't eating.

Which wasn't as awkward as the fact that my sister was. And was doing so at *my* table.

Or the fact that everyone else was tricked out in retro slum gear, just like her. I was the only person wearing anything with visible tech—the only person at the table, at least. I was dressed exactly like everyone else in the room. Normal.

But the clothes didn't explain why everything felt so wrong. You didn't claw your way to the top of the pyramid without knowing how to read people. You needed a radar, something to sense the smallest of fluctuations in the social field. You needed the skills to know, even with your eyes closed and your ears plugged, who was scheming, who was suffering, who was gaining on you, who was on the way out. If you couldn't figure out that last one, chances are, it was you.

It wasn't the kind of thing you could learn. You either had it or you didn't.

Except it turned out there was a third option: You had it, and then you lost it.

Part of it was them. No one could act normal, not while I was in the room.

Part of it was me.

The things I used to know about people, the things I *understood* . . . It wasn't a rational thing. It was just something I *felt*, like the way I could feel when someone was watching me.

I couldn't do that anymore either.

I felt like I'd gone blind.

It didn't help that I barely knew half the people at the table, especially the two grunters pawing Cass and Terra—

the reason, I quickly found out, they'd run off so quickly that morning. New season, new boys.

No sign of Walker.

No one asked me where he was.

Bliss had picked that day's b-mod, which meant—big surprise—everyone was blissed out. Everyone except me, since b-mods wouldn't do much for someone without brain chemicals to modify. I'd half expected them to opt for some retro drugs to match the retro clothes. Some of Zo's dozers, maybe, or even something alcohol based, like in the bad old days of hangovers and beer bellies. But no matter how in retro was, it couldn't offer anything that would kick in immediately and wear off by the end of the period. Advantage: b-mods. As far as I was concerned, bliss mods were bad enough when I was on them too, always leaving a weird moody aftertaste, like crashing after a sugar high. Staying cold sober while the rest of them blissed up? Infinitely worse.

"So do you have, like, superpowers?" That was Cass's mouth breather. It was worse when guys giggled. That just wasn't natural. "Are you an evil crime fighter now?" Cass glared at him, smacking his hand away when he tried to squeeze my bicep.

Terra tugged at my print-shirt. "You got a uniform on under here? For your secret identity?"

Zo blew out a laugh. It was the first time since the accident that I'd seen her with a real smile. "*I'm* the superhero."

She narrowed her eyes at Cass. "The power to wither with a single glare."

Cass clutched at her chest. "You got me!" She toppled over, tumbling into me. "Oh. Sorry." She sprang up, posture straight, arms assembled in her lap, a careful four or five inches away from mine. No one spoke.

"Apparently I have the power of awkwardness," I joked. Awkwardly. "Lia Kahn, super-buzz-killer."

No one laughed.

Terra's boy—Axe or Jax or something; it wasn't clear and since no one else seemed to care, I didn't either—grunted something about his balls itching, and how he'd prefer the power to scratch them without anyone seeing. Cass elbowed her guy, who was busy making an adjustment of his own. "How about *you* try that power sometime." She pulled his hand out of his lap—and didn't let go.

"Power," the guy repeated. "Pow-er. Weird word. Word weeeeiiiird." He wrapped his hairy arms around Cass, who dissolved into a shivering mass of giggles.

The bliss mod was kicking it up.

"What if we only walk in wouble-woo words," Bliss suggested, laughing.

Zo shrugged and flashed a sly smile. "Whatever works."

"Why?" Terra asked.

"Why wot!" her boy crowed.

"Where's Walker?" Bliss said, in a way that made me wonder if the whole *w* thing hadn't just been a convenient way of getting around to the question, except that Bliss wasn't smart enough to formulate such a plan, even when off the drugs.

"Walker's waiting," Cass said, and the others nodded, as if that made any sense.

"Wise Walker."

"Or Walker's whizzing!"

"What would Walker want?"

"*Who* would Walker want?" Bliss again.

"Walker wonders what's worse, waiting or wanting or wussing," Zo said in the tone of someone who knows she's won a game. Everyone else nodded at wordwise *Zo Zo*. Hail to the chief.

I stood up. "See you guys later."

"Wait!" Cass cackled. "We . . . uh, w—" The letter almost foiled her. Then, at the last minute, "We want Wia!"

Bliss pointed at me. "Whiner." Then giggled and shook her head. "Whatever."

Everyone lifted a glass, toasted. "Whatever!"

So I ditched the table and the cafeteria, and spent the rest of lunch outside, where I could be alone because it was too cold, at least too cold for anyone warm-blooded enough to care. Those of us running on battery power, on the other hand, could sit under a tree, wait for the bell, ignore the wind and the frost, because none of it—*none* of it—mattered.

Whatever.

• • •

That was the first day. And the next few weren't any better. My social life was hemorrhaging. And time, contrary to popular opinion, did not heal the wound. I retrofitted my wardrobe; I stuck it out through one lunch after another, b-mod haze and all. I did *not* ask Zo how she'd managed to weasel her way into every corner of my life or what had happened to her own life and the randoms she used to know and love. I didn't ask Zo much of anything. We shared a house, shared a lunch table, a set of friends, even—despite a lack of permission and my conviction that I was probably risking infestation from whatever hardy insects had survived all those decades in someone's moldy attic—her clothes. But we didn't talk. Which was fine with me.

I didn't talk to Cass or Terra, either, not about anything that mattered. And when I asked them about Zo . . . The first time we were alone, there it was, flat out: Since when don't we hate my sister? The conversation didn't get very far.

"After, you know, what happened," Cass stammered. "We were . . ."

"Upset," Terra said. "And worried about her."

"About you too, of course."

"But you weren't here."

"And you weren't linked in."

I waited for them to say they were just being nice—out of character, maybe, but not out of the realm of possibility. That Zo had been so distraught by "what happened" that they'd needed to comfort her, to include her, what any friends would do for a suffering little sister. They didn't.

"So no one knew what was going on with you . . ."

"And Zo just . . ."

"Surprised us," Cass said.

"She's different now," Terra said.

I wasn't buying it. "Seems the same to me." Even though that wasn't quite true either.

Cass looked away. "Maybe that's because you're different too."

After that, we didn't talk about it anymore.

Walker and I, on the other hand, did nothing but talk. Which wasn't exactly our strong suit. I didn't see him at school, not for days. That was no accident. He was avoiding me, and for a while, I let him. I wasn't stupid. It's not like I expected we'd just keep going like nothing had happened. Not right away, at least. He was weirded out, so for a few days, I let him hide. But I knew Walker, and I knew what he needed, even if he didn't. He needed me.

I staked out his car. He emerged from the building surrounded by people—girls, to be specific, but there was nothing new about that. Walker was that type; he got off on it. But that was fine, because he always ended up with me. As he did this time. The girls spotted me before he did, and faded away.

I watched him walk. It was more of a lope, arms swinging wide, legs sucking up pavement. Walker had never asked me out, not in any kind of sweaty-palmed, bumbling, would-you-like-to-whatever kind of thing, not that anyone did that, but if someone were going to, it wouldn't be Walker. When it happened, it had happened fast and unmemorably, as if all along both of us had known we would eventually end up together. There had been yet another party, yet another buzz. There had been a late-night, early-morning haze, a group of us sprawled on someone's floor, heads on stomachs, legs tangled, fingers absentmindedly intertwined, lids dropping shut until only two of us were awake, and while I hadn't been waiting up for him and he hadn't been waiting up for me, it seemed like we had. Like the whole night—the party, the group, everything—had been expressly designed to deliver us to this point, to an empty patch of carpet shadowed by the couch, to his arm oh-so-casually sprawled across my thigh, to whatever would happen when he slid toward me and I rolled to face him and our bodies ate up the space between. By which I mean, I had known him forever, but I had never wanted him—until that night, when I suddenly did. He was the one who acted. Brushed my hair out of my face. Kissed me, sleepy-eyed and loose-lipped, soft, and then, like we'd waited too long, even though we hadn't waited at all, hard. Afterward, when it was already obvious that this wasn't just another night, that this was a beginning of something, he pretended that he'd been planning it for a while, secretly pining and plotting. He wasn't lying, not to me, at least. I knew he believed it. But I also knew it had been the same for him as it was for me: lying there, fighting sleep without knowing why, knowing there was a reason to stay awake, something that needed doing, and then, somehow, just *knowing*.

And doing.

"You're avoiding me," I said, leaning against the hood of the car.

He shook his head no.

I shook my head yes.

He shrugged. "Been busy."

"You're *never* busy," I said.

"Things change."

Tell me something I don't know.

"Walker, I . . ."

"What?"

I let myself sink back against the car. It was a thing; it had no choice but to hold me up. "It's been a long week, that's all."

"You want to . . . talk about it?"

"Not really." And I wasn't even saying that because I knew he wanted me to, although he clearly did. Mostly I just wanted him to kiss me again, for real this time. But what was I supposed to do. *Ask?*

"So . . . you want to get something to eat?"

I just looked at him.

"Oh. Yeah. Sorry."

"No problem." He would learn; we would adjust.

"You want to come over, play some Akira?" he said.

We'd been into the game for months, although he liked it more than I did, especially since he spent most of his play on hunting ghosts in Akira's craggy moonscape, and zooming down the canyons and slithering through the worm-ridden tunnels always made me a little motion sick. Not that queasiness was much of a problem anymore, but boredom was. Generally after twenty minutes or so of busting virtual creepy crawlies while Walker flirted with slutty snake-women, their naked chests covered with shimmering scales and their users probably a thousand miles away, looking for a quick and easy love-link, I was ready for a nap. Or at least, I was ready to lie down. Usually, with the right combination of sulk and seduction, with Walker on top of me. And maybe that was the point.

"Sure."

And soon, side by side on his couch, goggled up and strapped in, we disappeared into the world of the game, his av and mine creeping down haunted hallways, hand in hand, touching without feeling, reality forgotten, or at least irrelevant, which was enough.

It was enough until it wasn't anymore, and then I slipped out of the game and back into the world. He stayed in, twitching, ducking his head, clutching the air, and grabbing for invisible demons, a careful space between us. I could have touched him then. He was too lost in the virtual universe to notice a hand on his leg, his lower back, his face. I'd done it before, more than once, making a game of it; how far could I go before calling him back to the surface, how deep had he sunk, how quickly could I reel him back in. But I didn't touch him, just waited for him to tire of the game, and when he did, I went home.

"No," the coach said when I finally found the courage to ask her. "I'm sorry, Lia. I wish I could, but . . . no."

"I know I'm out of shape, but I can get up to speed. I know I can."

"It's not that." She was slim and blond, and I wondered, as I often did, why she'd chosen coaching as her hobby instead of teaching or crafts. Something cozy and indoors, like most in her position, afraid of leathering their skin under the open sky. I got that she had to do *something*. It was a social imperative for the jobless rich, since the children of the wealthy weren't going to raise themselves (nor, obviously, be raised by the parents of the poor), but why opt for something that required so much actual work?

I suspected it was because, like me, she loved to run. Missed it, missed the uniforms and the competitions and the trophies and even the outdoors. I could imagine myself doing the same thing—except, of course, that I was destined for productivity. Let my spouse, whoever he turned out to be, ply his hobbies. I'd been informed from day one—still in diapers, spitting and drooling—that *I* would have a career. Eventually.

In the meantime I would run.

"Did you give my spot away?" I asked, glancing over at the

track. Zo was powering through her second mile. We had the same genetic advantages, I reminded myself. The same muscle tone, coordination, stamina—she'd just never bothered to use hers before. And meanwhile I'd used mine up.

"It's not that, either."

"What, then?"

"It's . . ." She looked me up and down, then grimaced, like it was my fault for making her say it. "Lia, I can't let you run with the team, not like this. It wouldn't be fair."

"What's not fair?" I asked. "It's not like I can run any faster."

"I have no evidence of that," she said. "As far as the league is concerned, you'd be running with an unfair advantage."

That was almost funny. "Trust me, there's no advantage."

"It's just not *natural*."

I couldn't believe it. More to the point, I couldn't *accept* it. I needed to run. "Jay Chesin runs with a prosthetic leg—*that's* not natural."

"That's different."

I closed my eyes for a moment. When I opened them, I caught her sagging a bit in relief, as if she'd spent the whole conversation waiting—in vain—for me to blink.

"What about the Ana League? I'd run with them if I had to." As far as I was concerned, it wasn't real running, not if you were chemically amping your strength and speed. I knew I'd never be able to keep up if I ran natural, but much as I loved my trophies, I didn't need to win. I needed to run.

The coach shook her head again. "They won't let you run either."

"But they're *anabolic*," I said. Paused, reminded myself not to whine. Be calm. Be rational. Be irrefutable. "It's a whole league for people who don't play fair. How can I be against the rules if there *are* no rules?"

"There are rules," she said, mouthing the official party line, even though everyone knew the Ana League was anything goes. "They wouldn't let you drive a car to the finish line . . . and they won't let *you* run. Not like this."

"But—"

"Lia, be realistic," she snapped. "You don't breathe. You don't get tired. For all anyone knows, you can run as fast as you want, as far as you want. Slotting you in would make a mockery of the whole race. Do you really want to ruin things for everyone else?"

I didn't care about everyone else. And until recently I'd never needed to pretend I did. When you're winning, no one expects you to care. They only expect you to keep winning.

"I guess not," I said.

"I really am sorry." Like we could be friends again, now that I'd let her pretend she was doing the right thing.

"Can I ask you something?"

"Yes." She looked like she wanted to say no.

"Is it actually written in the rules somewhere that . . ."

I still didn't know what to call the thing I'd become. ". . . people in my situation aren't eligible?"

The coach hesitated. "This particular . . . *situation* hasn't come up before. Not in this league."

"So you're just assuming, then."

"What are you getting at?"

"If the league didn't care—if I got my father to talk to someone and made it okay—would you want me back on the team?" I could have done it. I knew it, and she knew it. It's not about the money, my father always said. These days everyone has money. It's about the power. And he had that, too.

But that wasn't the question. I wasn't asking if I could bully my way back onto the team. I was asking whether she wanted me to.

This time she didn't hesitate at all. "No."

Friday morning was Persuasive Speech, a weekly dose of posture, comportment, and projection techniques intended to smooth our eventual rise into the ranks of social and political prominence. The road to power may have been paved with lies, but according to Persuasive Speech guru M. Stafford, said lies had to be carefully candy coated with a paper-thin layer of truth. Or at least, the appearance of truth.

M. Stafford, of course, rarely told us anything we didn't already know.

Of all the useless classes the Helmsley School offered—

and there was little else on the menu—none was more useless than Persuasive Speech. M. Stafford was big into tedious presentations on even more tedious current events, which didn't persuade us of anything except that we'd made an enormous mistake signing up for the class in the first place. A mistake, at least, for anyone who'd been expecting to learn something. For those of us expecting an easy A and plenty of time to lounge in the back of the room, linked in and zoned out while M. Stafford carefully ignored her snoozing audience, it fulfilled our every need.

So, all good. Except that while I'd been out "uh, sick"— that was M. Stafford's feeble euphemism—Becca Mai had transferred into the class, and M. Stafford had given my seat away. Which meant that Becca sat in back with Cass and Terra and Bliss while I was stuck at a broken desk in the front row, wobbling on the loose leg every time I shifted my weight and trying to pretend that Auden Heller wasn't aiming his creepy stare squarely in my direction.

I was—well, "sure" would be the wrong word, but let's say "willing to accept the possibility"—that Auden didn't *intend* to be creepy. He'd never been particularly creepy before. But then, he'd never been much of anything, except different, and not in the right way. Those glasses, for one thing. No one needed glasses anymore. At least, no one who could afford the fix, and no one without enough credit for that would have been allowed within fifty miles of the Helmsley School. There were net-linked glasses, of course, but those hadn't been popular since we were kids. Now anyone who wanted that kind of access (and that kind of headache) could just pop in a lens while everyone else went back to screens and keyboards. The only reason to wear glasses now—especially glasses without tech—was to look different. It was the same with his watch. They didn't even make watches anymore. FlexiViMs you could wrap around your wrist, or tattoo onto your forearm? Yes. But all the watch did was tell time, and—as I'd discovered one day a few years ago when one of Walker's idiot friends snagged the watch to see if it would make Auden cry—it didn't even do that right. A couple of miniature sticks swept out circle after circle, and you had to calculate the angles to even know the hour. And, yes, I was *smart* enough to figure it out, but why bother to do a math problem every time you want to know what time it is, when you can just get your ViM to flash the info and then move on with your life?

We'd been assigned to deliver a five-minute speech on a current issue that we felt strongly about. "We" didn't include "me." I'd been excused by virtue of my "uh, extended illness." I wondered how M. Stafford would, if pressed, describe my sickly condition. Did she consider death, in my case, to be a fatal disease?

Auden went first, stammering his way through some lunatic theory that the government could solve the energy crisis whenever it wanted, but preferred using the power shortage to control the cities and the poor, oppressed masses who lived there. He didn't explain where he thought all this magical energy was going to come from, or why, if the masses were so sad and oppressed, they never did anything about it. Everyone knew you could work your way out of the city if you wanted, and not just to a corp-town—although even that was better since you were guaranteed power and med-tech—but to a real life. If they didn't want to bother, how was that our problem?

Auden's conspiracy theories never came with much evidence or follow-through. I suspected he just liked getting a rise out of people with his flashy, if stupid, claims: *The corps are secretly running the country! The Disneypocalypse was an inside job! The organic farmers poisoned the corn crop and pinned it on the terrorists to scare people away from mass production! B-mods are the opium of the masses!* Apparently, if they made good slogans, they didn't have to make good sense.

Next up, Sarit Rifkin, whose speech on the importance of eating more red meat didn't include the fact that her family owned the county's only cattle farm and reaped credit for every steak sold. Cass detailed the criteria she used to select new shoes. Fox T. spewed five minutes of crap about his favorite tactics for racking up Akira kills. Fox J.—also known as Red-tailed Fox, less because of his long auburn ponytail than because of the time he and Becca started making out in her father's kitchen and Fox planted his ass on the stove, apparently so engrossed in the hot and heavy that it took him a full minute to realize the stove was *on*—got in about half a minute of arguing that chest lift-tucks should be mandatory for everyone overage and under a C cup before M. Stafford cut him off.

That was when Bliss, with her Fox-approved D cups, took the podium. She stood there for a long moment without speaking.

M. Stafford had the kind of voice you might use to talk to a mental patient, slow and measured and just a little too understanding. "Go on, Bliss."

Bliss shifted her weight. "I'm not sure I should."

"Are you sure you want to pass the class?"

Bliss reddened. Then glared at me, like she was daring me to blame her for going forward. "I wrote this last week," she said defensively. "Before I knew that—" She stopped. "I wrote this last week."

"Then you should be tired of waiting to deliver it," M. Stafford said. "Go on, we won't bite."

Bliss Tanzen *did* bite, I happened to know—courtesy of Walker, who had been out with her a few times before trading up.

She cleared her throat. "A mechanical copy, no matter how detailed or exact, can never be anything more than an artificial replica of human life."

I sat very still, face blank.

"It is for this reason that I argue that recipients of the

download procedure should not be afforded the same rights and privileges of human citizens of society."

I looked up, just for a second, long enough to note that everyone was staring at me, including M. Stafford. Everyone, with two exceptions: Bliss had her eyes fixed on her clunky speech. Auden had his eyes fixed on Bliss.

"You don't have to believe in something called a soul"— someone in back snickered at the word—"to believe that a person can't just be copied into a computer. They call it a copy because that's what it is—not the real thing. Just a computer that's been programmed to act that way."

M. Stafford wasn't going to stop her, I realized. Nor were Cass or Terra or anyone else. And *I* certainly wasn't going to say anything. *Four more minutes,* I told myself. Just tune her out and, when it's over, move on.

"Skinners can talk," Bliss said. Fox J.'s use of the term "tits" had been deemed too offensive for our sensitive ears, but apparently "skinner" was just fine. "But so can my refrigerator, if it thinks I need more iron in my diet. Skinners can move, but so can my car, if I tell it where to go. My refrigerator doesn't get to vote, and my car doesn't get to use my credit to buy itself a new paint job."

"She's not a car!" Auden said loudly.

I wanted to slink down in my seat—slink *under* my seat. But I stayed still.

"No interruptions," M. Stafford snapped. "We allowed

you the privilege of speaking your mind; please respect your classmates enough to do the same."

"My mind isn't filled with ignorant trash," Auden said. "And what about respecting *Lia*?"

I wanted to strangle him.

"You can stay silent or you can go," M. Stafford said.

Auden went.

M. Stafford looked at me, her face unreadable. "Anyone else?"

I wasn't sure if it was an offer or a warning. Either way, I ignored it. And when Bliss continued, I ignored her too.

When class finally ended, I stayed in my seat long enough to let everyone else drift out of the room. Then I waited just a moment longer, preparing myself for the inevitable onslaught of pity that would hit once I stepped into the hallway, Cass and Terra and random clingers assuring me that I shouldn't listen, that Bliss was a moron, that she was just jealous, that they were here if I needed to talk—which I did not. Nor did I need anyone's pity, but I would accept it with grace, because I had been well trained. Rudeness was a sign of weakness. Grace stemmed from power, the power to accept anything and move on.

But the hallway was empty. Only one person waited for me, rocking back and forth from one foot to the other, his fist clenched around the ugly green bag he always carried.

"You okay?" Auden asked.

I walked right past him, down the hall, around the corner,

all the way to the door that let out into the parking lot, where I could find the car and ride away. Let Zo figure out her own way home.

He followed. "She was wrong, you know."

I put my hand on the door, but didn't open it. I wasn't against ditching school, not in principle, at least, but I also wasn't about to let Bliss Tanzen drive me out.

"She shouldn't have said those things," he went on.

"It was an assignment," I said, my back to him, undecided. Outside meant blissful escape; inside meant more pretending, smiling dumbly as if I didn't hear the whispers that followed me everywhere. Inside meant going to lunch, facing Bliss and everyone who'd heard her. Everyone who'd sat quietly and listened. But outside meant running away, and I couldn't do that.

I wasn't the type.

"She was wrong," Auden said in a pained voice. "About the download, about you not being—"

I finally faced him. "First of all, she wasn't talking about *me*," I snapped. "*You* were the one who brought me into it, and second of all, thanks very much for that. You think I don't know she was wrong? You think I need someone like *you* telling me who I am? And now, like I didn't have enough problems, the whole school probably thinks we're—" *Rude enough*, I told myself, and stopped.

"We're what?"

"Nothing."

"Friends?" He spat out a bitter laugh, his face twisting beneath his stupid black glasses. "Don't worry. No one would think that." His black hair was short, almost buzzed, and his nose was crooked. Someone had done a really bad job selecting for him, I thought. It was one thing to sacrifice looks for athletic ability or freakish intelligence or artistic aptitude—everyone was, of course, only allowed to be so special and no more—but I happened to know he didn't have any of those things, or at least, not enough of them to justify his face. If I'd just seen him on the street somewhere, I'm not saying I would have assumed he was poor, but I wouldn't have assumed he was one of us.

And maybe that was his real problem: Credit or not, he wasn't.

"I'm not worried," I said. "And even if I was, it wouldn't be any of your business."

"I was just trying to help."

"If I were you, I'd focus on helping yourself. You need it more than I do."

"Meaning what?"

"Just look at you." The clothes: wrong. The face: wrong. The attitude: wrong. The tattered green bag that looked like something my grandmother would carry around: weird *and* wrong. "It's like you're not even trying."

"Trying to what?"

"Trying to be normal!" I lost it. "Look what you've got— and you're wasting it!"

A scowl flashed across his face, then disappeared just as quickly. "What I've got?" He raised his eyebrows. "You mean like a flesh-and-blood body? A 'normal' brain?"

"That is *not* what I said."

"Maybe I don't want to be normal," he said calmly. "Maybe it's okay that you're not."

"Who said I'm not?"

He just looked at me, like it was obvious, like I was stupid for even asking such a question when I was standing there forming a response with a brain that ran off the same wireless power grid as the school trash compactor.

"Why am I even talking to you?" I said, disgusted.

"You tell me."

"It was a rhetorical question." I brushed past him. He didn't flinch as our arms grazed against each other. "Just don't bother 'helping' again."

"Don't worry."

I didn't ditch school. I went back to class, kept my head down, paid attention. I went to lunch, ready to face Bliss, whether it meant an apology or a fight. But she wasn't there. Nor was Cass or Terra or their new boy toys or Zo or Walker. Becca, who would probably have spent the whole meal babbling about some species of frog she was intent on rescuing from extinction, wasn't there either. I found out later that they'd all cut out, grabbed lunch at Cass's place, and gotten an early start on the weekend partying. "I know we told you," Cass said later when I finally tracked her down. "You must have forgot."

Auden ate at an empty table tucked into a corner, half hidden behind a thick wooden pillar. I could feel him watching me.

I didn't eat, of course. But I took a tray of food and sat in the usual spot, alone.

It was the best meal I'd had all week.

DATE NIGHT

"Everything's okay."

"Y ou're going like *that*?" Zo asked, leaning in my doorway. The cat hissed at her from the foot of the bed. Psycho Susskind had, without my permission, made it his new home.

"What?" I braved the mirror again. Black retro shirt, baggy pants that looked like some kind of insect had gnawed off the cuffs, and—courtesy of an illicit raid through Zo's supplies— plum-colored lipstick and some kind of violet grease smeared across my eyelids. I looked like Zo. I also looked, as far as I could tell, like crap, but these days, so did everyone else who mattered. So at least I would fit in.

Zo rolled her eyes. "Nothing."

I shoved past her. "See you tomorrow."

"See you *tonight*."

I paused at the top of the stairs. "You're going?"

"Terra's picking me up in five," Zo said. "Is that a prob-lem?"

Like she cared. "No problem."

She looked like she wanted to say something else. But she waited too long, and I was out the door.

Walker's car was in the driveway.

"You're early," I said, slipping in beside him. "You've just been sitting out here?"

He nodded. "It's okay."

"If I'd known you were out here . . ."

"It's okay," he said again, and put an arm around me. His pupils were wide; he'd obviously gotten an early start on the night, tripping on something or a lot of somethings. But it didn't matter. Not if he was going to put his arm around me again.

"You ready?" He leaned forward, keyed in Cass's address, then paused, waiting for permission, like the old days.

I wondered what would happen if I told him that we should skip the party, that when he'd said he wanted to go out, I'd thought he meant the two of us, alone.

Before, I was the one who dragged us to parties. *Again?* he would whine, like a little kid, and it would be cute, but not cute enough to change my mind, so we would spend another night surrounded until the waiting got too intense, and then he would squeeze my hand or I would squeeze his ass and—signal sent, message received—we would sneak off together to one of the extra bedrooms or a closet or that spot between the trees or once, after everyone else had passed out, the glassed-in pool, our bodies glowing in the eerie blue of the underwater lights.

It was tradition, and keeping it tonight had to mean that he wanted to go backward. I wasn't about to risk a change.

I thought he might kiss me as we sped along in the dark; that was tradition too. But he stayed on his side of the car and I stayed on mine, and his arm rested on my shoulders, a deadweight that might as well have belonged to some invisible third passenger.

"Want to play Akira?" he asked.

"Not really."

"Mind if I do?"

"No."

Sometimes it felt like the body took over. That the body wasn't the stranger, I was—just a passenger, carried along wherever the body wanted to go. Because that wasn't me, letting Walker disappear into the network when I just wanted him to be with me—or, more to the point, wanted him to *want* to be with me. The strange voice that poured out of the strange mouth told him he could do whatever he wanted, I would go wherever he went, I didn't care, I was fine, everything was fine, it was all good. That wasn't Lia Kahn.

The car stopped in the usual place, at the bottom of the curving driveway that sloped up to Cass's guesthouse. Walker grabbed my hand before I could get out. He leaned close, and when he spoke, his stubble scratched against my ear; it didn't hurt. "Upstairs?" he said. "Later?"

"Definitely." I turned to face him, my cheek scraping

against his, but he pulled away just before our lips made contact. Even in the dark, his eyes were closed. "Later."

Inside, things were the same as always: bodies sprawled on the couches and across the greenish-gray carpet, writhing in the throes of whatever new b-mod mix Cass had cooked up; walls pulsing in time with the music; couples tangled up in each other; lonelyhearts on the prowl; screens encircling the room, set to flash up Cass's favorite vidlifes and a rotating selection of random zones; the lost dancers, gyrating to music that played only and forever in their heads; and in the glassed-in pool, girls with swanlike bodies skimming through the water, giggling, sputtering, chasing boys, chasing one another, the shifting patterns of their solar bikinis fading as the light disappeared.

The bikinis weren't the only tech. Sonicsilk, LBDs and LCD tees, net-skirts, girls in microminis smartchipped to grow—or shrink—when they bent over, gamers in screenshirts that broadcast their kills . . . Almost everyone was in something lit up or linked in, everyone, that is, except for me. And Zo, of course, who didn't count.

Bliss met us at the door, wearing a dress I'd seen before—a transparent fabric made opaque by the careful patterning of glowing light, but always, in its shifting translucence, offering the promise that if you watched closely enough, a glimpse of milky skin would slip through. She raised an eyebrow at my dead black shirt. Then leaned forward, voice lowered and fakely kind. "You should know, that retro look is totally wiped."

"Yeah," I said. "I got that." I turned to blast Walker for letting me walk in blind, not that he could be trusted on the subject, being barely able to dress himself, much less me, but I was decked out in freakwear and needed someone to blame. Too bad: He'd already slipped away, probably off to join the gamers or get zoned.

Terra drifted over, her face—like everyone else's—cosmetic clear, her shirt whispering melodies with every move. She stopped dead when she saw what I was wearing.

"Nice, uh . . . outfit," she said.

"You could have told me." It's not like we made some big announcement about which looks were in and which were out. But things got old fast, and when they did, either you knew—or you didn't.

Terra shrugged. "Since when do you need *me* to tell you what's wiped?"

Zo found me later, sitting in a corner, head tipped back toward the ceiling as if I were zoned. Anyone who knew anything knew that I wasn't in the business of getting zoned anymore, but it saved me from having to stare blankly at a wall or, worse, to make conversation.

Finally someone I could blame. "I can't believe you let me leave the house looking like this."

"What?" she asked innocently, perching on the side of the couch. "Like me?"

"You knew better."

"You're right," she said. "So why didn't you? Lia Kahn always knows what's cool, right? Lia Kahn decides what's cool. So what's *your* problem?"

I wanted to slap her.

"What's yours?" I asked instead. "If you knew retro was over, why come here like *this*?" I jerked my head toward her clothes, which were only slightly less gross than my own. But she was acting as if she didn't care that the look was wiped, and no one else seemed to care either. Like the rules were somehow different for her.

"Because maybe Zoie Kahn decides what's cool too," she said.

"You can decide whatever you want. It doesn't count if no one agrees. There's no such thing as a majority of one."

"Yeah, one's the loneliest number, so I heard," she said. "Two is working out a lot better for me these days."

"Two?" I scanned the room, as if Zo's new guy, if he really existed, would bear the mark on his face. "Who?"

She mouthed a curse, as if she'd broken something. "No one."

This was getting interesting. *"Who?"* Zo and I had never been the kind of sisters who stayed up all night, giggling in the dark about pounding hearts and stolen kisses. But she'd ruined enough of my dates with her tattling, her teasing, and, as she got older, her eavesdropping and clumsy stabs at blackmail. She was, and always had been, addicted to information about my personal life; the more personal, the better.

Karma's a bitch.

"I told you, *no one*."

"I'll find out eventually," I said. "You might as well tell me."

"Instead of wasting your time on my love life, maybe you should focus on your own," Zo snapped.

"Meaning?"

Zo tapped her wrist and I noticed that, like Auden, she was wearing a watch. Maybe *he* was her mystery man. Lame and lamer—they'd make a good match. "It's one a.m. : Do you know where your boyfriend is?"

"He's around." But nowhere I could see. I wondered if he'd gone upstairs without me, if he was waiting for me to find him. Or if he wasn't alone.

"He always is." Zo scowled and stood up.

"Seriously, why do you hate him so much?"

"I don't."

"You're usually a better liar that that."

"Believe whatever you want," she said.

I wanted to ask her something else. I wanted to ask her why she suddenly hated *me*.

I didn't want the answer.

"Later," she said, giving me a bitter half wave. "Terra's got some new boots she wants to show me. Weird, isn't it?" Zo smirked. "The way all your friends suddenly want *my* opinion?"

"They're just bored and looking for something different to play with," I shot back. "You're like their little retro *mascot*. Their token freak."

Zo shrugged. "Why would they need me for that? They've got you."

Venom released, she wandered off; I stayed where I was. I knew I should be circulating, but all I wanted to do was hide. Staying in place seemed like an acceptable compromise. And when I felt a pair of hands squeeze my shoulders, and a chin rest on the top of my head, I knew I'd made the right choice. I lifted my arms, let him grab my hands and pull me to my feet. "About time." I turned around. "What took you so—"

I yanked my hands away.

Cass's mouth breather leered. "Feels just like real hands," he slurred. "Dipper thought they'd be, like, stiff or some shit like that, but . . ." He slithered his fingers across my waist. I knocked them away. "Feels real enough to me."

Cass had always liked them dumb and pretty.

"You wanna know what's stiff?" He lunged toward me, resting his forearms on my shoulders, linking his fingers together behind my neck when I tried to squirm away.

"Fuck off."

He laughed. "I'd rather fuck something else," he said. "And I do mean *thing*. Come on." He plucked at my neckline. "I hear you've got all your parts under there, just like a real girl."

"I am a real girl, asshole."

"You want to prove it?"

I tried to knock his arms away, but they were too thick and sturdy, and the more I strained against them, the tighter his grip.

"Just because Walker's too chickenshit to take a test drive—"

This wasn't a dark and empty path winding through the woods, and he wasn't some Faither lunatic convinced that God had told him to screw my brains out—I had no reason to be afraid. But I wasn't thinking through reasons. I was thinking about this loser's grimy hands crawling all over the body—*my* body—and his breath misting across my face and his puny dick twitching at some fantasy of dragging me off and shoving himself inside me. All of which added up to not thinking at all. I punched him in the stomach.

"*Bitch!*" he wheezed, doubled over.

That's when Cass finally decided to show up. "What the hell, Lia?"

"She's psycho," the drooling pervert hissed, looping an arm around Cass. "Total nut job. Got pissed I wouldn't do her."

If the mouth had come equipped with saliva, I would have spit at him. "You sleazy piece of crap! Cass, come on." She was clinging to him, her arm tucked around his waist. "The perv was hitting on me."

The loser snorted. "Right. Liked I'd want *it* when I have *you*." He nuzzled his face into Cass's neck. She let him.

Terra popped up beside them, her boy in tow. The two guys smacked hands while Terra glared at me. "Trouble?"

"Trouble for Cass," I said. "She's dating an asshole."

"You were right about her," Terra's guy whispered loudly.

I turned on her. "What's that supposed to mean?"

"It means wake up, Lia," Terra snapped. "This isn't like before. You don't get to have every boy in the world drooling after you. Not anymore."

Cass rolled her eyes. "And contrary to popular belief—excuse me, *your* belief—they weren't all after you then, either."

"I never thought that—"

"Right." Cass choked out a laugh. "And you weren't hitting on my boyfriend just now."

"Why would I want this assface when I've got—"

"Walker?" Terra said with me. "You just keep telling your-self that."

"Walker and I are fine."

"Then take him with you when you go," Cass snarled. She tugged the mouth breather away, without looking back.

Terra shook her head. "She stood up for you. When you came back, and you were all—you know. She defended you. She said you were still the same person under there. That we should give you a chance, even if . . ."

"Even if *what*?"

She looked at me like it was pitiful, the way I couldn't figure it out for myself. "Even if it's *embarrassing*," she said, overenunciating. Slow words for my slow brain. "Being seen with you. Like *this*. And then you try to steal Jax?"

I hadn't even known that was his name. "I told you, *he* came on to *me*."

Terra shook her head. "I actually feel sorry for you. I mean, Lia was always self-absorbed, but whoever you are—whatever you are—could you be any more oblivious?"

"You know who I am," I pleaded. "Come on, Terra, you *know* me."

"Yeah, but there's an easy way to fix that." She walked away with mouth breather number two, leaving me alone again.

Walker found me by the pool.

"So it's okay? To get wet?" he asked, sitting down beside me.

I shrugged. I'd taken off my shoes and plunged my bare feet into the water. It was cold, or at least, I thought it was. Temperatures were still a challenge. "Everything's okay."

He dipped his feet into the water, then shivered. Cold—I'd guessed right.

"I heard what happened."

I shrugged again. That was an easy one for me, one of the first things I'd mastered. Maybe because it was so close to an involuntary twitch.

"You should have texted me," he said. "I was looking for you."

I'd been sitting out by the pool for almost an hour. He couldn't have looked very hard. "It's fine."

"So, were you, uh . . . you and that guy, you weren't—"

"You're seriously going to ask me that? You think I was lying too?"

"I don't know." He looked down, tapping his foot against the surface of the water, gently enough that it didn't splash. "I guess not."

Our shoulders were touching.

"You know what?" I said. "Just go."

He shook his head. Rested his hand on my lower back. Leaned in. "What if I don't want to?"

It felt like my first kiss.

In a way, I guess, it was. And just like back then, I wasted it, worrying about where to put my hands and what to do with my tongue and whether I should be moving my lips more or less—and then it was over. At least he didn't look too repulsed. His eyes were rimmed with red. But they were open.

Most people had vacated the pool area once I showed up. The ones who'd stayed behind were staring at us. We got out.

The grounds of Cass's estate were huge—and, once you got away from the guesthouse, mostly empty. We had a favorite spot, a clustering of trees at the top of a sloping hill—the same hill that, when we were kids, Cass and I had rolled down, shrieking as we bumped and slid, the grass and sky spinning around us. Walker and I stayed at the top. He was shivering.

"Nervous?" I asked. We sat facing each other, his legs

crossed, mine tucked beneath me so that I could rise up on my knees and reach for him.

He shook his head. "No reason to be."

He didn't ask if I was nervous.

Walker took a deep, shuddering breath, and then his mouth was on mine again, his hands at my waist, slipping beneath the black T-shirt. I stiffened. His hands on the skin— How would it feel? What would he think of the body when he saw it?

"You okay?" he whispered. His eyes were closed again, his face pinched, like he was expecting a blow.

"Okay."

"So, you can, like, do stuff?" he asked.

"I can do anything." I tried to force myself to relax.

Asking call-me-Ben about it, back in rehab, hadn't been the worst moment of that hell, not even close. But it had been humiliating enough.

"Can I get wet?" I'd opened with something easy. "Or will I melt or short-circuit or something?"

And call-me-Ben had had the nerve to laugh. "You're fully waterproof."

"What about sleeping?" Another lob. Working my way up to the real question. I barely heard his answer.

"The body will simulate the sensation of fatigue, as a signal to you that it's time to shut down for a few hours, give the system a rest. Tests show that it's probably a good idea to follow your normal schedule by 'sleeping' every night."

"Can I eat?" That was a no.

Just like there'd be no more bathroom breaks, no more tampons. At this point, call-me-Ben suggested I might be more comfortable talking to a woman, but by woman, I knew he meant *Sascha*, and I wasn't about to give her the satisfaction.

"What happens if I break?" I asked.

"You'll come to us," said call-me-Ben. "Just like you'd go to the doctor. And we'll fix you up. But if you take care of yourself, it's unlikely to happen. Although we attempted to emulate the organic form as much as possible, you'll find this body much more durable than the old one."

"Why?"

He looked surprised. "Well, for all the obvious reasons. It seemed economically efficient, not to mention—"

"No. I mean, why that, but no other differences? Why no superpowers or anything?"

Ben frowned. "This isn't a game. We're not trying to create a new race of supermen, no matter what the vids want to claim. This is a medical procedure. We want to supply you with a *normal* life, as much like your old life as it can possibly be."

"So . . . I should be able to do anything I used to do," I said.

"Within reason," Ben said. "Anything."

"What about . . . Well, I have this boyfriend, so . . . Could he and I . . . ?"

Call-me-Ben looked like he wanted to summon Sascha, no matter what I said. "As you've been told, your internal structure is—obviously—quite different. But the external structure mirrors the organic model completely."

I must have looked blanker than usual.

"You and your boyfriend will be fine," he clarified. "All systems go."

I didn't think to ask him how it would feel.

Now I knew: It felt wrong.

We didn't fit together: not like we used to. Our faces bumped, my elbow jabbed his chin, his legs got twisted up in mine, and not in a good way. Every kiss got broken by a murmured "sorry" or "ouch" or "not there" or "no, nothing, keep going" or, always, "it's okay," and we did keep going, his hands running up and down the body, my fingers searching his, trying to find the dips and rises they remembered, but everything felt different against the fingertips, distant and imagined, like I was lying in the grass alone, pretending to feel the weight of Walker's body on top of mine.

Things didn't get very far.

"Sorry," he said yet again, rolling off me. I pulled my shirt back on. It was one thing for him to touch the body, but I didn't want him to have to look at it while we were lying there. *I* didn't want to look at it. If I didn't have to see it, I could pretend. That was easier in the dark. "I can do this, I just need a minute."

"It's okay," I said. Like a parrot who only knew one phrase.

"I know it's okay," he snapped. "I just need . . ." He snatched a pill out of his pocket, popped it into his mouth. "It'll be fine."

"What was that?"

"Nothing. Just a chiller. Help me relax."

"*Another* one?" I knew he'd been popping them all night, and probably most of the afternoon.

"Don't worry about it." He rolled over on his side. "Okay. Ready?"

I pressed my hand against his chest, holding him in place. "You say that like you're gearing up for battle."

"What are you talking about?"

"It would just be nice if you didn't need to be totally zoned out before you could touch me."

"I don't *need* anything."

"Every time you come near me, you look like you're being punished."

"And what about you?" he asked. "I touch you, and you freeze up. It's like hooking up with— Forget it."

"What?"

"Nothing."

"Just say it," I insisted, and, maybe out of habit, he followed orders.

"With a corpse."

I sat up. "What a coincidence. Me being dead and all."

He sat up too, and hunched over his knees, cracking his

knuckles. "You have to admit . . . it's kind of weird."

"Oh, really? I hadn't noticed. Life has been oh-so-normal for me these last couple months. Not that you would know."

"What's that supposed to mean?"

"It means my life is shit," I spat out. "And where are you?"

"I'm here, aren't I?" Walker drove a fist into the grass. "What do you want from me?"

"I want you to be like you used to be."

"And I want you to be like *you* used to be," he shouted, "so I guess it's tough shit for both of us!"

Silence.

"You hate this," I said quietly. "Me. Like this."

"Lia, I didn't—"

"No." I sat very straight and very still. "Just admit it. The truth will set you free and all that."

He sighed. "Fine. I hate it. Not *you*. This. This whole thing. It's weird, it's gross, it freaks me out, but I'm doing my fucking best. I'm here, aren't I?"

"Because you feel sorry for me," I said.

"No."

Yes.

"Because you think you owe me something," I said.

"Don't I?"

Yes.

"Whatever it is, this isn't it." I stood up.

"Don't do this," he said.

"I don't need this," I said. "I don't need your *trying*. I don't need you *forcing* yourself to be with me, like I'm your personal charity case."

"I'm not telling you to go."

Which wasn't quite the same as telling me to stay.

"This is *you*, Lia. Giving up. If you walk away, just remember, that's on you."

"And if I don't walk away, I get stuck with someone who has to dope up before he can even look at me. I think I can do better than that."

"Yeah? Who?"

And that was the question, wasn't it?

Cass's mouth breather didn't count. He wanted to screw a mech-head, some kind of fetish fantasy, nothing real. It wouldn't count even if he weren't scum, which he was.

No one *normal*—and especially no one beyond normal, no one like Walker—would choose me, not the way I was now. But Walker was stuck with me, and I knew he would stay, mostly out of obligation, with a little nostalgia thrown in for flavor, because I knew Walker. I could keep him. I could sit down beside him and let him kiss me, ignoring the fact that it made him cringe. Ignoring the fact that when he touched me, it felt like nothing. Not because I couldn't feel his body on mine, but because the feeling was meaningless. It was like trying to tickle your own feet. Graze your fingers across your skin in the same places, with the same pressure, at the same speed, the mechanics all the same, but somehow the effect entirely different, the sensation lifeless. Not that I was ticklish at all, not anymore.

The old Lia Kahn wouldn't have hesitated. The old Lia Kahn knew she deserved better. But of course, the old Lia Kahn was hot. Her boyfriend couldn't keep his hands off her.

There was also the fact that I was probably in love with him.

"What am I supposed to do?" he said, still on the ground.

Not *The turtle is hungry.* Not *I'm sorry.* Not *I love you.*

Maybe I wouldn't have believed him anyway.

Maybe I would.

"I'm still Lia," I said finally.

"So? What's that mean? Staying or going?"

"It means you should already know."

LIFE SUPPORT

"I don't have issues, I have a life."

That was pretty much all it took to RIP my social life. Not
that I did much resting in peace. More like resting in
isolation and humiliation and doubt and regret. Just because you
can't take something back, doesn't mean you don't want to.

Just because you want to, doesn't mean you try.

By the time I got home and linked in that night, I'd lost
priv-access to Cass's and Terra's zones; I'd been blocked from
Walker's altogether. Everyone else followed their lead. I was
untouchable, on and off the network. People still stared; they
still whispered as I passed in the hall, with one big difference:
They no longer bothered to shut up when I got close. Instead
they got louder, so I could hear the words interspersed with
the giggles. Freak. Robo-nympho. Skinner slut. Cass spread
the word that I was a mechanical sex junkie, and her mouth
breather threw in some spicy details about my tendency to go
psycho when my lust was denied.

Walker didn't say anything, I was sure of it. But it was

obvious we were over. And rumors spread: I'd attacked him, torn his clothes off, tried to force him. I'd cheated on him with a toaster. I'd malfunctioned *in medias res*, blowing sparks in a *deus ex machina coitus interruptus* that saved him from a nasty mistake. I didn't deny any of it.

Neither did he.

Here's the part where I say that my friends were shallow bitches and I'm better off without them. That Walker wasn't good enough for me—that if he'd really loved me, he wouldn't have let me leave, not without giving at least a modicum of chase. That I learned a valuable lesson about true-blue friendship, or maybe that surviving on my own was more fulfilling than depending on people who, deep down, didn't really care.

Wouldn't it be nice to think so.

They were, in fact, shallow bitches. News flash: So was I. It didn't make me miss them any less. As for Walker . . . Life with a boyfriend? Far superior to life without. I probably shouldn't admit that, but what am I supposed to do? Lie? So my friends hated me. So my boyfriend hated touching me. So my life was one big game of let's pretend. Was that any worse than being alone?

Maybe it was, and maybe that's why I walked away. But I'm allowed to regret it.

"I don't get why I have to go in person," I complained. "Can't I just link in? What's the difference?"

My mother shook her head. "This is about growing

comfortable with your new physicality, dealing with issues of disembodiment and bodily alienation. You can't do that virtually."

"Physicality? Bodily alienation?" That did *not* sound like my mother.

"That's what the counselor said." My mother twisted the edge of her shirt, which she did when she was nervous, at least until my father noticed and forced her to stop. "She thinks this is crucial to a successful readjustment."

"Readjustment?" That was Sascha's term too, and I hated it. As if I'd emerged from a factory needing just a few minor alterations before I could rejoin my life. As if anything about this was *minor.* "I take it you're still quoting?"

My mother reddened.

My father, who'd been monitoring some board meeting as if we weren't even there, looked up from his screen. "You're going."

I went.

The group met in one of those buildings where they used to store paper books until no one wanted them anymore. You could tell because the shelves were still there, sitting empty, waiting for the world to change its mind and start printing with ink again—like that was going to happen. There were a lot of places like this, empty buildings that survived long after their purpose had died. Why go out for art, for drama, for literature, for fashion, when you could stay on the couch, safe from germs, weather, overexertion, crowds, annoying small talk, and get it all up close, personal, and on demand? I knew the corps had snatched up most of the useless land, keeping it around just in case. But I didn't know that *I* would be the just in case, me and all the mech-heads in a hundred-mile radius, forced to drag our not-quite-dead bodies to a not-quite-dead library and spill our souls. If we had any. Which, depending on who you asked, was seriously in question.

I was late. The other six were already there, their chairs aligned in a circle with an empty one waiting for me, right next to Quinn. Not my favorite person, but at least she didn't completely suck, which was more than I could say for the familiar face on the other side of the circle. Sascha offered up her best patronizing smile as I slipped into the seat. "Now that everyone's here, why don't we go around and introduce ourselves, so that our new members will feel more at home?"

Quinn slid a hand across her mouth, camouflaging her whisper: "If this is home, does that make her our new mommy?"

I smirked. "Kill me now."

"Lia, why don't you begin?" Sascha said loudly. It clearly wasn't a suggestion.

"Lia Kahn," I mumbled.

"Could you maybe tell us something more about your history?"

I shrugged. "I was born seventeen and a half years ago, on a dark and stormy—"

"I mean your recent history," Sascha said, all sweetness and light. "Is there anything you want to share about the circumstances that led you to be here today?"

"Circumstances." That was almost as good as "readjustment." Such a nice, neat word to sum up the smell of flesh crackling in a fire, the hours and days in the dark, the slices of frozen brain matter scanned in, tossed aside. Just a collection of unfortunate circumstances, nothing more. "You told my parents this was mandatory," I said. "And they bought it."

Sascha cleared her throat. "Okay . . . Quinn? Is there anything about yourself you'd like to share with the group?"

"Selected members of the group, maybe," Quinn said, glancing at the girl to her right, whose pale skin looked nearly white against the long strands of indigo hair. "I have plenty to offer."

Sascha moved on. Quickly.

The blue-haired girl was Ani, and had been a mech-head for almost a year. Judging from the effort she was putting into avoiding Quinn's gaze, she wasn't much into sharing. Aron and Sloane, who obviously knew each other—and, less obviously but still noticeably, played footsie beneath their folding chairs—were better behaved. Aron had traded in his disease-riddled, six-weeks-to-live body a few months ago; Sloane had tried to kill herself, but only half-succeeded, waking up immortal instead, courtesy of an ill-planned leap from a tall building that wasn't quite tall enough. They'd met in rehab.

And then there was Len. Perfectly proportioned and handsome, in that plastic, artificial way that we all were, but his looks didn't match the way he slumped in his seat, his limbs tucked into his body, his head dipping compulsively, flipping his hair back over his eyes every time it threatened to expose him. He slumped like an ugly boy nobody liked.

"Nobody likes me," he concluded at the tail end of a ten-minute pity fest.

"Can't imagine why," Quinn murmured. I turned my snort of laughter into a fake cough, which was an embarrassingly feeble attempt at subterfuge when you consider the fact that I didn't have any lungs.

"I hate this," Len said. "I just wish I could go back."

"But you've told us how much you hated your life before," Sascha said. "How you felt confined by the wheelchair, how you always felt that people didn't see you for who you are, all they saw was your body—"

"And *this* is supposed to be better?" Len exploded. "At least I *had* a body. At least when people stared at me, they were staring at *me*, not at"—he punched his fist into his thigh—"this."

"Everyone's a critic," Quinn murmured.

"At least it was your call," said the wannabe suicide. "You got to make a choice."

"You feel you weren't given a choice?" Sascha asked. I wondered how much she got paid for serving as a human echo chamber.

"I made a fucking choice," Sloane said. "This wasn't it."

Aron took her hand. "Please don't."

She pulled away. "What am I supposed to say? Thanks, Mom and Dad?" She scowled. "You know what happens if I try it again? They'll just dump me into a new body. I'm all backed up now, safe in storage. Even if I don't upload every night— They'd probably like that better, because then they get a clean slate. I wouldn't even remember trying to off myself again. Fuck, for all I know, it already happened, and everyone's just lying to me. They'd do it, too. They want me, they got me."

"You sound angry," Sascha said, always so insightful. "You blame your parents for not wanting to let their daughter die?"

Sloane rolled her eyes. "Wake up, Sascha. They *let* their daughter die. I'm just some replacement copy. And if I do it again, they'll make another copy. You think that'll be me? You think I'm her?"

"You *are* her," Sascha said.

"I know I'm still me," Aron said. "The same me I always was. I can feel it. But sometimes . . ."

Sascha leaned forward, eager. Hungry. "Go on."

"This is better than before. I get that," he said. "But . . . it's not just the way people look at me. It's like, I'm different now. My friends . . ." He shook his head.

Sloane shoved his shoulder. "I told you, they can't handle it? Whatever. Forget them."

"Yeah." Aron took her hand again, and this time she let him. I reminded myself I wasn't jealous. Two rejects seeking solace in each other. Nice for them, but it's not like I was looking to cuddle up with some freakshow of my own. "Sometimes I just think they're right. It's not the same."

"What's not the same?" Sascha asked.

"I don't know. Everything. Me. I'm not."

"Damn right," Quinn said, loud enough for everyone to hear her this time. "You're better, haven't you noticed? Or would you rather be lying around in a hospital somewhere, choking on your own puke and waiting to die?"

"I didn't say—"

"You said plenty," Quinn said. "You all did. Whining about wanting to go backward, like backward was some amazing place to be. Like you wouldn't be sick and your girlfriend here wouldn't be crazy and you"—she whirled on Len—"wouldn't be lame. In every sense of the word." Quinn stood up. "This is supposed to *help*?" she asked Sascha. "Listening to them whine about their *issues*?"

"What's supposed to help is sharing *your* issues," Sascha said. "And, yes, empathizing with everyone else's."

Quinn shook her head. "I don't have issues. I have a *life*. Something I'd advise the rest of you to acquire."

She walked out.

Quinn, I was starting to realize, had a thing for dramatic exits.

"Lia, you've been pretty quiet over there," Sascha said. "Do you want to add anything here?"

Everyone turned to look at me. I fought the urge to slouch down in my seat and turn away. I wasn't Len. I wasn't any of them.

"What do you want me to say?" I finally asked.

"Whatever you'd like," Sascha said. "You could weigh in on whether you wish you could go backward, as Quinn put it, or whether you'd rather look ahead."

I just stared at her.

"Or you could talk about how it's been being back at school. Any problems you might be having with your friends or . . . your boyfriend?" There was something about the way she said it that made me wonder what she knew.

"I don't have a boyfriend."

"When you were in rehab, you talked about—"

"I don't have a boyfriend," I said louder. "And I don't have any *issues* to discuss either."

"So you would say you've had no trouble adjusting to your new situation?" Sascha said. "You're happy? Nothing that's been said today rings true for you at all?"

I looked around the circle and suddenly saw how it would all play out. I would open up, confess all my fears about the future, I would empathize with Aron about feeling different, with Sloane about losing my ability to choose, even, maybe most of all, with lonely Len. With Sascha's help we would let down our guard, become friends, a ragtag group of survivors with nothing in common but our circuitry and our fear. We would go out in public, clumping together for strength in numbers, pretending not to notice the stares or the way crowds parted so as not to touch us—or maybe pressed closer, reaching out to oh-so-casually brush past so as to tell their friends they got a handful of real, live (so to speak) skinner. We would whine, we would confide, we would wish we could still cry, we would bond, we would hook up, make promises, break them, we would cheat and we would forgive, we would stick together, because we would know that we were all any of us had. And eventually we would tell ourselves we were happy. Well-*adjusted*.

"Something was true," I admitted, standing up. "You all need to get a life."

I prepared a story for my parents, something bright and shiny about how caring everyone had been, how wonderfully supportive—maybe so supportive that I'd been entirely re-adjusted and wouldn't need to go back. But it was a story I never got the chance to tell. Because when I got home, there was a strange man sitting on the couch, across from my father. A man I'd seen before.

My father beckoned, indicating that I should join them.

"This is the Honored Rai Savona," he said. "Leader of the Faith Party. He's come out here to apologize for the incident earlier when you first came home. The man who accosted you on our property?"

I hadn't told my father about the man in the woods—and I could tell from his look that he wasn't happy about it. But I knew he would never have admitted his ignorance to a stranger, and if I let it slip, things would be even worse. So I sat down and kept my mouth shut. The man kept his dark eyes on my father. I recognized him from the protest: He'd been the one in charge, the one who finally called it off.

"As I say, M. Kahn, his actions were in no way endorsed by the party, and he has been disciplined. A well-intentioned but sorely misguided soul. I take full responsibility for his trespassing and any damage he may have inflicted on"—he glanced at me—"your property."

"Are you talking about me?" I asked.

"Lia," my father snapped. "Manners."

"Because I'm fine, thanks for asking."

My father glared. "I appreciate your coming," he told the man. "And I trust you'll be keeping your followers off the grounds from now on? And away from my daughter?"

"There will be no more trespassing incidents," the man said. His voice was slow and rich, like honey poured out of a jar, the words pooling into a puddle of sickening sweetness. Except not so sweet. "And we'll maintain a respectful distance from . . . the recipient of the download process."

"By which you mean me," I said. "His daughter."

He took the challenge, finally turning to face me. "I'm sorry," he said, and, to his credit—or maybe to his acting teacher's credit—he sounded it. More than sorry. Heartbroken. "I bear you no ill will."

"No, you just don't think I'm a real person."

"I think looks can be deceiving," he said. "My reflection in the mirror may *look* exactly like me. Talk like me. Move like me. But that doesn't make it anything more than a copy. Nothing beneath the surface."

"Your reflection can't think for itself. It can't do anything you don't do."

"Just like you can't do anything your programmers didn't program you to do."

"No!" He was wrong. He had to be wrong. "I'm not a copy. I'm not a computer. I'm a *person.*"

"A person is created by God," he said. "Gifted with a natural body, a divine soul. A person thinks and feels, is born and dies. A *person* has free will. You, on the other hand, are a machine. Built by man. *Programmed* by man. You may look like a person and act like a person; you may even, in your own way, believe you're a person. But, no, I don't think you are."

"I have free will." I was, for instance, willing myself not to walk across the room and punch him in the face.

"You have a computer inside your head, a computer designed to operate within a set of man-made parameters. To react a certain way to one set of stimuli, a different way to another."

"If I'm just a computer, reacting mindlessly to *stimuli*, how come I'm free to make any decision I want?" I picked up one of my mother's glass miniatures, a crystal pig that was sitting on the coffee table, watching the argument play out. "I can decide to throw this at the wall or to put it back on the table. No one programmed me one way or another. *I* decide."

"You're arguing you have free will because you feel like you have free will?"

"Yes. Which proves my point. If I were just some mindless computer, how could I feel anything?"

"And how do I know you do?" he asked. "How do I know you're not just programmed to act like you do, to act like you have thoughts and beliefs—the belief in your identity, the belief in your free will, the belief in your humanity?"

"Because I'm telling you, I *do* have those beliefs."

"And that's exactly what you'd say if you were programmed to behave as if you were human. You would be programmed to respond to questions such as mine with the assertion that you made your own choices. Even when logic dictates that it's not true."

"You're wrong."

"I hope not," he said. "Because if you really *can* think in some way, feel in some way that I can't fathom, my heart goes out to you. Nothing is more tragic than believing yourself to be something you're not." He turned to my father. "I apologize if I'm speaking out of turn, but this *thing* is not your daughter. It has your daughter's memories, it emulates your daughter's personality, it may actually believe itself to be your daughter. But, much as you want it to be so, it's not. Your daughter is gone."

"Get out of my house," my father said quietly. You'd have to know him to recognize the tone as thinly masked fury.

"M. Kahn, I speak not to offend, but to help guide you to the truth about—"

"*Out!*" He grabbed the glass pig out of my hand and flung it against the wall, just over the Honored Rai Savona's head. *"Now!"*

The Honored Rai Savona didn't bother to duck. But he made a speedy exit, brushing glittering flakes of glass out of his hair as he left. Once he was gone, my father and I sat in silence.

"So, why do you think he calls himself that?" I asked. "'The Honored.'" Not because I cared, but because I couldn't think of anything else to say, and I didn't want to leave. This was the first time we'd been alone together since the accident. My father had already turned back to his screen. If I didn't fill the silence soon, the moment would end.

"He says it's a sign of respect for his 'flock,'" my father said, without looking up from his work. "Nondenominational, all-inclusive." He snorted. "And, of course, a handy way to get respect in name if you can't get it in deed."

It was confirmation that father didn't respect the man who'd called me inhuman. Confirmation I shouldn't have needed.

"We won't tell your mother about this," he said, like it should be obvious. Which it was.

"Of course."

More silence.

"Can I ask you a question?" I asked, thinking of the support group, of Sloane, the fabric of her skirt clenched in her fists. Sloane, who had wanted to die.

My father nodded.

"What if, hypothetically, something happened to me?"

He still didn't look up. "What would happen?"

"I'm just saying, what if," I said. "If I got . . . hurt."

"Then they'd fix you," he said brusquely. "I thought they explained all that to you. Nothing to worry about."

I had to edge toward it slowly, to give myself time to back away if I lost my nerve. "But what if it was bad? What if it was something they couldn't fix?"

"Then we'd get you a new body," he said, like it was nothing. Something I'd done before; something everyone did. "If you're worried about the expense, don't. It's all included in what we paid for the initial procedure."

"No. No, it's not that. I'm just . . . What if I didn't want it? A new body?"

He looked up. "What does that mean?"

"Well, what if, when something happened—I mean, if something happened, I just wanted . . ." *Not that I would want that. I wouldn't,* I told myself. It was the principle of the thing;

it was knowing I had the choice. "What if I'd told you ahead of time. No new body. What if I just wanted this one to be it?"

"Then we'd get you a new body," he said, with the same matter-of-fact inflection he'd used the first time.

"No, you don't understand, I mean—"

"No, Lia. I *do* understand." With my father it was always hard to tell the difference between disinterest and rage. Both were delivered in the same rigidly controlled voice, his lips thin, his face expressionless. "You're underage. Which gives me legal control over your medical condition. And I would prefer said condition remain 'alive.' So, in your hypothetical scenario, you'd be overruled."

It *was* just hypothetical. But he didn't ask for reassurance on that front. "Until next year," I said instead.

"Because?"

"I turn eighteen," I reminded him. "Then it's my call. Legally."

He gave me a thin smile. "Legally. Yes. If one were to play by the rules."

"You taught us to always play by the rules."

He nodded. "Necessary. Until you're in a position to make the rules. Which I am."

"So you're saying—"

"Lia, in case you hadn't noticed, I'm trying to work." He tapped the screen. "Which means I don't have time for your ridiculous hypotheticals."

"Sorry. Yeah, of course." I stood up. Backed out of the room. "Later, maybe. Or, whatever." So he didn't want to talk to me. Even about this. So what?

But then he spoke again. Without looking at me. Barely loud enough for me to hear. "I'm saying I won't let you die. Will *not*. Not again."

Upstairs, I sat on the edge of my bed, alone again. I didn't want to be dead, I knew that. Even living like this . . . It was living. It was *something*. I couldn't imagine the other option. I tried, sometimes, lying in bed, thinking about what it would be like: nothingness. The end. Sometimes I almost caught it, or at least, the edge of it. A nonexistence that stretched on forever, no more of me, no more of anything. The part I couldn't grip was all the stuff I'd leave behind, the stuff that would stay here and keep going when I was gone.

When I was a kid I used to wonder if, just maybe, the world existed only for me. If rooms ceased to exist when I stepped into the hallway and people disappeared once they left me, the rest of their lives imagined solely for my entertainment. Other times I used to wonder if other people thought—I mean *really* thought—the way I did. They said they did, and they acted like they did, but how was I supposed to know if it was true? It was like colors. I knew what red looked like to me, but for all I knew, it looked different to everyone else. Maybe to everyone else, red looked like blue, and blue looked like red. It was, I had to admit, just like the

Honored Savona had said. How could you ever know what was really going on in someone else's head?

What I'm saying is, when I was a kid, I knew I was real. I just wasn't sure anyone else was. And even if I didn't think that way anymore, I still wasn't convinced that the world could go on without me.

I didn't want to die.

But that wasn't the point. The point was now I *couldn't*. My father wouldn't let me.

Zo peeked into the room, hesitating in the doorway. "I heard," she said.

Big surprise. "That's what happens when you eavesdrop."

Zo scowled. "I wasn't—whatever. Forget it."

"I'm sorry." Not that I was, not really. But I didn't want her to go. "This day just sucks."

"Yeah." She looked like she didn't know what to say. Neither did I. Zo and I had never talked much before, and now we didn't talk at all.

"You think he's right?" I finally asked.

"What, Dad?" She shrugged. "What's the difference? You planning on another accident? Or should I say"—she curled her fingers into exaggerated quotation marks— "*accident*?"

I wondered, again, why she seemed to hate me so much. But I couldn't ask.

She might answer.

"Not Dad," I said. "The Faith guy. About—you know. All of it."

"There's no such thing as a soul," Zo said. "So I kind of doubt you have one."

"But the rest of it? About me being just a machine, fooling myself into believing . . . You think he could be right?"

She hesitated. Too long. Great—another answer I didn't want to hear.

"Forget I asked," I said. "Of course he's not right. I'm just—"

"I don't think you're fooling yourself," Zo said slowly. "And I don't think . . . I don't think it's true what he said. About it not being natural. What's natural anymore? Besides . . ." She glanced toward the window. The fog—or smog or haze or whatever it was—was bad today, so thick you couldn't even see the trees. "Nature sucks."

I laughed. She flinched.

"What?" I asked.

"Nothing." Zo shifted her weight. "I'm just not used to it yet."

"My laugh."

"Your whole . . . Yeah. Your laugh."

"Remember when Mom decided she wanted to be a singer, and she made us sit through her rehearsal?" I didn't know what had made me think of it.

A smile slipped onto Zo's face, like she couldn't help it.

"And we just had to sit there while she butchered that stupid song over and over again. What the hell was it called?"

We both paused. Then—

"'Flowers in the Springtime'!" Together.

She giggled. "Everything was going fine until you made me laugh—"

"*I* made *you* laugh?"

"You made that *face*!" she said accusingly. "With your cheeks all puffed up and your eyebrows scrunched. . . ."

"Yeah, because I was holding my breath, trying not to laugh at *you*, looking like you were having some kind of seizure."

"Okay, but how could you not laugh, when she kept singing that stupid song—"

"'Flowers in the springtime, apples in the trees,'" I warbled in a falsetto. "'Your hand in my hand, gone weak in my knees.'"

"She sounded like a sick cat," Zo sputtered.

"Like psycho Susskind, that night we left him outside in the thunderstorm."

Zo shook her head. "Like psycho Susskind, if we threw him out the window. Howling for his life."

"And when you started laughing—"

"When *you* started laughing—"

"I thought she was going to kill us both."

Zo grinned. "At least that was the end of her singing career."

"Career," I said. "Yeah, right. A bright future in breaking

glasses and shattering eardrums." I shook my head. "And remember when Walker showed up that night, I had to explain why I was grounded, but that just started me off laughing again, and then *you* started again, and we couldn't get the story out? I wonder if I ever did tell him what that was about."

"You did," Zo said flatly. She'd stopped laughing. "You texted him later and told him."

"Oh. Right, okay. How do you even remember that?"

"I have to go," Zo said. It was like the last few minutes hadn't happened. "I'm late."

"Where are you going?"

"What do you care?" she snapped.

I didn't say anything.

She sagged against the doorframe, just a little, not enough so most people would notice, but I was her sister. I noticed. "I'm going out with Cass, okay? Is that a problem?" But she didn't ask like she really wanted to know.

"It's fine," I said. "She's your friend now, right? Go."

"I wasn't asking for permission."

"Fine," I said again, even though it wasn't.

"Fine," she said. And she left.

I wanted to get into bed and shut down, forget the day had ever happened. But there were two messages waiting for me. That was bizarre enough, since pretty much no one was speaking to me anymore, not unless you counted the randoms I only knew from the network, and even if I did count them, they'd mostly faded away, since I wasn't doing much zone-hopping these days. When you ignored the randoms for long enough, they tended to get a clue.

The most recent text was from Quinn.

I'm going. And so are you.

It didn't make sense. Not until I saw the one that had arrived just before it, addressed to both of us. From an anonymous sender.

Congratulations, you passed the first test.

Then there was a time, a date, and an address.

Ready for phase two?

ONE OF US

"If you can't remember something, did it really happen?"

The car took an unfamiliar route, depositing me at some smallish house a little too close to the city for my comfort. There was a security field around the property, which lifted as I drove through. No one was waiting outside for me. I wondered if Quinn had already arrived. Or changed her mind about coming in the first place. It was, after all, slightly insane, showing up at a random spot in the middle of nowhere just because some anonymous message told me to. It was more than slightly insane to do so without telling anyone where I was going. But I had come this far; I was going in.

After all, what was the worst that could happen? It's not like I could die.

I knocked. When the door opened, the blue-haired girl from the support group stood behind it. *"You?"* I asked, surprised. The girl—Ani, I remembered—had spoken even less than I had at the session, revealing only that, aside from the technicolored hair, she was kind of blah.

"Sort of me," she said softly. "But not just me. Come in." She stepped aside.

The place was crawling with them. Mech-heads. Skinners. Freaks. And I mean, crawling, literally, since a few of them were on the floor, writhing against the cheap carpeting—or against one another—their eyes rolled back, their fingers spasming. It was as if they were tripping on Xers, but I knew they couldn't be, because they were like me.

No, I thought, trying not to stare, although they wouldn't have noticed. *Not like me.*

The house was sparsely furnished: white walls, gray floor, a couple of cheap couches set at haphazard angles to the walls and each other, and not much more. Ani took a seat on one of them, settling back against Quinn's arm. Quinn looked like she was home. There was an empty space next to them. I didn't sit. On the other couch slumped a tall, lanky mech-head with brown eyes, brown hair, and a sour look on his waxy face. And next to him, staring at me with flickering orange eyes, someone familiar. Jude something, one of the earliest skinners. A year ago he'd been everywhere on the vids, hitting parties, crashing vidlifes, popping up on all the stalker zones. And then, a month or two later, people had gotten bored—or he had—and he'd disappeared. A month was longer than most insta-fame lasted; he'd been lucky.

He'd also been a brunet. But now he was . . . something else. His hair gleamed silver, and the color bled down his face, streaking his forehead and cheeks with a metallic sheen. His bare left arm was etched with the snaking black lines of a circuit diagram. But his right arm, that was the worst of it. The pseudoflesh had been stripped away, replaced by a transparent coating that glowed with the pulse and flicker of the circuitry underneath.

He wasn't the only one. The writhing freaks were all streaked with silver, their skin painted with whirling diagrams or stripped away, wiring exposed. One had even decorated his bare skull with an intricate vision of the cerebral matrix that whirred beneath the surface. As Ani leaned forward on the couch, her shirt rose on her back, exposing a patch of bare, silvery skin.

"Stare all you want," Jude said. "It's important to know what you are."

"What *you* are. A bunch of freaks," I muttered. "What did you do to yourselves?"

"Not freaks. *Machines*," Jude corrected me. "And we didn't do it. We're just embracing it."

"You think this is funny?" I asked, disgusted. "You want to turn us all into a joke?"

"Not a joke," Jude said. "A machine."

"I'm no machine!"

Jude glared at Ani. "I thought you said she was okay."

"She is," Ani said, glancing at Quinn. "When her friend—"

"We're not friends," Quinn and I said at the same time. Only Quinn laughed.

"She sounded like she got it," Ani said. "And she walked out on the session. Seemed like a good sign."

"What is this?" I asked. "Some kind of stupid spy game? You go to those meetings and what, report back? To *him*?"

"Well, she's not stupid," Jude said. "There's that."

I stood up. "*She's* out of here."

"Stay," Ani said. "You belong here."

I shuddered. "I don't think so."

"It's better than Sascha's crap," Quinn said, stroking the silver streak on Ani's arm. "They know what they are. What *we* are."

"This isn't who I am," I said, backing away.

"It's who we all are." The guy next to Jude spoke for the first time. "Like it or not."

"Let her go, Riley." Jude flicked a lazy hand toward the door. "This is a place for people who want to look forward, not back. She's obviously not ready to do that. Not if she's still whining about what she was and denying what she *is*."

"I'm not denying anything."

"Your sentence is a logical impossibility," Jude said. "Not to mention inaccurate. Come back when you've figured things out. We'll wait."

"I hope you can wait forever."

Jude laughed. "What, you think you'll make it out there? With the orgs?"

"The what?"

"Orgs—organics. Nasty little piles of blood and guts. Humans. You know, the ones who hate you."

"No one hates me," I said.

"Yeah, you're not in denial at all." Jude shook his head. "Come back when you've grown up a little." He looked younger than me. But he was a skinner—looks meant nothing. "Well? What are you waiting for? Be a good little mech and get out."

"You're throwing me out?" Unbelievable.

Sorry, Quinn mouthed. But she stayed where she was.

"Have fun with your orgs," he said with fake cheer. "Take care of yourself."

"Take care of your mental problems," I advised him.

And left.

There was a mech-head sitting on the edge of the front porch. I winced as the door slammed behind me, afraid it would catch his attention. I'd talked to enough skinners for one day. Maybe for life.

But the mech-head didn't look up. He was hunched over, his fist wrapped around a switchblade, and he was carving something into the porch's rotting wood, except—

I gasped.

He wasn't carving the wood. He was carving his arm. The knife flashed as the point dug in again, slicing a gash from his wrist to his elbow. He shivered.

And then he finally looked at me, his lips drawing back in

a sickening smile. His teeth were coated in silver.

"Feels good." His voice was a sigh. "I mean, feels bad. But that feels good, too. You know?"

I shook my head. I didn't know.

But . . .

Pain, I thought. *I miss pain.*

I shook my head harder.

He tossed the knife and caught it neatly, gripping the blade. Then, like a knight making an offering to his queen, extended it to me. "You'll like." His teeth gleamed. Not like the knife handle. It was inky black, sucking in light. "You'll see."

"You're crazy," I whispered. I couldn't get my voice to work right. Just like I couldn't make myself walk away. "You're all crazy."

He just nodded.

And the knife was still there, waiting.

I didn't want it.

I did *not*.

"I'm not one of you," I said louder. Backing away. "I don't belong here."

The mech-head just shrugged and started carving again.

They were all psycho, I told myself. Freaks. Nothing to do with me. Nothing *like* me.

I'd been wrong to come; I'd been stupid.

I'd been stupid a lot, lately. But that was over. And smart

decision number one? Leaving this place, these . . . *people*.

Leaving—and never coming back.

One month passed.

See how easy that was? From point A to point B in three little words, skimming over everything that happened in between. As if it were possible to do that in real life, as if you could just shut your eyes and open them a moment later only to find: One month passed.

It's not. Days pass slowly; minutes pass slowly. And I had to live through them all. I went to school, most days, at least. I lingered in empty classrooms after the bell, then hustled to the next class at the last minute so I could slip in the door just before the teacher started droning. And again for the next class, and again. I ate lunch outside, alone, in a spot behind the lower school building where no one was supposed to go. No one ever knew I was there, because the biosensors deployed to catch students wandering astray couldn't catch me. I went directly home at the end of every day, taking the long way around to the parking lot so I wouldn't have to pass by the western edge of the track and see Zo and the others running heats across the field.

It got colder.

I didn't notice. Some afternoons I shut myself in my room, linking in and sending my av on missions across the network, avoiding the zones of anyone I used to know, racking up kills on Akira, thrashing players who lived on the other side of the globe and had no idea they were playing against a machine.

I skipped dinner. Even when my mother begged; even when my father ordered. And neither tried very hard. They didn't want me there either, stiff and still at the table, watching the mouthfuls of risotto or filet or chocolate mousse disappear. Then there were the nights when I slipped down to the kitchen, snagged a brownie or a cookie or anything chocolate, mashed it up with a fork, and tried to swallow it, washing it down with a swig of water in hopes of forcing something past the grate at the base of my throat. Not because I wanted to taste any of it—not that I *could* taste any of it—but just to see what would happen. Nothing happened.

I didn't upload, not anymore. It was supposed to be a daily routine; it was supposed to be my protection against the finality of death, every experience stored, every memory preserved, so that when the next accident came along, I—the essential *I*, the mysterious sum of seventeen years of days and nights and the best quantum computing credit could buy—would remain intact. But what was the point? If the worst happened, and I had to start over again, what would I need to remember? Waiting out the minutes behind the school until it was time to slog through yet another vapid class? Or maybe the moment Walker saw me, froze, then turned abruptly and zagged off in the opposite direction? Not quite treasured memories. So I let them slip away.

Nights, I ran. Factory specifications recommended that I stop running when the body reported its fatigue; that I "sleep" when the normal people slept. But I couldn't stand the way it felt. It would be one thing if I dreamed, but there were no dreams. It would have been okay even if there was just darkness. I had spent plenty of time in the dark. But shutting down meant surrendering to a blank; closing my eyes and opening them again, immediately, only to discover that hours had passed. When you sleep, your body marks the time. Yesterday dies in the dark; tomorrow wakes. Eyes open, you know. The body ages, the hourglass empties, death approaches, time is devoured but not lost. It wasn't like that for me, not anymore. I couldn't shut down without feeling like I was losing myself all over again, night after night. So instead I ran.

I ran through the woods in the dark, full out, without fear that I would stumble over the uneven ground or the broken branches blown across the path, running faster, maybe hoping I would fall, just to see if it would hurt, and if it did, maybe that would be all right, because feeling something was better than nothing. But I never fell. And I never stopped when I was tired. The body told me it was wearing down, but I didn't ache, I didn't cramp, I didn't wheeze. The body's monitoring system flashed red warnings across my eyes; I ignored them. The coach, before she'd thrown me off the team, had always said that running was 90 percent mental. That was for humans, I decided. (*Orgs.* The word popped into my head, but I ignored it, because that was Jude's word, Jude and his freaks, not mine.) For me it was all mental; the body, and whatever it wanted, was irrelevant. So I ran for hours, for miles, until I got bored, and then I ran farther until eventually I retreated to the house to wait out the dawn.

One month passed.

It happened on a Tuesday.

I was crossing the quad, the grassy, open-aired corridor between two wings of the school. There was an enclosed hallway too, and most people used that, not wanting to spend any more time outdoors than necessary. I preferred the cold.

I didn't feel strange before it happened. I didn't feel much of anything, which was the new normal.

Everything was normal. One foot in front of the other. One step, then another. And another. And then—

Not.

I was still. Left foot forward, flat on the ground. Right foot a step behind, rising up on its toe, about to take flight. Arms swung, one forward, one back. Head down, as always.

Move, I thought furiously. *Walk!*

The body ignored me. The body had gone on strike.

Being a human statue didn't hurt. It didn't wear me out. It felt like nothing. I felt like nothing. Like a pair of eyes, floating in space.

I couldn't speak.

And, like most statues, I drew a crowd.

"What the fuck!" more than one person exclaimed, laughing.

A couple people poked me. One almost knocked me over before another grabbed my side and steadied me on frozen feet. Laughing, all the time. Several of the guys helped themselves to a peek down my shirt.

Walker and Bliss passed by, hesitated, then kept walking. She's the one who paused. He pulled her away.

I stayed where I was.

"You think she can hear us?"

"Who broke her?"

"Don't you mean who broke *it*?"

Someone balanced a banana peel on my head. Someone else approached my face with a thick red marker. I couldn't feel it scrape across my forehead. But I could see his satisfied smirk as he capped the marker and stepped away.

Maybe, I thought, I was being punished. Maybe the Faithers were right, and I wasn't supposed to exist at all. I wasn't sure if I believed in God, but if He or She or It or Whatever was pissed off to see me wandering around all soulless and abominable, this seemed like a pretty effective start to the divine retribution.

"You think she's stuck like this forever?"

I thought so. The absence of body felt absolute. I was pure mind. I was floating. I was wishing I could float away, when the crowd parted, and Auden Heller came barreling through.

"Get away," he hissed at them. No one moved. "Get the fuck out of the way!"

Auden wasn't big enough to take on a hostile crowd; he was barely big enough to take on a hostile individual, and he was facing plenty of them. But they were facing Auden, half-crazed behind his thick black glasses. Maybe they saw something worth avoiding or maybe they'd just gotten tired of laughing at the frozen freak. Maybe their markers had run dry. For whatever reason, they got out of his way.

Auden wrapped his arms around my waist.

I don't need you to save me, I thought furiously.

"I hope this doesn't hurt you," he murmured.

Nothing hurts me, I thought.

I didn't expect he'd be strong enough to pick me up. He was. He carried me, my body stiff, my feet a few inches off the ground, my face staring blankly over his shoulder, watching the crowd, still laughing, recede into the distance.

"You'll be okay," Auden said quietly as we crossed the quad. "They'll know how to fix you."

I wondered what made him think I could hear. Or that I cared.

I wondered why he was bothering to help.

He brought me to the school's med-tech, but of course, that was useless. I didn't need first aid; I needed a tune-up. The tech voiced my parents, who must have voiced BioMax. Maybe they even went straight to call-me-Ben. And I waited, propped up in a corner, still frozen. Auden waited too, sitting in a chair next to my body, holding my hand.

"I'm coming with you," he said when the man arrived to take me away.

The man shook his head.

"Yes," Auden insisted.

The world flipped upside down as the man hoisted me over his shoulder. My face slammed into his back, and I was stuck staring at his ass.

"How do I even know you're legit?" Auden asked. "You could be trying to kidnap her or something. It's not like she can stop you."

"It's not like you can either, kid." The man, large enough to multitask, shoved Auden out of the way, using the arm that wasn't holding me.

"Let them go," the school tech told Auden. "He knows how to help her."

No one knows that, I thought.

The man carried me outside, out to the parking lot, past another crowd of jeering wannabes probably already posting shots to their favorite stalker zones. He carried me to a car and loaded me inside.

"Kid's right," the man muttered, folding me into the back. "I could do anything. Who'd know?"

His hand lingered on my leg, which he'd had to twist to fit into the narrow space. My limbs were rigid, but not as frozen as they'd seemed. With a little effort, they moved when he moved them. He rubbed his finger in a slow circle along the skin of my calf.

I can't even feel it, I told myself. *So it's not really happening. It's not really my body.*

"Almost forgot," he said, chuckling. He raised up my shirt, reached underneath. I watched the fabric undulate as his hands crept up my torso. I couldn't feel him massaging the patch of skin just below my armpit or carefully peeling it back to reveal the fail-safe, an input port that functioned only with BioMax tech and a well-protected access code; an emergency shutdown. But I knew what he was doing. And no matter how much I willed myself to stay awake, I knew it wouldn't work.

Don't, I thought uselessly.

There are some moments you'd rather sleep through, pass from point A to point B without awareness of the time passing or the events that carry you from present to future. And it's mostly those moments in which it's smarter—safer—to stay awake.

Don't.

"Sweet dreams," the man said.

Please don't.

Lights out.

"Don't," I said, and I said it out loud, in a different place, a familiar cramped white room, a too-bright light in my eyes, call-me-Ben's face inches from mine. I was back on floor thirteen.

"There you go," he said. "All better."

"What happened?" I remembered the car, I remembered the man's hands on my body, under my shirt, I remembered his sour smile, and then . . . I was here, awake, with call-me-Ben. As if no time had passed.

"I'd suspect someone hasn't been taking very good care of herself," he said. "And your system . . . Well, think of it like this: In an organic body, too much wear and tear, overexhaustion, and malnutrition weaken you, make you susceptible to bugs. This body, when mistreated, can fall prey to the same problem. Not germs, of course." He laughed fakely. "But every system can be crashed by the right bug—under the right circumstances. A temporary disconnect between your body and your neural network. Shouldn't be a problem again if you take care of yourself."

But that wasn't what I needed to know. "How did I get here? Who was that guy?"

"The man who brought you in? Just one of our techs."

"He knocked me out."

"He initiated a shutdown," said call-me-Ben. "Standard protocol. I'm sure it couldn't have been very pleasant, frozen like that. We didn't want to cause you any more discomfort than necessary."

"He just brought me here?"

Ben nodded. "Straight here, and we fixed you right up. We'll run a few more diagnostic tests, and then you should be able to go home."

"How long?"

"Shouldn't take more than—"

"No. How long was I out?"

Call-me-Ben checked the time. "About five hours, I believe. But they didn't start working on you until I got down here. So it only took an hour or so to fix you right up. Just a minor problem, nothing to worry about."

Five hours gone. Turned off.

And four of those hours lying in a heap somewhere, limp and malleable, like a *doll*, while the man, or anyone else, carted me around, did whatever he wanted. Or maybe did nothing. Maybe dumped me on a table somewhere, like spare parts in storage, and walked away.

If you can't remember something, did it really happen?

No, I decided.

Or even if it did, it didn't matter. The body wasn't *me*, not when the brain was shut down. They treated it like a bunch of spare parts, because that's all it was. It wasn't me.

Which meant whatever happened, nothing happened.

Nothing happened.

"You have to start taking care of yourself," Ben said. And there was something about the way he said it that made it seem like he knew what I'd been doing, all of it. It was the same tone Sascha had used when she mentioned my boyfriend. A little too knowing, like he had to restrain himself from winking. "Will you promise me you'll do that?"

"Can you guarantee this won't happen to me again?" I asked.

"If you stop pushing yourself so hard? Yes, I can guarantee it. So can *you* guarantee *me* this won't happen again?"

"Yes."

I didn't care what I had to do: I would never be that helpless again.

TERMINATED

"Computers think; humans feel."

When I finally got home, there was a message from Auden waiting at my zone. His av was weird, like him, a creature with frog legs and black beetle wings. It chirped its message in Auden's voice. "Are you okay?"

I ignored it.

But the next day at school, when he found me eating lunch behind the low stone wall, I let him sit down.

"You're not supposed to be here," I said.

"Neither are you."

"But they can't catch *me*." I nodded toward the biosensors. "No bio, ergo, no sensing."

Auden shrugged. "And they don't care about catching me. No one's paying attention."

"How do you know?"

He unwrapped a slim sandwich with some suspiciously greenish filling. "Where do you think I used to eat? Before you took over my territory, so to speak."

"Oh."

"'Oh' is right."

"So I guess I should thank you or something," I said. "For yesterday."

"I guess you should." There was a pause. "But I can't help noticing that you didn't."

I wasn't sure whether to laugh or shove the sandwich in his face. I certainly wasn't saying thank you.

"So what's in the bag, anyway?" I asked instead.

"What bag?"

I rolled my eyes. "That bag." I pointed to the green sack he always toted around. "Or is it just your security blanket?"

Auden flushed. "Stuff. Nothing important."

"Really?" I doubted it and reached for the bag. "Let me—"

"Don't!" he snapped, snatching it away. His fists balled around the straps.

"Okay, whatever. Sorry." I held up my arms in surrender. "Forget I asked."

"Look, I'm sorry, but . . ."

"I mean it. Forget it. I don't want to know."

I wasn't sure if I was mad at him or he was mad at me. Or if neither of us was mad. There was an uncertain silence between us, like we were deciding whether to settle in and get comfortable or to leave.

"What do you want from me?" I asked.

"What makes you think I want something?"

"We don't even know each other, and you keep—you know, sticking up for me. Being *nice*. And now you show up here. What is it?"

"So you think if someone's nice to you, it means they want something?" he asked. "Interesting."

"What's so interesting about that?"

"If I were a shrink, I might wonder what it means for your relationships with other people and what you expect to get out of them," he said.

He was so deeply weird. "What the hell is a shrink?"

"They were like doctors, for your moods. Someone you talked to when you were feeling screwed up."

"Why would you *talk* to some random when you could just take a b-mod to feel better?"

"This was before b-mods, I think," he said. "Or maybe for people who didn't want them."

"Sounds kind of stupid, if you ask me." Who wouldn't want to mod their mood, if they could? Something to make you happy when you wanted to be happy, numb when you wanted to be numb? I missed them more than chocolate. And what did I get in exchange? Eternal life, for one thing.

And to help with the feeling-screwed-up part? I supposed there was always Sascha.

I missed the drugs.

"And, by the way, my relationships are just fine," I said. "At least I *have* relationships, unlike some people."

"Oh, excuse me," he said with exaggerated contrition. "I forgot— You're *popular*."

For some reason, maybe because it was so far from reality, maybe because he made being popular sound like a fatal condition, maybe just because there was nothing else to do but cry and I was a few tear ducts short, I laughed. So did he.

"People are idiots," he said when he caught his breath.

"You don't have to say that."

"I'm not just saying it. Those girls you used to hang out with? Superficial bitches. And the guys—"

"Stop," I said.

"They're not your *friends*," he said. Like I needed a reminder. "They dropped you."

"I noticed. Thanks. But they're still . . ." I shook my head. "So is that what you think of me, too? Superficial bitch?"

"I think . . ." For the first time he seemed not quite sure what to say. "You're different now. And that interests me."

It wasn't an answer.

"So that's why you helped yesterday? I'm, like, some kind of scientific study for you?" I said bitterly. "Something neat to play with?"

"Why do you have to do that?" he asked.

"What?"

"Turn everything into something small like that. Mean."

"Are you trying to be my shrunk again?" I said.

"Shrink."

"That's what I said."

"I just want to know what it's like," he said. "Being . . ."

"Different?" I suggested. "It sucks."

"No. I know what it's like to be different." He wound the strap of his bag around his fingers. "I want to know what it's like to be *you*. To be downloaded. To have this mind that's totally under your control, to know you're never going to age, never going to die, this body that's perfect in every way . . ." He looked up at me, blushing. "I didn't mean it like that. I mean, I just . . ."

"Don't worry," I said. "No one's meant it like that. Not since . . . before."

He blushed a deeper pink. "You do, though," he mumbled. "Lookgoodlikethis." It took me a second to decipher what he'd said. "Better than before. I think, at least."

The body couldn't blush. Not that I would have blushed, anyway, just because Auden Heller gave me a compliment. The Auden Hellers of the world were always giving compliments to the Lia Kahns of the world. It's what they were there for.

But it was the first time in too long that I'd really felt like a Lia Kahn.

"Thank you," I said. "For yesterday, I mean."

"So what *does* it feel like?" he asked eagerly.

"Like . . . not much." It wasn't that I didn't want to explain it to him. I *did*, that was the strange part. But I didn't know how. "Everything's almost the same, but not quite. It's all a little wrong, you know? It sounds different, it looks different, and when it comes to feeling . . ."

"I read that every square inch of the artificial flesh has more than a million receptors woven into it, to simulate organic sensation," he said.

"If you say so." I hadn't read anything; I didn't want to know how the body worked. I just wanted it to work better. "But maybe a million isn't enough. I can feel stuff, but it doesn't feel . . ." I brushed my hand across the surface of his bag. This time he didn't pull it away. "It's like if I close my eyes and touch the bag, I know it's there. I know it's a rough surface, a little scratchy. I *know* all that, but I can't . . . It's just not the same. It's like I'm living in my head, you know? Like I'm operating the body by remote control. I'm not *inside* it, somehow."

Auden nodded. "The sensation of disembodiment, an alienated dissociation common to the early phase of readjustment. I read about that, too."

"That doesn't mean you understand," I snapped. "You don't know what it's like."

"I know I don't," he said. "But I want to, believe me."

I almost did.

The final note, a fever-pitched, keening whine, seemed to stretch on forever. It didn't fade, didn't swell, just sliced through us, a single, unending tone until, without warning, it ended. For a second everything froze—and then the applause crashed through the silence. A thunder of cheers and screams. The band went nuts, jumping up and down, smashing instruments against the stage, waving their arms in an obvious signal to the fans: more applause, more shouting, more, more, more. Only the lead singer stayed frozen, her mouth open like she was still spooling out that final note, this time in a register too high for us to hear. I felt like she was looking at me.

"Nothing?" Auden asked, stripping off his gear.

"Nothing." I dumped the earplugs and goggles on the pile of crap next to his bed. "But that's what I figured."

Auden had thought that maybe some live music—or at least, as live as it gets these days—would penetrate in a way the recorded stuff couldn't. That maybe it would get my heart pounding, even though I didn't have a heart; my breath caught in my throat, even though I didn't have any lungs; my eyes tearing up, even though I didn't have any ducts . . . You get the idea.

We both knew it was a long shot.

But I'd been willing to give it a try. And even though it hadn't worked—even though the music made me feel cold and dead inside, just like always—it was better, having Auden there. This time it didn't feel like a disappointment, or like I'd lost yet another piece of myself. It just felt like an experimental result—not even a failure, because when you're experimenting, every new piece of information is a success.

That's what Auden said, at least.

And that's what he called them: experiments. At least

going to a virtual concert was more fun than sticking my head in a bucket of ice water to see how long I could stand the cold. (Result: longer than Auden could stand waiting for me to give up.) We'd spent the week "experimenting," trying to see what I couldn't do—and what I could. It wasn't like before, on my own, when I'd pushed the body until it broke. This wasn't about testing limits, Auden said. This was about getting to know myself again. Because maybe that would lead to liking myself. Just a little.

I laughed at him for saying that—it was a little too Sascha-like for my taste. But I went along with the experiments. Partly because I didn't have anything else to do—or anyone else to talk to. Partly because I wasn't sure he was wrong.

"What's it like?" he asked now. "Linking in with your mind?"

"I don't know." He was always asking me that: "What's it like?" And I never had a good answer. *What's it like to breathe?* I could have asked, and stumped him just as easily. *What's it feel like to dream, to swallow, to age?*

"I mean, how do you do it?"

I shrugged. "I don't know. I just think about linking in, and the network pops up on my eye screen."

"But *how*?"

"Same way I do anything, I guess. How do I shut down at night? How do I stand up when I want to?" I asked, wishing we could change the subject. "How do *you*?"

Auden looked thoughtful. "I just do it, I guess. I want to, and it happens."

"Well, same thing," I said, even though we both knew it wasn't.

"So how come you can't do more?"

"More like what?"

"Like, you still need a keyboard," he said. "Why can't you just *think* commands at the network and make stuff happen? Like you did with the language hookup."

I'd told him all about the computer that had spoken for me, how horrible it had been. Except he didn't get the horrible part; he thought it sounded cool.

"I just can't," I said. "It's not the same thing."

"It should be," he argued. "If they have the tech to do it in the hospital, that means they have it, period. They could have wired your brain right into the network. It'd be like telepathy or something."

"It'd be weird, is what it would be," I said. "And they were trying to make us normal."

It had been call-me-Ben's favorite word, Sascha's too. *You are normal.* Or at least, *as normal as we can make you.*

"You've got to get over that," Auden said.

"What?"

"The normal thing."

Because I wasn't. "Thanks for rubbing it in."

"But you've got something so much better," Auden said,

and I knew where he was going. He had the same dreamy look in his eyes that adults always got when they talked about how I would never age.

"I wasn't afraid of getting old," I said.

"What about *not* getting old?" Auden asked. "What about dying? You always act like it's nothing, Lia, but it's everything. *You can't die.* What about that is not amazing?"

"I don't know. I never really thought about it much. Before, I mean." I'd never known anyone who had died. At least not anyone who mattered. Everyone dies, I got that. But I'd never quite believed it would happen to me. And now it wouldn't. That didn't seem amazing. Weirdly enough, it just seemed like the natural order of things. "I guess I've never really been too afraid of it. Death."

He paused and looked away. "Maybe you should be."

Somewhere below us, a door slammed.

Auden flinched. "Shit. What time is it?"

"Almost six. Why?"

"Nothing. Forget it. You should go."

I'd come to his house every day after school for a week, but I'd always left by sunset—until today.

Footsteps tramped up the stairs.

I put my hand on the door, but before I could open it, Auden grabbed my arm. "Wait," he whispered.

I shrugged him off. "What? I thought you wanted me to go."

"Yeah, but not . . ." He shot a panicked glance at the window, like he was trying to decide whether to push me through it. Anything to get me out of the house before whoever was out in the hallway came into the room. Before they saw me.

"Are you *hiding* me?" I asked loudly. "Embarrassed or something?"

He put his finger to his lips, silently begging. I couldn't believe it. At school he acted like he didn't care what anyone thought. He kept telling me that I was better off being different, if my only other option was being the same. I didn't believe him, but I'd believed that *he* believed it. At least, until now.

"Auden, you actually got a girl in there with you?" a man's voice called from the hallway. "Aren't you going to introduce us?"

"Just me," Auden called back weakly.

Screw him.

I twisted the knob. Opened the door.

The man in the hallway didn't look anything like Auden. He was blond and handsome, his features perfectly symmetrical, green eyes, rosy cheeks, square chin. He could have starred in a pop-up for a gen-tech lab. And the two little girls clutching his hands were just as picture-perfect. Their blond hair was tied back into pigtails; green eyes sparkled; identical dimples dotted their identical cheeks.

Auden had never mentioned having sisters.

He'd never mentioned much of anything about his family, and I'd never thought to ask.

The man shook his head, looking disgusted. "I should have known."

"Don't," Auden said quietly.

"Girls, go to your room," the man said. But the girls didn't move. They were staring at me. *"Now."*

Their giggles drifted down the hallway, then disappeared behind a door.

"Get it out of here," he said, glaring at me.

I bared my teeth. "Nice to meet you, too, M. Heller."

"This is disgusting," he said to Auden. "Even for you."

"We weren't—"

"You bring this on yourself, you know," the man said. I couldn't think of him as Auden's father. Not with the ice in his eyes. "If you would just try a little harder, you wouldn't have to resort to . . . *that.*"

"We're leaving." Auden grabbed my wrist and tugged me into the hall, past his father.

"Didn't you learn anything from what happened to your mother?"

Auden froze. "Don't." His voice had gotten dangerous.

"You're just like her, you know."

Auden stood up straighter. "Thank you."

His father snorted. "Take that out of here," he said, and even though he was no longer glaring at me, I knew what— who—he meant. "And you can take your time coming back. Tara's cooking a special dinner for me and the girls."

"Family bonding," Auden said bitterly. "How sweet. And I'm not invited?"

"Can you be civil?"

"Unlikely."

"Then enjoy your evening," the man said. "Somewhere else."

We didn't talk until we were out of the house.

And then we didn't talk some more.

Auden walked me to my car. I got in, then left the door open, waiting. After a moment, he climbed in too. His hands clenched into fists.

"You don't embarrass me," he said finally. "*He* does."

I didn't know what to say. "Parents are just . . ."

"It's not parents," Auden said furiously. "Just him. Parent. Singular."

"Your mother . . . left?"

"Died."

"I'm sorry."

"Why? You didn't kill her."

I looked away.

"I'm sorry." He touched my shoulder, hesitated, then drew his hand away. I didn't move. "It's been a long time, but I still . . ."

"Yeah. I get it." I didn't, not really. My mother wasn't dead; my father wasn't evil. I couldn't get it, any more than he could get what it was like to be me.

It was weird, how many different ways there were for life to suck.

"I'm sorry for what he said. He shouldn't have treated you like that."

I shrugged. "I'm getting used to it."

"You shouldn't have to."

True. But there were a lot of things I shouldn't have to get used to, and if I started making a list, I might never stop.

"So Tara's your stepmother?" I asked.

"She's the new wife."

"And the girls . . . ?"

"Tess and Tami. The perfect little daughters my father always wanted."

I wasn't sure if I was supposed to keep asking questions, but I didn't know what else to do. "Your mother was the one who wanted a son?"

He snorted and, for the first time, he sounded like his father. "No one wanted a son."

"I don't get it." *Everyone* got what they wanted these days, even if you barely had any credit. Looks, skills, personality, that was all more expensive, but sex was basic. Check box number one for a girl, box number two for a boy, and that was it. Case closed.

"My mother . . ." Auden squirmed in his seat. "It's going to sound weird."

"Since when do you care about that?"

"My mother was sort of old-fashioned," Auden said. "She didn't . . . Well, she thought genetic screening was, uh, tampering with God's work." He paused, waiting for me to react. For once I was glad that my face's default expression was blank.

Because what kind of lunatic fringe freak didn't believe in gen-tech?

"I mean, she let them do the basics," he said quickly. "Screen out diseases, mutations, all that stuff, but as for everything else . . ."

"You're a *natural*?" I asked, incredulous. Maybe I shouldn't have been surprised. I'd even wondered a few times, back when Auden was just another weirdo to avoid, when it seemed like no one would choose to have a kid like him. It would explain the crooked nose, the slightly lumpy body, and all the rest of it. But it was still hard to believe. Families like ours just didn't do things like that.

He blushed. "Pretty much." He turned his head toward the window, looking back up at the house. "Tara doesn't even know, although I'm sure she suspects. When she decided to get pregnant, my father made sure he got everything he wanted. I always kind of thought that's why he went for twins." He laughed bitterly. "So he'd have an extra, like a replacement for the kid he should have had, when he got stuck with me instead."

"I'm sure he doesn't—"

"Yeah. He does."

"So your mom . . . She was a Faither?"

"No!" he said hotly. "Not all believers are Faithers. Just the crazy ones."

"Yeah, but how do you tell the difference?" I muttered.

It just slipped out.

Auden glared. "It's not crazy to believe in something."

"My father says—" I stopped.

"What?"

"Nothing."

"Lia." His expression hadn't changed, but there was something new in his eyes. Something fierce. *What?*

I sighed. "My father says that believing in something without any proof is, at best, sloppy thinking and, at worst, clinically delusional."

"Well, my mother said that in the end, all we have is belief," he countered. "That you can't *know* what's out there, or who. And that denying the possibility of something bigger just means you've got a small mind, and you're choosing to live a small life."

"So I've got a small mind?"

"I didn't say that."

"No, your mother did," I snapped.

His face was red. "Well, I guess if she were here, you could ask her yourself. Too bad she's not!"

There was a long, angry pause.

"I'm sorry," I said finally. And I was, although I wasn't sure for what.

"This is why she wasn't a Faither," he said, his voice quiet. "She didn't think it was her business to tell other people what to believe. She was just happy believing herself. She said it made her feel like . . ." He looked down. "Like she was never alone."

I was almost jealous.

"Do you?"

"What? Feel like I'm never alone?" He barked out a laugh. "Not quite."

"No. I mean, believe."

He shrugged, still looking away. "I don't know. I used to try. When I was a kid, you know? I wanted to be like her. But . . . I guess you can't *make* yourself believe in something. Sometimes I think I do, I think I can feel it deep down, that certainty . . . but then it just disappears. That never happened to her. She was so *sure*." Auden shook his head. "I've never been that sure of anything."

"Maybe she wasn't either," I suggested, "and she just made it seem that way. Maybe that's what believing is—pretending to be sure, even when you're not. Ignoring your doubt until it disappears."

"Maybe." He didn't sound convinced. "Too bad I can't just ask her, right?" He tried to laugh again. It didn't work.

"You miss her."

His answer was more of a sigh than a word. "Yeah."

And maybe I could understand a little, after all. I'd never lost a parent—but I'd lost plenty. I knew about missing things.

"Auden, can I—can I ask you something?"

He nodded.

"All that stuff your mother believed in, about tampering with God's will and . . . all that. You don't . . . I mean, everything they did to me, you don't think . . . ?"

"No!" He shook his head, hard. "I know that was— I mean, I know she wasn't . . ." He pressed his lips together. *He doesn't want to insult her*, I thought. *Even now.* Like he thought she could still hear him.

But maybe I got it wrong. Because that really would be crazy.

"I don't agree with her," he said finally. Firmly. "I think it's incredible, what they can do. And what they did. For you. But . . ." He rubbed the rim of his glasses. "You want to hear something weird?"

I smiled. "Always."

"You know how I wear glasses?"

"Yes, Auden, I've noticed that you wear glasses," I said, hoping to tease him out of the mood.

"Ever wonder why?"

"I just figured . . ." I didn't want to tell him I'd figured he was a pretentious loser trying to look cool. "That you liked old things. All that stuff you're always talking about. The way things used to be."

"That's part of it, I guess. I do like that stuff."

"Because of your mother?"

"Well, sort of. But also because—I don't know. It was all different back then. There was more . . . room."

"More room?" I echoed. "Are you kidding? I thought you were supposed to be good at history. *No one* had any room back then, when they thought they had to live all crammed into the same place, all those people stuck in the cities. . . ." I shuddered. It freaked me out just thinking about it. Made me feel like the walls were closing in.

"No, I don't mean more room for people. I just mean more room to *do* something. Change the way things worked. You could be important. Now . . . I don't know. No one's important."

"Everyone's important," I said. "At least if you've got enough credit."

"And if you've got no credit, you might as well not exist?"

"I didn't say that."

"Yeah, but you thought it," he said. "Everyone does. And so all those credit-free people just end up in a corp-town or a city, and no one really cares, because that's just the way it is."

"But that *is* the way it is," I said, confused. "And they don't care, so why should you?"

"How do you know they don't care? Do you actually *know* anyone who lives in a corp-town? Have you ever *been* to a city?"

"Have you?" I countered.

I could tell from the look on his face that he hadn't.

"I don't want to fight," he said instead of answering.

"Then stop insulting me!"

"I wasn't— Look, I'm just saying, things weren't always the way they are now. But people act like they were. Like the past doesn't matter, because everything's always been the same. And like it should always be the same."

I didn't want to fight either. "So that's why you wear glasses? To change the world."

He took them off. His eyes were bright green, like his father's. "No, that's what I'm trying to tell you. I don't just wear them because I like old stuff. I actually . . . I need them."

"No one needs glasses anymore."

"Trust me." He squinted at me. "Without them, I can barely tell whether your eyes are open or shut."

"I don't get it. Why not get your eyes fixed?"

"I don't know. I guess wearing them reminds me of my mom. Like it's what she would have wanted."

That was . . . I didn't want to think it, but that was sick. "What if you got sick or something?" I asked. "Would you not do anything about *that*? Would your mother want you to—" *Die,* I was going to say. But I didn't. Because for all I knew, that's what had happened to her. "—just stay sick?"

"Of course not! I'm not crazy. It's just this one thing. Just the eyes," he said. "So, I guess you think it's pretty weird."

"Well . . ." I had the feeling he didn't want me to lie. "Yeah. *Very*. But maybe I get it. A little."

"I should go," he said, opening the car door.

"Where? Your father said . . ."

"Yeah. I know what he said. But it's my house, too. And"—he shrugged—"not like I have anywhere else to be."

I probably should have stayed—or invited him to come with me. But I was supposed to be home for dinner, and I couldn't picture bringing him along. Meals were bad enough without a stranger at the table, watching us not speak to one another.

I let him out of the car. "Good luck," I said, even though he was just going home.

"You too." Even though I was doing the same.

I saw Auden at school after that, but we didn't talk much, not like before. Not that I was avoiding him or anything. We just . . . didn't. Talk. And there were no more "experiments."

Then a few nights later, I came home, linked in, and: account terminated.

That was it. Two words flashing red across a blank screen. They linked to a text from Connexion, the corp that carried my zone.

A determination has been made that the owner of
this account, Lia Kahn, is for all intents and purposes

deceased. Although Connexion acknowledges that the entity now designated as "Lia Kahn" retains legal rights to the identity under current law, the corporation has been afforded a wide latitude in this matter. As of today we will no longer extend continuing access to recipients of the download process. As per standard protocol in cases of the deceased, when the next of kin has made no request for continuing access, the account of Lia Kahn has been deleted. We apologize for any inconvenience this may have caused. Have a nice day!

It was gone. All of it. My pics, my vids, my music, every voice and text I'd ever received or sent, every mood I'd recorded, everything I'd bought, read, watched, heard, played, all gone. Any evidence of the friends I'd had or the relationship I'd walked away from. Gone. The av I'd hidden behind since before I was old enough to pronounce the word. Gone. Proof that Lia Kahn had ever lived—still lived. Gone.

Terminated.

I panicked.

Which I guess is why I didn't scream for my father, who could probably have voiced someone at Connexion and bullied them into giving back what they'd stolen from me. I just linked into a public zone, I voiced Auden, and I told him I needed him.

Then I sat on the edge of my bed, waiting, wondering

what I'd been thinking, and whether he would come and what good it would do if he did, and whether I should voice him again and tell him to forget it. And I tried not to think about how my entire life had been deleted.

Psycho Susskind nudged his head against my thigh, then started licking my hand. He rolled over, and I rubbed my fingers along his belly, knowing he would pretend to enjoy it for a minute, then twist around and snap at me, tiny fangs closing down on the heel of my hand. He did, and I let him. "Think I liked it better when you hated me, Sussie." But I scratched him behind his ears, and I let him curl up on my lap.

Auden showed up. Zo let him in, which was lucky, because it meant no explaining. She didn't talk to me any more than she had to, which worked for me. So Auden was alone when he stepped into my room, hesitantly, with that look on his face that guys get when they think you're going to cry.

Even though he knew I couldn't cry.

"It's all gone," I said, even though I'd already told him. "They wiped me."

"It's just your zone." He stayed in the doorway, his eyes darting around the room, like he was trying to memorize everything in case the lights suddenly failed—or in case he never got to come back.

"It's my *life*. And you know it."

If I could cry, that's when I would have done it. But instead I hunched over and covered my face with my hands.

He sat down next to me, his hands clasped in his lap, like he was afraid of touching me. He'd done it before, but maybe that was why he didn't want to do it again. Who wanted to touch the dead girl?

"It could be worse, Lia."

"Is that supposed to be *helpful*?"

"No, I just mean . . ." He turned red. "I meant that this is bigger than just losing your zone, and maybe you're lucky that's all it was. Connexion's not the only corp that's trying this. I read there was this one guy who almost lost all his credit when—"

"I don't give a shit about some guy!" I exploded. "This is about *me*!"

Even I knew how hateful that sounded. But I couldn't take it back.

"What's going on?" he asked quietly.

"I'm pretty sure I just told you."

"There's something else, right? More than just the zone?"

"Like that's not enough?"

And here's the thing. That *was* enough. Maybe it was a little shallow to feel like my whole life was wrapped up in my zone, but that's how I felt. The network was the only place where I could pretend I was normal. Hidden behind my av, no one would guess what I really was. Losing it all like that, without warning? It was enough to be upset about.

Except that maybe he was right. There was more.

"Come on," he said. "What?"

"It's just . . . They said they terminated the account because I was dead. I mean, because Lia Kahn was dead, and I was . . . something else." I held my hand up in front of my face. It was so strange, the way I could hold it like that, without trembling, for hours. And I knew I could: We'd done an experiment. "I didn't tell you"—I hadn't told anyone—"but this guy was here. A while ago. This guy named Rai Savona."

"Such an asshole."

I should have known Auden would recognize the name. He knew everyone in politics; he actually cared. Yet another weirdness.

"He was here to—Well, it doesn't matter. But he said . . ." I didn't know why it was so hard to talk about. Maybe because the guy had made a pretty good argument. And maybe once Auden heard it, he wouldn't disagree.

"Everything that guy says is a joke," Auden said. "You should ignore it on principle."

"Is that what your mother would have done?" As soon as it was out I wanted to take it back.

"She believed, but she wasn't a Faither," he said in a monotone. "And I'm not her."

"He said I wasn't human, okay? He said I was just pro-grammed to *think* I was human, but humans had free will, and all I had was programming." It sounded even worse out loud than it had echoing in my head.

Auden raised his eyebrows and tilted his head, like, *Is that all?* "So what?"

"So . . . what if he's right?"

"Do you *feel* like you're programmed to act in a certain way?"

"Well . . . no," I admitted. "But he said that didn't matter. That I could be fooled into thinking I was free, but really I'm not."

"He's right."

I'd thought I had prepared myself for the worst, but when it happened, I knew I'd been wrong. Auden kept going.

"But it's true for him too. And for me. How do you know that I have free will? How do *I* know that I have it? Yeah, I feel like I make my own decisions, but who knows? He's the one who thinks God is in charge. How does he know God isn't jerking him around like a puppet? How does he know we aren't all just machines made out of blood and guts and stuff?"

"It's not the same." I knocked the side of my head. "There's no blood in here. No guts. Just a computer. It's not the same."

"No, it's not the same," Auden agreed. "But maybe it's better."

"Yeah, how?"

"You mean aside from the whole immortality thing?"

"Aside from that." Why did no one seem to get that living forever was only a good thing if life didn't suck?

Except you uploaded last night, an annoying voice in my head pointed out. *And the night before that.* No matter how crappy my life got, it was still my life. And sometime in the last couple weeks—sometime after meeting Auden, I tried not to think—life had become worth preserving again. Maybe even worth living. Too bad I still wasn't sure I could call it that.

If even I wasn't sure this counted as life, how could I expect anyone else to be?

"All that stuff you complain about," he said slowly. "Not feeling things the same way? Maybe it's a good thing. You don't have to get so screwed up by how you feel, like the rest of us do."

"'Us' humans, you mean?"

"I *mean*, maybe it's not a bad thing to have some control over your emotions. To be able to *think* once in a while instead of just act on animal instinct."

Human instinct, I thought but didn't say. *Computers think; humans feel.*

But he was trying to help.

"You think I don't get it," he said. When I was actually thinking how weird it was that he got me so well. "So maybe you should talk to someone who does."

"I am *not* going back to that so-called support group." I'd told him all about Sascha and her little losers club. "No way."

"I wasn't talking about the support group. Not the official one, at least."

"Oh." I'd told him about the rest of it too. The girl with the blue hair and the boy with the orange eyes. The silver skin. The house filled with living machines who wanted me to be just like them. But I hadn't told him everything. I hadn't told him about the knife. "Not there, either."

"You have to go back sometime," he said.

"Why?"

"Aren't you curious?"

"Not really."

"Okay." But I could tell he knew I was lying. "But I don't think that's why you're staying away."

"Tell me you're not shrinking me again."

"I think you're scared."

"Am not," I said like a little kid.

"Are so," he said, playing along.

"Am *not*."

"If you say so." He shrugged, and then turned to the screen. "You want to get started?"

"What?"

"Signing up for a new account with a different corp. Creating a new zone. Building a new av. Isn't that why I'm here?"

I flopped back on the bed. "What's the point? They'll probably just come up with some excuse to take it away from me again."

"You know what av stands for?" Auden asked weirdly.

"Avatar. I'm not stupid."

"Yes, but do you know why it's called that?"

"I'm guessing you're going to tell me," I said. More old stuff. Like the past ever helped anyone make it in the future.

"It's Sanskrit for—"

"I don't know what that is."

"A dead language," he said. "Really, really old. And 'avatar' is Sanskrit for 'God's embodiment on Earth.'"

"So?"

"So maybe, if you think about it, you're kind of like an avatar," he stammered. "Like, the ultimate avatar. You know? This incredible body that's been created as a vessel for Lia Kahn. Your embodiment on Earth."

"So you think my body's incredible?" I asked, smirking. Sometimes I went on autoflirt. Force of habit.

He blushed so hard I thought his blood vessels might actually burst. "That's not—"

"I know," I said quickly. "It was just . . ." Tempting to imagine that someone could still think of me that way. Even if it was only Auden. "Let's do it," I said. "New zone. New av. New everything."

JUMP

"You'll never be the same."

I'll go with you," Auden offered the next time we had what I soon began to think of as the Conversation.

"No, you won't," I said, "because I'm not going."

"Stop saying I'm scared!" I insisted for the hundredth time the following week. "There's nothing to be scared of."

But all that got me was a smug smile. "That's what I keep trying to tell you."

"It's not like I need more friends," I tried later. "I've got you, don't I? That's enough."

"Your flattery is embarrassingly transparent," he said. "Don't think it's going to work." But I could tell by the pink glow on his cheeks that it had.

"Why do you care so much?" I finally asked after one Conversation too many.

"Because I know, deep down, you want to go."

"Except I don't," I pointed out. "So try again."

"Okay . . . Maybe, deep down, *I* want to go."

That was a new one. "Why?"

"Aren't I allowed to be curious?" he asked. "You keep telling me I can never understand what it's like to be a mech-head without actually *being* one. Fine. But maybe this is the next best thing."

"You're serious?"

He crossed his arms and nodded firmly.

"You really want me to go, just so that *you* can go?"

He nodded again. "Consider it a personal favor."

I wasn't sure if he was telling the truth or if this was just his way of letting me change my mind without admitting that, deep down, I couldn't stop wondering about the house of freaks and their fearless freak leader.

"Okay," I said. "We'll go. But only because you asked nicely. And because I'm sick of you asking at all."

Auden grinned. "Whatever you say."

We took Auden's car. The coordinates Quinn gave me led us to a deserted stretch of road about an hour from his house, just a strip of concrete bounded on each side by a dark and desolate stretch of trees.

"You sure about this?" Auden asked as we parked the car on the shoulder and set out into the woods.

"*Now* you want to turn back?" *Say yes,* I thought.

"I guess not," he said.

We disappeared into the trees.

The night was black. Auden led the way, silhouetted against the beam of the flashlight. We followed the GPS prompts, hurrying along the narrow, bumpy path, twisting through the trees, ducking under branches, Auden shivering despite his thermo-reg coat. I couldn't feel the cold.

"You sure we're not lost?" I asked.

He peered down at his dimly lit ViM. "According to the GPS, we're almost—" He froze as the trees gave way to a riverbank dotted with people.

No, not people.

Skinners.

Although, in the dark it was harder to tell the difference.

They were lying in the grass, their flashlight beams playing against the trees, the water, the dark canopy of the sky. Beyond the treeline the night glowed with a pale, reddish light, just bright enough to cast flickering shadows on the fringes of my vision. As if, while watching, we were being watched.

Auden was still shivering. "Maybe we should—"

"Let's do this," I said, and started toward the group. He followed, careful to stay a few steps behind.

Most of them ignored us, but a few figures climbed off the ground as we arrived.

"No way," one of them said, a tall, slim guy I didn't recognize. "You can stay, but *he* goes."

"Lia, you shouldn't have." Quinn appeared at my side and

leaned in, her lips brushing my ear. "He's not supposed to be here," she whispered.

"This place is just for us," a girl's voice said. I thought it was Ani—especially when she threaded her arm through Quinn's—although it was too dark to see whether or not her hair was blue. "It's all we've got." She jerked her head toward Auden. "*They* get everywhere else."

Jude stood in the middle of the pack, silent. Watching.

Auden inched closer to me. "Maybe I should get out of here, let you—"

"You're staying," I said. "He's staying. And he's not a *they*." Just like I wasn't an *us*.

"He's an org," the first guy said. "He doesn't belong here. And if you can't get that, neither do you."

"He goes, I go."

The guy shrugged. "Fine."

"She stays," Jude said suddenly. His voice was deeper than I remembered. "They both do."

There was no more argument.

After his pronouncement Jude wandered away. We were good enough to stay, but apparently not good enough to talk to. They all ignored us, except for Quinn and Ani, who sat down again, tangling their legs together. We joined them.

This is it? I thought. Some lame, food-free picnic in the woods?

Quinn did most of the talking, at least at first. Everything was new to her; everything was exciting. Life was amazing. Wonderful. She couldn't get enough. I wanted to dig up a couple clumps of grass and cram them in my ears. Or, better yet, in her mouth.

Finally I couldn't stand it anymore. "So, Ani, what about you?" I asked. "What's your story?"

She looked uncomfortable. "I . . . I'm not sure what you mean."

"Why the download?" I asked. "What happened to you?"

"I . . . uh . . ."

"We don't ask those questions here." Jude loomed over us, his face hidden in shadow. "The past is irrelevant."

"Typical," Auden muttered.

"What?"

"I said, *typical*," Auden said, louder. "That you would think the past doesn't matter. It's a common mistake."

Jude sat down; Ani and Quinn leaped aside to make room for him. It should have made him less intimidating, down on our level. But somehow it had the opposite effect. Maybe it was those glowing eyes. "The past is irrelevant to *us*," he said, stretching his legs out and resting back on his elbows. "What we *were* has nothing to do with what we *are*. Not that I'd expect an org to understand that."

"Speak for yourself," I said. "I'm the same person I was."

Jude laughed.

"I think what Jude's trying to say is that the sooner you

forget about your org life, the sooner you can realize the full potential of being a mech," Quinn said, darting a glance at Jude. He gave her a small smile. She beamed.

"This is why I didn't want to come," I murmured to Auden.

Jude leaned forward. "Then why did you?"

"None of your business."

"Maybe you got bored pretending you still fit in to your tiny, claustrophobic org life," he suggested. "You're looking for a better way."

"Better?" I sneered. "If this is so much better, if you're all so superior, then why doesn't *everyone* want to be a skinner?"

Ani gasped.

"We don't use that word here," Jude said quietly. "We're *mechs*. And proud of it."

There was a long pause.

"Sorry," I said, only because I felt like I had to.

"As for your question, I don't *care* whether your rich bitch friends recognize my superiority. Some of us can make judgments for ourselves, without just valuing whatever the masses decide is cool that minute."

"I don't—"

"But don't worry," he said. "Even the rich bitches will catch on. Sooner than you think."

I stood up. "*This* rich bitch is leaving."

"So soon? Such a shame."

"All that crap about embracing potential, and *this* is what you come up with? A supersecret society that meets at midnight to—What? Sit around in the mud, gossiping? Lucky, lucky me to get a membership. I'll pass."

Jude shook his head. "You really don't understand anything, do you? This is just the staging ground. You can go if you want, but you'll be missing the main event." He stood up too. We stared at each other, and for a moment it felt like we were alone in the night. Then he shouted. "Ready?"

As one, the skinners—*mechs*—stood up and began walking along the riverbank. I looked at Auden, who shrugged. "We've come this far," he pointed out.

We hung back, but followed the group along the river, tramping through the mud for a little over a mile, a rumbling in the distance swelling to a roar, until we finally rounded a bend in the river—and stopped short at the edge of a cliff. The river tumbled over the side, thundering down the rocks into an explosion of whitewater below. Far, far below.

"It's a forty-foot drop," Jude said. He peered down the falls. "Eighty thousand gallons of water per second. Welcome to your new life."

The other mechs—there were seven of them—lined up along the edge.

"What are they doing?" I shouted, over the roar of the water. "Are you all insane?"

"It's incredible, Lia!" Quinn shouted back. "You'll love it."

I shook my head. "They're going to kill themselves."

"Not possible," Jude said. "They—we—can't die. Can't drown. So we get a little bashed up on the way down. Trust me, it's worth it."

Someone jumped.

One moment there were seven shadowy figures standing on the rim, the next, there were six. And a human-shape form disappeared into the churning water. I didn't hear a scream.

A moment later two more leaped into the air. They were holding hands.

"You're more durable than an org," Jude said. "This won't hurt you—not much, anyway. Although, I should warn you, it *will* hurt."

"So what the hell is the point?" I asked. Another mech took the jump.

And then there were three.

"The *pain* is the point," Jude said. "At least for some of them. For others, it's the rush. Like adrenaline or Xers, only better. Intense feelings—intense *pain*—it's the only kind that feels real. And for some of us . . ." He paused, just long enough to make it clear that he was talking about himself. And maybe about me. "It's about facing the fear—and conquering it. Mastering all those sordid animal instincts and rising above them. And having a hell of a good time on the way. Don't tell me you're not tempted."

I looked over the edge, just as Quinn and Ani jumped,

their arms around each other's waists. Way down at the bottom, I could see the water churning, but not much else. It was too dark to pick out any individual features, like bobbing swimmers. If any had survived.

"You can't actually be thinking about doing this," Auden said. "It's crazy."

"Crazy for *you*," Jude snapped. "You're not like her."

"And *she's* not like you," Auden said.

"Don't hold her back just because you can't move forward."

"Better I should let her jump off a fucking cliff?"

That was enough. "No one *lets* me do anything!"

Auden rubbed the rim of his glasses. "Lia, I'm just saying—"

"If *I* were an uninvited guest," Jude said. "I'd keep my mouth shut."

"Would you both shut up!" I shouted. "I need to think." They opened their mouths, but I walked away before either of them could start arguing again.

There was no one left on the edge of the falls. There was just me and the rushing water.

I'd never been much of a swimmer.

It was crazy. *Jude* was crazy. But what he'd said about the rush, about the pain . . . It made sense. Sascha had said the same thing about strong sensations flooding the system, fooling it into accepting them as real. Maybe it wouldn't matter that I had no goose bumps, no heartbeat—not when I was plunging over a forty-foot drop with eighty thousand gallons of water slamming me into the rocks. There wouldn't be time to notice what was missing. There would only be the body, the water, the fall. The fear.

To feel something again, to *really* feel . . .

I peered down, trying to imagine launching myself off the solid ground. I would bend my knees. Flex my ankles. Shut my eyes. Then in one fluid motion thrust myself up on my toes, off the edge, into the air, arms stretched up and out, and for a long moment, maybe, it would feel like flying.

Then I would smash into the water. And together, the water and I, we would crash to the bottom.

I can't die, I whispered to myself, testing the words on my tongue. They still didn't seem real. *I can do this.*

I *wanted* to do it.

A hand wrapped around mine. "We can go together," Jude said. "On three. You won't be sorry."

I didn't say anything. I didn't move.

"One . . . two . . ."

I ripped my hand away. And then I jumped—the wrong way. Into the shallow pool trapped behind a ridge of rocks, just before the falls. The water was nearly still, and I let myself sink to the bottom, settling into the packed mud. Everything was a murky black. And silent.

It was the first time I'd been underwater since the accident.

I could stay there forever, I realized, hiding out. Because I didn't need to breathe.

I had never felt more free.

I had never felt less human.

I launched myself off the bottom and exploded out of the water, scrambling onto dry land, soaking. Auden tore off his coat and wrapped it around my shoulders. I let him, although I wasn't cold. And he was still shivering. I grabbed his hand without thinking and squeezed tight. It was so warm, so human. I didn't want to let go.

Jude watched, disgusted.

"We're leaving," I told him.

"This is a mistake."

"This *was* a mistake," I said. "I'm fixing it."

Jude came closer, close enough that I could see his eyes flashing, his silvery hair glinting in the dim moonlight. "You don't belong with him. With them. You're strong, they're weak. *He's* weak."

"You're wrong," I said.

"Tell yourself that if it helps."

"What do you even care?" I asked. Auden squeezed my hand.

"I don't. But I can't stand waste." Without warning Jude's hand shot out and gripped our wrists, tight enough that I couldn't pull away. "And you're wasting your time, pretending that the two of you are the same." Something flashed in his other hand. The gray metal of a knife. "Don't believe me?" Jude's grasp tightened. He dragged the edge of the blade across my palm, then Auden's.

Auden gasped. Blood beaded up along the narrow cut, then dripped across his skin, thin red rivulets trickling from his hand to mine.

I didn't bleed. The knife had barely punctured the artificial flesh, and the shallow scratch was already disappearing as the material wove itself back together. Self-healing. Whatever pain there'd been in the moment was already gone.

Jude let go.

A moment later, so did Auden.

"You can pretend all you want," Jude said, looking only at me, talking only to me. "But you'll never be the same."

Auden walked me to my door. We had driven home in silence.

"I'm sorry that was so . . . I'm sorry I made you go," he said as we stood on the stoop. I wasn't ready to go inside.

"No. I'm glad we did."

"Liar." We both laughed, which helped, but only a little.

Auden rested his hand on my arm. "Lia, what that guy said, it's not true."

"No. I know." I ducked my head. He rubbed his hand in small circles along my arm, which was still wet. "He's crazy. They all are."

"Especially him," Auden said with a wide-eyed grimace that made me laugh again, harder this time.

"Thanks for coming with me. Really. I'm glad we went. At least now I know. And"—it was the kind of thing I usually hated to admit, but for some reason I didn't mind admitting it to him—"I couldn't have done it alone."

"Like I would have let you."

I gave his chest a light shove. "Like you could have stopped me."

"He was right about one thing, you know," Auden said quietly. "You are strong."

I didn't know what to say.

So I hugged him. His arms closed around me. I shut my eyes and pressed my face against his chest, imagining I could hear his heartbeat. Imagining I could hear mine.

"What's this for?" he asked, his voice muffled. I wasn't sure if it was because my ear was against his coat or his lips were against my hair.

"For nothing. Everything. I don't know." I held on.

But I opened my eyes. And over his shoulder, I raised my hand to where I could see it, still spattered with Auden's blood.

"Lia, there's kind of something I've been wanting to—"

"I should go inside," I said, letting go.

He backed away, and locked his hands behind his back. "Right. Well, good night."

Auden left quickly, but I didn't go inside, not that night. I'd learned my lesson about taking care of myself, and I'd been following a normal schedule—an *org* schedule, Jude probably would have said, his lip curling in disgust—shutting down for at least six hours every night. But not that night.

That night I sat outside, leaning against the front door, eyes open, wide awake as the reddish glow of night faded to the pinkish glow of a rising sun, remembering the thunder of the water, wondering what might have happened if I'd had the nerve.

If I had jumped.

TURNING BACK

"Maybe I wasn't programmed to want."

I hate it," I told Auden as we walked to class. The hallway was mostly empty, but not empty enough.

"What?"

"The way they all stare at me."

"No one's—"

"Spare me," I said.

"Okay. They're staring. But at least they notice you," he said. "Would you rather be invisible?"

I didn't want to tell him that he *wasn't* invisible, that all those people he hated were perfectly aware of his existence. They just chose to ignore it. "Let's blow this off," I suggested.

Auden looked doubtful. "And go where?"

"Who cares? Anywhere but here."

"We only have a couple more hours to get through . . ."

Since when did a couple hours of hell qualify as *only*? "Whatever. You stay. I'm going." I turned on my heel and headed quickly down the hall, but not so quickly that he couldn't catch up, which he did after a couple steps. He always did.

"You win," he said. "Where to?"

"Out." I pushed through the door at the end of the hall, wishing I could smell the March air. It no longer got much warmer as winter shifted to spring, but there was still something different in the air, something sweeter—fresher. Or maybe that's just how I like to remember it. "Then we'll come up with something."

But we wouldn't.

The exit we'd chosen was tucked at the end of a mostly unused corridor and opened into the alley behind the school, usually packed with delivery trucks, repair units, garbage compactors, and the steady trickle of students who'd elected to seek their education elsewhere for the day and preferred to do so without getting caught. But that afternoon it was empty except for a couple groping each other against the brick wall, her tongue shoved into his mouth, her back to the wall with her shirt creeping up to expose a bare, flat middle while his hands pawed her skin, snaking beneath her skirt. His fingers found her neck, her arms, her abs, her hair; hungry, grasping, needing, she sighed, he groaned, they breathed for each other. I couldn't see their faces.

I didn't need to.

I recognized the sound of him first, eager panting punctuated every so often by unprompted laughter, like a little kid, like an unexpected joy had overwhelmed him. I recognized his hands. Especially the way they crept beneath the skirt, massaging bare thigh.

It took a moment longer to identify her, although it shouldn't have, even without her face. I knew her arms, her legs, her sighs, her lanky blond hair. I'd just never known them like this. Or maybe I didn't want to know.

I let the door slam behind us.

They sprang apart. Walker looked up. Gasped. My sister took a deep breath and opened her eyes.

She looked like she'd been waiting for me.

I couldn't look at them. I couldn't look at Auden, either. I couldn't stand the idea of him—of anyone—seeing me see *this*. I wanted to run the scene backward, slip back into the school, back to the hallway, back to class, like none of it had ever happened. Some things were better not to know.

Because once you knew, there wasn't much choice. You had to deal.

Somehow.

"I'm sorry," Walker said. His hand was resting on her lower back. Like he was trying to keep her steady. *Her.*

"It just happened," he said.

"I didn't want to hurt you," he said.

He was still touching her.

"I don't know how it started," he said.

Enough.

"*I* know." My voice was steady. That was easy. My legs weren't shaking. My stomach wasn't heaving. My heart wasn't pounding. I was steady. "You shoved your tongue into her mouth. My *sister's* mouth. That's how it started."

"You're wrong," Zo said. And she was steady too. "I shoved my tongue into *his* mouth. That's how it started."

"Zo," he said, like he was pleading. "Don't."

"Why not?" she said. "Aren't you sick of this? How long were we supposed to wait?"

"How long?" I didn't want to know what the words meant.

I knew what the words meant.

"How long, Walker?" I asked.

He looked down. So this wasn't the first time. "After the accident . . ."

I wished for a stomach, so I could throw up. But there was no way of getting it out. It was all inside of me, stuck. Rotting.

"I was upset, and she was upset, and it helped to, you know, talk. To each other. And one day, we . . . we just . . . It wasn't supposed to happen."

"So, just to be clear. I almost *died*," I said, still calm, still steady, "and while I was learning how to walk again, fighting to *survive*, you were back here, *fucking my little sister?*"

"We weren't doing that." Zo paused. "Not then."

"This is disgusting," I said. "You're disgusting."

"Lia—"

Zo put her hand on his arm, and he stopped talking.

Apparently she was the boss. I'd taught her well. "I told you this would happen," she said quietly. "Just let it go."

"Oh, you *told* him this would happen?" I laughed bitterly. "What, that I'd have the nerve to get upset about my boyfriend screwing my sister?"

"I'm not your boyfriend anymore, Lia. You made that clear."

"Lucky you, right?" I spat out. "So you could ditch me and go back to the one you really wanted." Now it made sense. Why he hadn't wanted to touch me, why he hadn't wanted to be with me. Why he hadn't wanted me. Maybe it wasn't me.

It was *her*.

"We stopped for you," he said. "I was willing to try. I told you that."

Right. Because he pitied me.

"Give him a break," Zo said. "You don't know what he was willing to give up for you."

"I guess I do know, now," I said. *"You."*

I didn't ask if they actually thought they were in love. I didn't have to. I didn't care.

"Why?" I asked. Not Walker; he wasn't worth it. I asked her.

"I don't know," she said lamely. "It just happened." But she was lying, I knew that. Nothing "just happened" to Zo. It wasn't the way she ran her life.

I didn't have to push it. I could let this be like all the other times, when I just let it go, when I pretended things between us were the same as before, that she was just being Zo, nothing more, nothing less. I could keep pretending.

Except I *couldn't* keep pretending. Not anymore.

"I mean, why do you hate me this much?"

Her expression didn't change. "I don't hate you."

"You've got a weird way of showing it."

"What do you want from me?" Zo asked. "You want me to give him up? For *you*?"

That would be a start.

"Blood is thicker than water, right?" she said, her lip curling into a sneer.

"Well, yeah."

"Then show me," she said flatly.

"What?"

"Your blood."

The anger was a flood, drowning my words.

"I can't believe you," I finally choked out. "Literally, I can't believe this is happening. You're my *sister*. How the hell can you do this to me?"

"It's not my fault he doesn't want you anymore. None of this is my fault."

"It's all your fault!" I screamed. "*You* should have been the one in that car. It should have been *you*!"

The world froze.

I'd never said it out loud before. I'd promised myself. I

wouldn't say it, I wouldn't think it, I wouldn't feel it. I *would not* blame her. I wouldn't process the ifs. *If* she'd been in the car, *if* she'd died that day instead of me. I would still have my body. I would still have my boyfriend. I would still have my life.

I couldn't take it back.

Walker put an arm around her shoulder.

"Sorry to disappoint you," she said slowly, her voice cold. "But it wasn't me. It was you." I didn't know what she was thinking. We were sisters, but I never knew what she was thinking. She wrapped her arm around Walker's waist. "Let's go," she murmured. He nodded.

"I'm sorry," he said again, over his shoulder as they walked away.

She never turned back.

I don't know how I ended up on the ground. But suddenly that's where I was, sitting with my back to the wall, only a few feet from where they'd been kissing.

Auden sat next to me. I still couldn't look at him. Not that I wanted him to go—but I didn't want him to stay, either. I didn't want anything except to not know. My brain was a computer: It should have been possible to delete.

"He's not good enough for you," Auden said finally.

I wanted to laugh. Such a lame cliché. True—but still lame.

"And your sister . . . You know she didn't mean what she said."

"She meant it," I said flatly. Zo had only told one lie that afternoon—that she didn't hate me. Because obviously she did. Fine. That made us even.

"Okay, so she's a bitch and he's an asshole." Auden looked hopeful. "Does that help?"

I had to laugh. "No. But thank you."

"Do you think— No, never mind."

"What?" I asked.

"It's none of my business."

"Auden, I think we've just established you're the only one I've got. So if it's not your business, then whose would it be?"

"I was just wondering . . ." He hesitated. "I mean, you're obviously upset."

"You noticed."

"Is it because you still . . . I mean, if Walker wanted to get back together, would you . . . ?"

"You want to know if I'm still in love with him?" I asked.

He nodded. "But like I say, it's not really my business, so . . ."

"It's fine." I just wasn't sure how to answer. "I'm over him, I think," I said, and it felt true. "If he was with someone else, anyone but—" I couldn't say it out loud. Instead I lowered my head and pressed the heels of my hands over my eyes. "What he said, about being willing to try? He was. And what if he's the only one who . . . What if no other guy . . . I mean, who would want me like this?"

His hand brushed my neck, flitted to my shoulder, then disappeared. "He's not the only one."

"Whatever."

"No. Lia. I've been waiting to—I mean, I didn't know how—I have to tell you—" The hand was back, resting firmly on my shoulder this time, heavy. "He's not the only one who would. Want you. Like this."

Shit.

"Auden, you don't have to—"

But he wouldn't stop.

"I know you probably don't see me like that," he said, talking quickly, like if he paused for breath he wouldn't get himself going again, although I guess that was too much to ask for. "But I think you're amazing and when I'm with you, it's like we really understand each other, you know, and I think you're beautiful, you're more beautiful like this than you ever were before—"

Not now, I thought, furious with him, furious with myself. *Not now, when I need you. Don't do this.*

"I know I shouldn't say anything, I know, I always say something, I always ruin things, I should just let it happen, but I can't let you think that no one would—because I would, I do, I just . . ." His entire body had gone rigid. "What do you think?"

"I'm a little . . . This has been a weird day for me," I said, stalling. "You know, with—" I glanced toward the spot they'd been leaning against, where I imagined I could still see their afterimage bright against the bricks.

"I know." He shook himself all over. "I know. It was stupid. Bad timing."

Damn right. But, "No, it's okay."

"It's *not* okay. It's stupid. I shouldn't have thought—"

I kissed him.

Because he wanted me to. Because he *wanted* me. Because no one else did. Because he'd saved me, more than once.

Because why not?

And in the fairy tale that's it, the end, happily ever after.

In the fairy tale they never mention the part about your tongues scraping against each other or your foreheads bumping or your nose getting bent and flattened or his tongue just sitting there in your mouth, limp and wet, and then spinning around like a pinwheel, bouncing back and forth between your fake palate and your porcelain teeth. In the fairy tale they never mention how it tastes, although to me it didn't taste like anything at all.

I'm not saying he was a bad kisser.

I'm not saying he was great, because he wasn't. But I'm not saying it was his fault, even though maybe it was. Or maybe it was mine.

I'm just saying it was bad.

Worse than bad. It was nothing. Like kissing my own balled-up fist, as I'd done for practice when I was a kid. I wanted not to care, to just go with it, because it would have been so easy, it would have made him happy, and it would have made me . . . not alone.

When our faces separated, he was smiling, his eyes glazed and dewy, his mouth half open, like he wasn't sure whether to speak or to lunge in for another round.

"I'm sorry," I said as gently as I could. "I can't."

"Did I do something wrong?"

"No!" I said quickly. "I just don't think it's a good idea."

He sagged, a deflated balloon. "I should have known you would never . . . not with me."

"It's not that," I said. "It's just too much right now."

"You don't have to say that," he said bitterly. "I know I'm not Walker. I do have a mirror, you know. I get it."

"It *not* you." I wanted to touch him, to shake him. "Everything's so . . . screwed up. And I'm"—I gestured down at myself, at the body—"I'm different. *We're* different, and I don't think the two of us . . ."

"Is this about what that guy said? Jude?" Auden's fingers flickered across the bandage on his palm. "I told you, he doesn't know what he's talking about."

"It's not about what he said. It's what I know. This wouldn't work. And if it didn't . . ." Now I did touch him—I took his hand. He pulled away. "I don't want to mess this up, what we have. I can't risk that."

"Why not?" He was edging toward a whine. "If you really want something, sometimes it's worth taking a chance."

But what if you really *didn't* want something?

"It's not going to work, Auden."

"Because you don't *want* it to work," he snapped.

"Because it won't!" Why couldn't he just let it go? "Stop pushing it!"

"I know you're scared," he said. "I'm scared too. But we can try this together. We *can*."

I needed to make him stop. And I was pretty sure I knew how to do it.

"Why do you really want this so bad?" I asked in a low voice. "Is it me, or is it this stupid body?"

His eyes widened. "What?"

"Admit it, you're obsessed with what I am, with what it's like being a mech, with everything about it—"

"Because I'm your friend," he protested. "Because I care!"

"But that came later. You were obsessed before—before you even knew me. You couldn't stay away."

"So I was curious! So what? And you know I was just try-ing to help."

"Maybe—or maybe you've got some weird mech fetish. And you can't stop until you know how *everything* works, right?"

He drew himself up very straight and very still. "I can't believe you would say that."

I couldn't believe it either. And I couldn't keep going, even if it was the one thing guaranteed to drive him away. Because

I didn't want him to go away. I just wanted him to shut up and leave it alone.

"I didn't mean it," I admitted.

"I would never . . ." I could barely hear him. "That's not who I am."

"I know."

Then neither of us said anything. We just sat with our backs to the wall and our shoulders almost, but not quite, touching.

"I shouldn't have pushed," he said, finally cutting through the dead air.

"I shouldn't have said that to you. That was cruel."

Another long pause.

"We would never have been friends, would we, if it weren't for your accident," he said, asking a question that wasn't a question. "We probably would have graduated without ever having a single conversation."

I kept staring straight ahead. "Probably."

"And even if we had talked . . ."

"You would have hated me," I said. "Shallow, superficial bitch, remember?"

"You wouldn't have bothered to hate me. It wouldn't have been worth it to you."

I didn't deny it.

"But I'm different now," I said. "Everything's different."

"I know. But would you keep it that way?"

"What do you mean?"

"If you had a choice, if you could go backward. Would you want to be the old Lia Kahn again, with your old life and your old friends—or stay like this, who you are now?" *Stay with me,* he didn't say, but it was all over his face.

"Auden—"

"Don't lie," he said. "Please."

I didn't even have to think about it. "I'd go back. Of course I'd go back."

"Even if it meant losing—"

"No matter what it meant," I said firmly. "If I could have my body back, my *life* back, don't you think I'd want it? No matter what?"

"No matter what." He stood up. "Good to know."

"Auden, that's not fair. You can't expect me to—"

"I don't expect anything."

"Don't go," I said. "Not like this."

"I can't stay," he said. "Not like this."

He left. I stayed. *Maybe I should have tried,* I thought. *Maybe it wasn't him. Maybe it was me.*

Before, rejecting guys had been easy—and I'd had a lot of practice. Before, I knew what it felt like when it felt right. I knew what I wanted. And I knew there would always be someone new who would want me.

Before.

He's just not my type, I thought. *Too scrawny. Too intense. Too weird.*

But I couldn't be sure. Walker was my type—and I didn't want him, either. Not really. Not anymore.

Maybe I wasn't programmed to want. Maybe that was just something else lost, like running, like music. Something else that had slipped through the cracks of their scanning and modeling. Maybe it was one of those intangibles—like a soul, like free will—that didn't exist, not physically, and so wasn't supposed to exist at all.

CONTROL AND
RELEASE

"Nothing was left but an absence."

The waterfall wasn't loud enough to drown out my thoughts. But it was a start. I found myself a wide, flat rock near the bank, a few feet from where the water plunged over the edge. The place looked different in the light. For one thing, you could see the bottom clearly. Which made it look even farther away. Beyond the rumbling white water, the river ribboned out flat and calm again, but not for long. There was another precipice, another plunge, another fall. From where I sat, I couldn't see whether it was as long or as deep; the river just dropped away. I took a pic—not of the second waterfall, but of the empty space beyond the river, the air where there should have been land. It was crap—a little crooked, like I'd tried an artistic shot and failed miserably when, in fact, I just hadn't cared enough to steady the lens. I posted it to my new zone anyway. Anything to fill up the empty space.

A mist rose from the gushing water. I was tempted to stand

by the edge, wave my hand through the dewy cloud, but that seemed too close. I might have fallen in; I might have jumped. I stayed where I was, watching the water, trying not to think about Auden and Walker, and especially not about Zo.

But I couldn't help hoping that one of them might voice me to apologize, to tell me I'd misunderstood and the whole thing was a hideous mistake. One hour passed, then two. No one did.

"You probably shouldn't jump in the daylight. Too easy to get caught." Like the waterfall, Jude looked different during the day. Every silver streak, every black line etched into his skin, stood out in sharp relief. And seeing him against the pastoral backdrop made him look all the more machinelike.

"What are you doing here?" I asked, jumping up as he sat down.

"I should ask you that," he said. "Last I checked, this was my place."

"Oh, so now you own the river?"

"Sarcasm doesn't scare me. Fire away. I'm staying."

"Enjoy," I said. "I'm going."

"After I came all this way? I would have thought a girl like you would come equipped with better manners."

"So you're stalking me now? How'd you know I was here?"

"I know all." He smirked.

"I'm leaving."

"Okay, wait!" He spread his arms wide in truce. "Your zone, okay? You posted the pic. I recognized the view."

"You've been lurking on my zone?"

"What can I say? I have a lot of time on my hands," Jude said.

"Use it for something else," I snapped. "Stay out of my life."

"Maybe I don't want to. Maybe I think you're worth a little extra effort."

I couldn't believe it. Not another one. Not today. At least this time around I wouldn't have to worry about letting him down easy. "Look, I'm flattered—Well, I'm not, actually, but let's say I am. I'm not interested, okay? So—"

"You think *I'm* interested?" He burst into laughter. "You really are an egomaniac, aren't you? I mean, I knew you were spoiled and self-absorbed, that's par for the course. But this? Please. Trust me, I'm not into the chase. When I want something, it chases *me*."

And *I* was the egomaniac?

Still, I sat down again. He had some kind of agenda, that was obvious. And if it wasn't the expected one, that was interesting. Or at least interesting enough to distract me from the things that actually mattered.

"So why are you here?" I asked.

"Brought you something."

"What?" Like I cared.

"Just something to help you let go."

"What makes you think I have any interest in doing that?"

He smiled. "Because letting go, that's the key. If you're too scared to let go, you'll never be in control. Not really."

"Is that supposed to make sense?" I asked. "Let go so I can get control? Do you even listen to yourself talk, or do you just spit out this crap at random?"

"It's all connected," he said, so disgustingly pleased with himself. So sure. "People only fear letting go because they fear they won't be able to get the control back. That they'll keep going until their urges and instincts destroy them."

"But *you* know better?"

"I know you're afraid of what you've turned into, but only because you don't know what it is, not yet. And because you don't understand it, you think you can't control it."

"You're wrong."

"You're a *machine*," he said. "And that means absolute control—or, if you so choose, absolute release. You have the power to decide if you let yourself." He pulled something out of his pocket, small enough to fit snugly in the palm of his hand. "You wanted to know why I came looking for you? To give you this."

He tossed the object at me, and I caught it without thinking. It was a small, black cube with a tiny switch on one side and a slim, round aperture on the other. Harmless.

"It's a program," he said.

"For what?"

"For you. Or for your brain, at least. You can upload it wirelessly through your ocular nerve."

"That's not possible." No one at BioMax had said anything about additional programming; no one had hinted that I might be able to . . . reprogram myself.

You have a computer inside your head, the Faith leader had said. *Programmed by man.*

Normal people—*human* people—didn't adjust their programming. They didn't rewire themselves with chips and wireless projections. They just changed. Or they didn't.

"Anything's possible if you know the right people," Jude said smugly, like he said everything.

"What's it do?"

"Let's call it a vivid illustration of my point."

I faked a laugh. "You want me to stick something in my brain based on *your* predictably vague recommendation?"

"I don't care what you do," Jude said, and the way he said it, I almost believed him. Not that it mattered. "Think of it as a dream."

"We don't dream."

He gave me a knowing smile. "Yes. That's what they told you."

"You're lying."

"Maybe," he said. "Only one way to find out. You say you're not afraid, right? Prove it."

I tossed his little black box back to him. "Just how stupid do you think I am?"

He smirked. "You really want an answer to that?"

"Excuse me for not just buying all your crap without question, like one of your brainwashed groupies."

"I don't have to brainwash them," Jude said. "They know the truth when they hear it."

"Unlike me?"

"Apparently."

"So that's what this is?" I asked. "You've made it your own personal mission to convert me?"

He laughed. It made him look like a different person. No, that's not quite right. It made him look like a *person*. "See what I mean?" he said. "Total egomaniac. You should really get that checked out."

"You're here, aren't you?" I pointed out. "Following me?"

"Maybe I was just in the mood to talk."

"To me?"

He looked around at the wilderness. "Seems like my only viable option."

I shrugged. "So talk."

"Let's start with: What's wrong?" he asked.

He almost sounded like he really wanted to know. Not that it mattered. "No. I'm not talking about me."

"Because?"

"Recovering egomaniac," I reminded him.

He grinned. "The first step is admitting you have a problem."

"And the second step is acknowledging that other people do too. So let's start with you. Why are you following me? *Really.*"

He shook his head. "No cheating. That's still about you."

"Fine. How about: Where do you live? What do you do all day when you're not stalking me? How did you end up a mech—"

"I told you before," he said, the joking tone gone from his voice. "The past doesn't matter. All that matters is what I am now, and that's everything I want to be."

"Come on, how can you say that?"

"Easy. It's true." His eyes flashed.

Everything I wanted to be had died in that car crash.

"You really don't miss it?" I asked. "Not at all?"

He smiled wryly. "There's not much to miss. We weren't all like you."

"What's 'like me'?"

"Rich," he said, ticking it off on his fingers. "Treasured. Sheltered. Deluded."

"Is this fun for you? Insulting me every time you open your mouth?"

"A little."

I started to get up again, but he grabbed my arm. "Okay, I'm sorry," he said. "Don't go. Please." I glared, and after a moment he let go. But I sat down again.

"You think this is some kind of punishment," he said. And again it almost sounded like he cared. Or at least that he understood.

"I don't—"

"You *do*," he said. "Because you don't let yourself see the possibilities. All you can see is what you've lost."

Everything.

"Some of us didn't have that much to lose," he continued with less intensity than usual.

"You do realize you're being ridiculously vague, right?"

"You want something concrete?" he asked. "How about the way it feels to walk for the first time?"

There was something new in his voice, something ragged and unrehearsed, like he'd gone off his script and wasn't sure how to find his way back. He sounded like I felt: lost.

"Or to know that nothing can ever hurt you again, not for real?" he continued. "How about never having to be afraid?"

I was afraid all the time.

If he knew how that felt, if he could understand that and had found a way to fight back, maybe I'd been wrong about him. About it all.

"That's why, isn't it?" I said softly. "Why you don't talk about before."

He looked away. "I told you. The past is irrelevant for us."

"I'm not talking about *us*. I'm talking about *you*." Without knowing why, I wanted to touch him, to rest my hand on his hand, his knee, his shoulder. I wanted contact. "I'm talking about whatever happened to you. Want to talk, Jude?" I said. It wasn't a question, it was a challenge. "Talk about that. Talk about how you ended up here. How you're just like the rest of us." I paused, not sure I should keep going. And when I did, it was in a whisper. "Broken."

He raised his eyes off the ground and looked at me. "I'm *not* broken. And I don't need your pity."

Pity hadn't even occurred to me. Why would it when we were the same? "I'm not—"

"Save it for yourself," he said, his eyes flashing again, a yellow-orange that looked like flame. "Drown in it, for all I care. *I* don't need it. I know what I am. I'm *proud* of what I am."

"So that's why you did *this* to yourself?" I asked. "Turned yourself into some kind of . . ."

"Freak?"

"I wasn't going to say that."

"Because you're a coward," he said.

"Shut up."

"Afraid to say what you think. Afraid to do . . . *anything*. Afraid to accept the truth."

"*Shut up.*"

"You can't face facts about what you've become, and so you're missing it."

I had never met anyone so disgustingly smug. "You don't know anything about me."

"I know enough," he said. "I know all you care about is what people think, and whether you look *cool.* Guess what? You don't. Not to *them*."

"Why are you so obsessed with all this us-and-them crap? There is no *them*. There is definitely no *us*."

"Why are you so determined to lie to yourself?" he retorted. "*They* know you're not one of them. When are you going to wake up?"

"What the hell do you want from me?" I shouted. It was too much. It was too much for one day, too much on top of everything. I couldn't deal. I shouldn't have to. "You want me to walk away from everything, to pretend the past never happened and that I'm not the person I know I am?"

"That would be a start!"

"I'm not going to destroy myself." I tried to make my voice as cool and cutting as his. "Not for you. Not for anyone."

"That job's done. You don't have to do anything. Just acknowledge the wreckage and walk away."

I stood up—and this time, although he grabbed my arm again, I didn't hesitate. His fingers wrapped tight around my wrist. He was the only mech I'd ever touched. "Don't come looking for me again," I said. *"Ever."*

"Trust me," he said coldly. "I won't have to."

"I'm going now." I didn't move.

"I'm waiting." He was still holding my wrist.

"Screw you." And then, somehow, my hand was on his

chest. His fingers tightened on my wrist. He yanked me toward him. Or I lunged. He grabbed my waist. Or I dug my hips into him. Whatever he did. Whatever I did. Our faces collided.

Our lips collided.

I clawed at his shirt, digging into the fabric, struggling for the fake, silvery skin that lay below. His lips were rough; his kiss was rough. Hard and angry, or maybe that was me, hating him, *wanting* him, wanting his hands on my body—anyone's hands on my body—even if it didn't feel the same, it felt right, it *felt*, for the first time since the accident and the fire and the darkness, I *felt*, and I sucked at his lips, and he bit down, a sweet, sharp pain, and I imagined I could taste the iron-tanged blood on my tongue.

But there would be no blood.

I shoved him away.

For the second time that day I wished I could throw up.

He came toward me; I jerked away.

"*Don't* touch me."

I couldn't believe I had done it.

I wanted to do it again.

I had to get away.

"Don't do this," he said, an edge in his voice. "Don't question it, not now, not when you're so close."

"To what?" I spat out. But I knew. To him. To grabbing him again. To his body. To our bodies, together.

To *feeling*.

I took another step back.

"To letting go," he said. I couldn't believe he was back to that, spewing his bullshit, like I was a dutiful member of his flock. "I told you, it's the key to accepting what you are—"

"Spare me." I hated him. This wasn't about me, I realized. Not for him. This wasn't about need, about raw *want*. Not for the high and mighty Jude, who'd risen oh so far above all those nasty org instincts. This was just about his stupid campaign. His pathetic philosophy. This was just about him being right. About me being wrong.

"Don't do this," he said again, closing his hands over mine. But I was done.

"Go." I felt as cold as I sounded.

"You don't want that."

I met his eyes. They were, as always, unreadable. Like mine. "You. Don't. Know. What. I. Want." Nice and slow, so he would understand.

"Maybe not." Jude shook his head. "But neither do you." He pressed something into my palm—the sharp-edged cube, the one he'd called a dream. "Not yet."

I looked down at the tiny black box, turning it over and over in my hands.

When I looked up again, he was gone.

I'm not stupid.

I wasn't stupid then, either.

I didn't trust him. I didn't trust his little black box or his mysterious "program" or his unshakable convictions. Least of all those.

On the other hand, I didn't have much to lose. And I had too much I wanted to forget.

I uploaded the program.

There was a brief burst of flickering light, then nothing.

For several long minutes, nothing.

Then the world started to glow.

Pain first. Pain everywhere. Nowhere. I was nowhere. It burned. I burned. Pain like the fire, pain like the flames peeling away my skin. Hot, searing hot. Then cold, like ice. Steel.

I was standing. I was spinning. I was lying on my back. I floated in the sky. Stars shot from my fingertips. Trees bowed at my feet. I was leaping off a cliff, I was in the water, in a whirlpool, sucked below. I was drowning. I was flying.

I was in the black. But the colors shimmered. They exploded from the dark. *I* was color. I was light. I pulsed green, I sang out purple, I screamed red. I cried blue. The monsters swarmed out of the deep. Spider tentacles and red eyes, and they wanted me to die, and I wanted to die, and I was death, black and empty, bottomless, null.

• • •

I would destroy them. I would destroy them all.

It began at the center of me, at the center of it all, small and warm and glowing, a sun, and it swelled. It grew. I tingled with its warmth. There were no words, not for this. This was beyond words. This was cool grass brushing a bare neck. This was dark-chocolate ice cream melting on a tongue. This was his body, heavy on mine, his breath in my mouth, his skin on my skin. It was everything, it was life.

It was over.

Nothing was left but an absence. And his voice, which I understood, as I came back to myself, was only in my head.

"If you're listening to this, I suppose that means I was right. You're welcome."

I was lying on my back. I didn't know how I'd gotten there. The sky looked close enough to touch, but I knew that was just the heavy, gray clouds. I reached out anyway. Nothing but air.

"You've just experienced an electrical jolt to your limbic system—or at least, the circuitry that mimics an organic limbic system. It overwhelmed all the mood-simulating safeguards, cycling through a random series of preprogrammed emotional stimuli. Take the most intense b-mod you've ever experienced, multiply it by a thousand, and—Well, I guess now you know what happens."

I closed my eyes. I felt like I had a headache, but that wasn't possible. I didn't get headaches, not anymore. Still, something felt swollen and tender. Fragile. Fuzzy. I wanted the voice to stop.

"Direct stimulation of the cortex is the best way to simulate intense emotion and sensation in mechs. It supplies you with the somatic responses you miss while conscious, all those nasty animal responses to emotion. Some say it makes you feel like an org again."

I had never felt so empty. I wanted it back, all of it. I needed it. I wanted to live in that world of darkness and light, where I had been frightened. Angry. Happy. I had been alive there, and I wanted to return. I wanted to stay.

"*I* say it's better than the orgs will ever know. And admit it or not, you agree."

I wanted him to shut up. I wanted him to keep going. I wanted him to come back, I wanted a body to match the voice, hands and shoulders and neck and lips. I hated myself for wanting it.

"See you soon."

IN THE DARK

"Touch me and I'll kill you."

What's this for?" Auden asked when I gave him the box wrapped in silver foil. He'd been avoiding me for days, but I finally cornered him at lunch. He'd found himself another secluded corner to hide in, far away from mine.

"I just wanted to," I said, feeling a little awkward. I couldn't say I was sorry, not really, because then we would have had to get into what I was sorry for. And neither of us wanted to touch that because we both knew: I was sorry for not wanting him the way he wanted me. But that meant I couldn't tell him the other part of the truth, that I needed him. It didn't matter if he was an org and I was a mech; it didn't matter what Jude thought. Jude who was like me, but didn't understand me at all. Who knew nothing.

Auden opened the box. He pulled out a gray bag with a smart-strap that would heat up whenever a new message came in. The front flap had a full-size screen and the back doubled as a pocket and a keyboard, perfect—as the pop-up had said—

for the stylish guy who needs to link on the go. Not that Auden was stylish, or did much of anything on the go, but it looked good. Definitely better than the ragged green sack he toted around everywhere. *I* might not have been cool anymore, but my taste still was.

He looked confused.

"Thought you could use a new one," I said.

Auden didn't take it out of the box. "You shouldn't have."

"I wanted to," I said again.

"Really, you shouldn't have." He sighed, and finally picked up the bag, flipping it open and glancing inside before placing it back in the box. He didn't even notice the smart-strap much less the board and the screen. "But thanks, I guess."

It looked like the symbolic approach wasn't working. Did he not get that I was trying to spare him even more embarrassment? Shouldn't he be *grateful*?

Especially since, when you think about it, *he* was the one who should have been apologizing. I wasn't the one making unreasonable demands or throwing a temper tantrum when I didn't get what I wanted.

But I'd lost the moral high ground when I'd given in to Jude. Even if Auden didn't know—could *never* know—I knew.

"I'm sorry about before," I said. If he really wanted to talk about it, then fine. We'd talk.

"You don't have to—"

"I wish it hadn't happened."

"I shouldn't have said anything," he said.

"No, I'm glad you did." Lie. "We should be honest with each other." Lie number two. "And what I said? About wishing I could go back to the way things were before? I can't . . . I can't take that back. But, Auden, you have to know, you're the only good thing that's happened to me since the accident. The *only* thing." Truth.

Except for yesterday, some rebellious part of my brain pointed out. *Except for Jude. Except for what he did. And what he gave me.* But that was nothing. That was already forgotten.

Lie number three.

"You don't have to say that," Auden said.

"I do." I smiled nervously. "Are we okay? I really need us to be okay."

"Me too," he said, and gave me a tight hug.

Now or never, I decided. "So, now that we're friends again . . . any chance you want to do me a favor?"

Auden let go, laughing. "Now I get it. That wasn't a gift, it was a bribe."

"No! Well . . . maybe a little."

He sighed. "What do you need?"

"Jude and the rest of them are going out again tonight." I winced at the expression on his face, stranded somewhere between suspicion and disgust. "I want to go. I thought maybe you'd come with me."

"Back to the waterfall? Are you crazy?"

I shook my head. "They're doing something else tonight. I don't know what. It's some kind of big secret."

"Maybe you didn't hear me the first time: Are you crazy?"

"You're the one who talked me into going last time," I pointed out. "Remember all that stuff about facing up to my fears, meeting people who were like me and could understand what I'm going through?"

"Remember how it turned out that Jude was an asshole and all his little followers were daredevil nut jobs who thought killing themselves might be a fun way to pass the time?"

"They weren't trying to kill themselves," I said.

"They were doing a pretty good imitation of it."

"Auden, you know it's different for us."

"*Us?* Since when—"

"You know what I mean," I snapped. "It wasn't that dangerous. They were just having fun."

"Exactly. What kind of person thinks that's fun?" He scowled. "A seriously messed-up person. Or a person who can't think for himself."

"Or maybe a person who's not a person at all. Is that what you're trying to say?"

"No!" Auden sighed. "You know I don't think that way about you. I just don't get why you'd want to go back. What's the point?"

I wasn't sure why I wanted to go back.

It wasn't because I wanted another dose of whatever Jude

had to give me. I'd promised myself it wasn't because of that.

"They're trying to test their limits," I told him, "and to explore the possibilities of this thing. To enjoy it a little. Is that so bad?"

"When did you start talking like that?" he asked.

"Like what?"

"Like . . . I don't know. Like *him*."

"Look, if you don't want to go with me, I'll go by myself," I said, annoyed. "No big deal."

"It is a big deal," he said. "Whatever they're doing, I'm sure it'll be dangerous. And stupid. I'm not letting you go by yourself."

"I don't need you to protect me," I said, even though that's exactly what I'd asked of him—and I'd asked knowing he would never be able to say no.

"Too bad. That's what you've got."

"What's the point?" Auden asked.

"Because we *can*," Jude said. "Because why not?"

Auden pulled me away from the group. He was still carrying his hideous green bag. "This is a bad idea."

"You're the one always talking about the people stuck living in the cities," I said. "Don't you actually want to *see* one?"

"Not like this," he mumbled. "Not by ourselves. At *night*." But I knew I had him.

There were ten of us, including me and Auden. Again, no

one had wanted him to come along, but I'd insisted, and Jude had gone along with it. As before, everyone else went along with Jude.

"You can leave, if you want," I offered, and I was almost hoping he would take me up on it. I wanted him there, I did. But even I knew he didn't belong.

Auden shook his head. "You know the city people; they hate mechs more than anyone," he said. "Most of them die before they hit forty, and you're going to live forever. You really think that's a good combination?"

"I think Lia trusts me," Jude said, appearing behind us and resting his hand on my shoulder. I shook it off. "Maybe you should give her a little more credit."

I glared at him. "Don't touch me."

He just smiled. "I'll give you two a minute," he said. "We're leaving in five. Stay or go."

Once he was gone, Auden gave me a weird look. "What was that?"

"What?"

"The two of you."

"*What?*"

"Nothing." He headed back toward the group of mechs waiting for their field trip to begin. "Let's just go."

We took two cars. Jude and Auden sat in the front seat of ours, not talking. I squeezed into the back with Quinn and some guy whose name I didn't hear the first time—and didn't get much chance to ask a second time, since he spent most of the ride with his tongue down Quinn's throat. I looked out the window.

The skyline carved dark, jagged chunks out of the sky. The car sped along swooping bands of concrete, a purposeless, unending sculpture of roads that dipped over and under one another, splitting, merging, crisscrossing; so much space and all of it empty. Even without the curfew no one would be stupid enough to enter a city at night. And no one who lived there had a car. That would have guzzled too much fuel; that would have made it too easy to get out.

We parked on a narrow street. Without a word Quinn and the other mech began collecting armfuls of debris from the gutter while Jude pulled a stained beige tarp from the trunk and draped it over the car. The gutter trash went on top.

"Best way to keep it safe," Jude explained. Across the street the passengers of the second car were doing the same.

It was eerily quiet. The dark buildings shot up on all sides, and I reminded myself that at least some of them were full of people, staying warm, staying dry, staying off the streets after curfew. But everything was so still and empty, it was hard to imagine that anyone was alive here. The group moved stealthily, stepping lightly, staying clustered in a pack. Only Auden breathed.

"What now?" I whispered.

"We look around," Jude said. "And we try not to get caught."

Caught by who? I wanted to ask. But I didn't really want an answer.

This city had been lucky. No major bombings, so no radioactive debris. Too far east for the Water Wars, too far north for the flooding. They'd gotten hit by the Comstock flu strain, but no worse than any of the other population centers, and in the last bio-attack, before the cities cleared out for good, they'd lost less than a million.

They'd been lucky.

Not lucky enough for anyone to stay, at least voluntarily, but that much was true for all the cities. Who would be crazy enough to stick around an energy-poor, germ-ridden death trap if they had enough credit to get the hell out?

We wandered down the broad, empty avenues, flashlight beams playing across the pavement. I tried to imagine what it would be like to live in a place where the lights went off two hours after sunset, where you could only link in once a day if you were lucky enough to find a screen that worked, where the punishment for energy theft was death.

I couldn't.

There wasn't enough to go around, I reminded myself. Of anything. There wasn't enough energy for everyone to stay wired all day, every day. There wasn't enough fuel or enough road for everyone to own cars. There weren't enough cows—at least not enough free-range, grass-fed cows, now that you weren't allowed to raise anything else—for everyone to eat

meat. There wasn't enough space for everyone to have a kid. Either we would all have to suffer—or some would have to sacrifice.

I was just glad it was them and not me.

I was also glad my power cells were fully loaded. There was no wireless web of energy here, and if something happened, if I somehow got left behind, there would be nowhere to recharge. After a few days I would just . . . fade out.

"Those used to light up," Auden whispered in my ear, pointing at the thick, empty screens papered across almost every building. "Like giant pop-ups. Telling people what to buy."

"What a waste of energy," I whispered back. Maybe these people deserved to live in the dark.

Our feet crunched with every step. Crushed glass, I decided, as we passed broken window after broken window. Everything here was broken.

I wanted to go home.

A distant howl cut through the silence.

"What was that?" I whispered, freezing in place.

"Just a dog." Jude didn't bother to whisper. "Fighting it out for who gets to run the place. Like the rats and the roaches haven't already won." He turned sharply to the right, leading us down another wide avenue, its gutters flowing with trash. Auden was breathing shallowly and, for the first time, it occurred to me how the place must stink, with its mounds of garbage heaped on urine-stained pavement. "This way."

Two blocks later we heard the scream. High-pitched, piercing, it went on and on and—it stopped. It didn't fade away. It just stopped.

That was no dog.

We went deeper into the city, and I tried not to wonder how we would find our way out.

Jude stopped short in front of a building so tall it blotted out most of the sky. "Last stop for orgs," he said, staring at Auden.

Auden glared back. "Meaning?"

"Building's locked down, and all those biosensors . . ." Jude smirked. "You don't want to start panting and get us caught, now do you?"

"I'm supposed to wait out here while you . . . do what, exactly?"

"Just taking a look around. We'll be back before you get too scared."

"I'm not scared," Auden said fiercely.

Jude shrugged. "Great. Then you don't mind if we—"

"You're not going with them?" Auden half-said, half-asked, grabbing my arm.

I paused. "I don't have to. I can wait down here with you . . . if you want." I knew I should stay.

But I didn't want to.

"No." Auden closed his eyes for a moment. "You're the one who wanted to do this. So you should do it. All the way."

Jude chuckled softly. "Funny, she never struck me as an all-the-way kind of girl."

I ignored him.

"You sure?" I asked Auden.

"Yeah. Go." He gave me a weak smile. "Be careful."

"You too."

Jude and one of the other guys, the tall, brooding one named Riley, bashed open one of the doors, and we crept inside. It was even darker in there, a broad space smudged with shadows. A screen glinted in the beam of someone's flashlight, and then another and another. This is where the city people came to link in, I realized. It explained why the building was locked down. It didn't explain what we were doing there.

Jude led us to a bank of elevators, and we waited as Riley pried open a control panel and dug his hands into the mess of wiring.

"Isn't the electricity shut off?" I asked.

"They keep it running low-level in this building," Jude said. "For the hardware. Easy to tap into if you know what you're doing."

"And he knows what he's doing?" I said, nodding toward Riley.

"He knows a lot of things. You don't hear any alarms going, do you?"

I shook my head.

"Thank Riley."

A few seconds later the elevator doors popped open. The group stepped on, but when I tried to follow, Jude held me back. "We'll take the next one," he said.

Before I could argue, the doors shut, and we were alone.

"What do you want?" I said.

"What do *you* want?"

Another set of doors opened, and we stepped into the small space. Together. The doors shut behind us, and the elevator whooshed up the shaft. Jude turned to face me, backing me into a corner.

"Touch me and I'll kill you," I hissed.

He just laughed. "A, you've really got to train yourself to stop thinking in outdated terms, like life and death, and B, I have zero interest in touching you. Not at the moment, at least."

I promised myself I had no interest in touching him, either. "So what the hell is this about?"

He pressed his hands flat against the elevator walls, one on either side of me, locking my body between his arms. "I thought you might have some questions. About your little . . . experience by the waterfall."

"I don't know what you're talking about."

He smirked. "I think you do. And I think you loved it. I think you came back for more."

I didn't say anything.

"Better be careful." It sounded more like a threat than a

warning. "Don't want to end up lost inside your own head. Better to get your thrills out here, in the real world."

"Is that what we're supposed to be doing, wandering around this trash heap of a city?" I asked. "Am I being thrilled? I hadn't noticed."

Jude dropped his arms. "That's how you want to play it? Fine."

The elevator swept up and up.

"Where'd you get it?" I asked.

He didn't bother asking what.

"As *human* as possible," he said bitterly. "That's the BioMax party line. But it doesn't mean they don't have the technology to make us different. To make us better. They just don't want to give it to us. Not officially, at least."

"Make us *better*? How's some crazy intense b-mod trip supposed to make me better?"

He raised his eyebrows, and I realized that now there was no denying it. I'd uploaded the program, and he knew it.

"There's more where that came from," he said. "But only if you're willing to look."

The doors opened. We were on the roof. Three dark silhouettes tiptoed along a railing at the far edge, wobbling in the wind. There was plenty of wind, ninety-eight stories up.

"They're not jumping," I whispered in horror. "Tell me they're not jumping."

"No, *we're* not jumping," Jude said. "Just playing around.

Admiring the view. Enjoy." And he slipped into the shadows.

I circled the roof, weaving through abandoned solar arrays and broken satellite dishes. The world above was no less shattered than the world below. The three mechs on the railing swung themselves over the thin metal barrier and began scaling it from the outside. I passed Quinn in a dark corner, wrapped around the guy whose name I would probably never know. Riley and Jude argued against the skyline. I veered in the opposite direction and found myself standing next to Ani, her blue hair black in the darkness. She'd folded herself over the railing, elbows propped on the metal, eyes fixed on the dead buildings that stretched beneath us. My eyes had adjusted to the night enough to pick out a few of the closest ones, but beyond that, there was nothing but a field of shadow.

"Hey," she said, without turning her face away from the nonview.

"Hey."

"So, what do you think?"

I shrugged. "Not much to see."

"I mean about the whole thing," she said. "Tonight."

I shrugged again. "Seems like a lot of effort just to go somewhere we're not supposed to be. What's the point?"

"Jude says there doesn't always need to be a point. Sometimes it's just about having fun." Ani glanced over my shoulder. I turned to see Quinn and the guy, still going at it. "See? Fun."

"Maybe it's none of my business, but . . . that doesn't bother you?"

"Why should it?"

"I guess I just thought you and Quinn were . . ."

"We are. Sometimes." She smiled faintly. "But this is all new for her. She wants to . . . you know. Play."

"And that's okay with you?"

"Jude says we have to learn not to lay claims on one another anymore," she said. "He says monogamy's impractical if you're planning to live forever."

"Seems like Jude says a lot."

Ani beamed. "He's amazing."

"And you always listen?"

She shook her head. "You don't understand."

"What?"

"Where we come from. Where *he* comes from."

"So tell me."

"How do you think he knows his way around here so well?" she asked.

I hadn't really thought about it.

"He used to live here," Ani said. "Before."

"Really?" I leaned forward. I'd never met anyone who had actually *lived* in a city. "I mean, I knew he was . . ." I wasn't sure which word would make me sound least like a spoiled rich girl. Everyone knew that the first mechs had been volunteers from the cities and the corp-towns. What everyone also knew,

although no one said it, was that you'd be crazy to volunteer for something like that unless you had no other choice. "Do you know what happened to him? Why he volunteered?"

Ani looked alarmed. "I'm not supposed to be talking about the past," she said. "He'd kill me."

"I thought we were supposed to forget about our mortal fears," I teased. "Retrain ourselves to accept immortality. Isn't that what 'Jude says'?"

She shook her head, hard. "The past doesn't matter," she said, almost to herself. "It's better forgotten."

"Easy for some people," I said quietly. "Not so much for others."

Ani flopped forward against the railing again. "I don't miss it, if that's what you're thinking. I'd never go back."

"Are you from around here too?" I asked, hoping I wasn't pushing too hard. I didn't want to scare her away.

"No. Farther west than that." There was more than a little pain in her smile, but her voice stayed flat. "My parents are from Chicago."

"Oh." *From* Chicago, not *in* Chicago. No one lived *in* Chicago, not anymore. And most of the ones who'd lived there the day of the attack weren't living, period. The initial blast had only taken out a couple hundred thousand, but then there had been the radioactive dust. And the radioactive water. And the radioactive food. A radioactive city, filled with radioactive people. Who had, pretty quickly and pretty gruesomely, started getting sick. I hadn't seen the vids, but then, it wasn't really necessary. In school they made us watch footage of Atlanta. And Orlando.

Once you've seen one ruined city, you've seen them all.

I didn't know how to ask the obvious question, but it seemed rude not to try. "Are your parents, uh, are they . . . did they . . ."

"Still alive." Ani's mouth twisted. "At least, as far as I know. Which isn't very far."

"You're not in touch?"

She shook her head.

"Is it because of . . . what happened to you?" I glanced down at her body, and she got the idea.

"I wish." She hesitated. "How much do you know about the corp-towns?"

I shrugged. "Just that it's a good place to live, if, you know, you need a job. And that if you live there, you get stuff you need." Stuff like food, electricity, med-tech—stuff you wouldn't get in a city. Not unless you stole it.

"You get it," she agreed, "but only if you follow the rules."

There was a code of good behavior, I knew that. But it made sense to me. If the corporation was running the town, supplying houses and schools and doctors and lights, didn't they deserve to make the rules?

"And only if you're willing to give *other* stuff away," she continued.

"Like the voting thing?" I rolled my eyes. "Big deal." Residents of corp-towns sold their vote to the corps. Seemed like more than a fair trade. Most people I knew weren't planning to vote anyway. Who cared which b-mod addict fame whore pretended to run the country next?

"Other things, too," Ani said. "Things for the good of the community. Like minimizing medical costs."

"Seems fair."

She looked down. "When you're from Chicago, having a kid is not a good way to minimize medical costs."

"Oh." You could take the people out of the radioactive city—but you couldn't take the radioactivity out of the people.

"Yeah. Oh. They signed a contract. So when they decided to have me . . ."

"They got kicked out?"

"Not until I was born." The pained smile was back again. "Then it was straight back to city living for them. And their adorable legless wonder."

I forced myself not to look down at her long, slender legs. "You were born without . . ."

"Among other things." Her grip tightened around the railing. "Radiation poisoning really spices up the genetic soup."

"I'm sorry."

"Yeah. So were they." She shrugged. "After a few years they ditched me. Headed for the nearest corp-town, I guess."

"And you never—"

"Ten years." She shook her head. "Not one word. Guess they wanted to forget I ever happened."

"I really am sorry," I told her. It seemed like such a lame thing to say. "It must have been . . . hard for you. On your own."

Ani shrugged, keeping her eyes fixed on the skyline. "There are places. For people like me. No doctors, of course. And not much food or . . . anything. But . . ." She shook her head. "It doesn't matter. Anymore. Let's just say that when they shipped me off for the download, I didn't care what they were going to do to me. It couldn't have been worse than where I was."

"So how did you get to volunteer?"

She laughed. "Lia, what makes you think we volunteered?"

"I didn't—I don't know—that's what they said. I believed it." Which sounded totally feeble. But it was the truth.

"It doesn't matter. Jude's right. None of that matters now. We're better off."

She said it, but I couldn't help thinking she wasn't done talking. Not yet. If I could find the right question to ask. "Did you know him? Before?"

She hesitated. "Not in the place. No. But later, in the hospital. When they were doing all the tests, deciding which of us they wanted. Jude was there. Riley too. They were friends from before. And the three of us . . . It just worked, you know?" She pulled a nanoViM from her pocket and flicked the screen to life. "You want to see something?"

I nodded.

"You can't tell them I showed you," she said. "Ever."

I nodded again.

In the picture, three teenagers grinned at the camera. Two sat side by side in wheelchairs, their cheeks sunken, their bodies withering away. The girl had no legs. The boy had all his limbs, but they were twisted and gnarled. Useless.

"Jude," Ani said, tapping his hollowed face.

The guy standing behind looked like a giant next to their fragile, wasted bodies. "Riley?" I guessed. "He looks pretty healthy."

She flicked off the screen. "He was."

He was also black. As was the boy who had become Jude. The girl's skin was lighter, more caramel than chocolate, but still radically darker than the body she wore now. Ani saw the question in my face.

"What? Did you think we were *white*?" she asked in disgust.

I guess I hadn't thought at all. "I don't get it. Why didn't they . . . I mean, it's not like they couldn't . . ."

"We were the first," she said in a more bitter tone than I'd ever heard her use. "An *experiment*. So they used what they had, and what they had were standard-issue bodies for their standard-issue rich white clients. *You* get a new body, you get to customize. *Us?* We get something off the rack. We get *this*." She looked down, now aiming the disgust at the body she'd been assigned. "You think I like this?" she asked. "You think I like the fact that my parents wouldn't even recognize me, if they ever—" She choked it off. "Not like that's going to happen." She slipped the ViM into her pocket. "It doesn't matter. Jude says that race is irrelevant, since it's not like we even have skin anymore, not really. He says being a mech is like being part of a new race." She lowered her voice. "But I know he hates it too."

"And Riley?" I asked, thinking of the tall, silent boy who never seemed to smile.

Ani shrugged. "Who knows? Hard to tell *what* he's thinking, right?"

"I guess." I paused. "So, when you said he was healthy, before, did you mean—"

She shook her head. "No," she said firmly. "I guess it's okay for you to know where I came from. I mean, that's my business. But if you want to know about them, ask *them*."

"Okay. I get it." A lot of good it would do me, though. Jude had already made it clear he wasn't in the question-answering business. At least not when it came to questions I actually wanted the answers to.

"I don't even know much myself," she said in a softer voice. "He's serious about the whole forgetting-the-past thing. Even before the download, he and Riley didn't talk about where they came from. Not *ever*."

I thought about the picture, the boy's body curled up in the wheelchair, his legs and arms strapped down, his neck looking too frail to support his head. And then I thought about Jude, passionate and proud. I thought about his firm grasp, and the way it had felt when his broad arms embraced me. "I guess I can maybe understand that."

Ani gave me a shy smile that suddenly made her look about ten years old. "I'm glad you came up here, Lia. Alone, I mean."

"Not like I had much of a choice. If Auden had set off the alarms—"

Ani laughed. "There are no alarms," she said, like it should have been obvious. "Jude just said that."

"Are you kidding me?" I asked, picturing Auden standing nervously on the curb in front of the building. Alone. Where I'd left him. "Why would he lie like that?"

"Don't be mad," she said quickly. "He just wanted you to see what it was like with us. You know. On your own."

I turned to face the view again, resting my forearms on the railing, staring out and trying to imagine a city filled with lights. "It's not so bad, I guess."

I probably should have been mad.

But I wasn't.

As we made our way back to the car, Auden and I hung behind the rest of the group.

"Have fun up there?" he asked, sounding a little sullen.

I shrugged. "It was okay."

"Hope you two found some time to be alone together."

"*Us* two?"

"You. *Him*." He glared at Jude's back.

I forced a laugh. "Don't make me throw up."

"You can't," Auden said flatly. "Remember?"

"Like I could forget."

"You seem to have forgotten that he's crazy. Dangerous."

"You've got no reason to think that," I said. "You're just—" But that was a sentence that didn't need finishing. "He's not so bad." I didn't know why I was bothering to defend him.

No wonder Auden was freaked. *I* was a little freaked. But it didn't mean something was going on. Just because I didn't totally hate Jude, didn't mean I— Well, it didn't mean anything.

"You tell yourself that if it helps. If that makes it easier."

So he *was* jealous, even though there was nothing to be jealous about—and even though he had no right to be. Auden didn't own me. "Something you want to ask?"

"None of my business," he said.

"Except you obviously think it is," I pointed out. "Unless you're still mad about what happened between the two of us."

"You mean what *didn't* happen."

"So you are mad."

"No."

"Passive-aggressiveness is incredibly lame," I said. "You do realize that, right?"

"How am I being passive-aggressive?"

I plucked at the fraying strap of his green bag. "What'd you do, throw the one I gave you in the trash? Light it on fire?"

"It's new," he said defensively. "I didn't want to bring it tonight, mess it up."

"Whatever. None of my business, right?"

"It was my mother's," he mumbled, so quietly that I thought I must have heard him wrong.

"What?"

"The bag." He pressed it tighter to his body. "It was my mother's."

And I'd given him a bright, shiny new one, suggesting he throw the old one in the garbage where it belonged. What a lovely gesture. "Why didn't you just tell me?"

"I didn't want to talk about it. I *don't* want to talk about it." He stared hard at me. "We don't have to talk about everything, do we?"

I looked away. No. We didn't.

We walked the rest of the way in silence. The city was silent too, at least at first. And then I heard something. A scuffling, shuffling noise. Like careful footsteps, creeping behind us.

I didn't say anything.

It was probably my imagination, just like the shadows flickering in every alley we passed. It was probably nothing.

Once we reached the cars, Jude loaded us all in—all except for a mech named Tak. I hadn't talked to him much, partly because he scared me a little. It wasn't so much the spikes around his neck or the patchy transparent casing on his face that revealed a layer of chunky wiring and circuitry. It was his eyes, which somehow looked even deader than mine. I told myself it was just a trick of the light.

Jude nodded at Tak. *Ready?* he mouthed.

Tak nodded back, and Jude tugged the tarp back across the car, leaving a corner of one of the windows unblocked. Then he jumped inside and slammed the door behind him. "Everyone scrunch down in your seats," he ordered. "It's safer."

"But what about Tak?" I asked.

"Down," Jude said. "You'll see."

I saw.

"I'm here, motherfuckers!" Tak screamed so loudly we could hear him through the thick windows. He stood in the middle of the empty street, as if waiting. "Come and get me!"

Nothing happened.

He screamed again and again until the words faded, replaced by an incoherent roar. And then, heeding his call, two figures emerged from the darkness, clothed in rags. One carried a knife. The other, a gun.

We couldn't hear what the men said. But through our corner of window, we could see Tak laugh. The men advanced.

I grabbed Jude's arm. "We have to *do* something!" I whispered, panicking.

"He can deal," Jude said calmly. "Just watch." And, like a coward, I did.

The man on the left raised his gun.

Tak laughed again. "Can't kill me, motherfuckers!" he shouted. "No matter how hard you try!" Then he raised his arms out to his sides. "I fucking dare you!"

The gunshot was like thunder.

The men ran away before Tak's body hit the ground.

"Now!" Jude shouted. "Before the cops!"

As Auden and I clung to each other, Jude and Riley jumped out of the car, grabbed Tak's body, and slung it into the back. Onto us. They piled into the car themselves, and suddenly we were speeding away.

"Awesome," Tak gasped, his head in my lap. There was no blood, but the wound was oozing something green and viscous. I didn't want it touching me.

"Hurts?" Jude asked, programming in a new set of coordinates as the city fell away behind us.

"Like fuck," Tak said, thumping his shoulder where the bullet had slammed into him. "Gonna be a bitch to get this one out."

"What the hell is going on?" I said. "You did that on purpose. You let them shoot you! We all could have been—"

"Killed?" Jude asked wryly.

"I wasn't going to say that."

"Because you're learning." Jude twisted around in his seat to look at me. Me, not Auden, who had turned pale and was pressed up against the window, like he wanted to jump out of the car, speeding or not. "We all have our little daily pleasures," he said. "Tak's happens to be pain. Violence, too. And fear, of course."

"Fuck fear," Tak shot back. "Just a gun, right?"

Jude smiled. "But mostly pain. Or at least, a digital simulation of such. A quick trip to BioMax and he'll be all better, won't you?" He patted Tak on the shoulder; Tak screamed at the touch. "I would think you'd have a little more understanding now that you've seen for yourself how addictive this sort of thing can be."

"It's not the same and you know it!"

"What are you two talking about?" Auden asked, eyes wide.

"Nothing," I said quickly. "Just bullshit. His usual."

"That's right, look down on us, like we're crazy, like you're *so* different." Jude sneered. "I hear the land of denial's lovely this time of year."

"It's not so easy for some of us! Your life may have sucked, but mine didn't. I'm not ready to give it up yet."

"Like you know anything about my life."

"I know tonight was a little trip home for you," I spat out, so angry and freaked out that I forgot about the promise I'd made to Ani. "I know you probably like this better than your wheelchair."

Jude hit manual override, and the car skidded to a stop. "Who told you?"

I was glad Ani wasn't riding with us. "Nobody."

"Get out." Jude said quietly. "And take the org with you."

"What?" We were in the middle of nowhere, a long, dark stretch of highway bounded by nothingness. "No way!"

"Get. *Out*." Jude reached back and opened the door. "You love running away when things get intense, right? So let me help you. *Run*."

I didn't move.

"Now!"

The scream was pure rage. I leaped out of the car, letting Tak's head slam against the seat. Auden jumped out behind me. The car sped away before the door was fully shut.

And then we were alone.

"Now what?" Auden asked. "We walk back from . . . wherever the hell we are?"

There was no way I was ready to tell my parents what I'd been doing—and I was guessing Auden didn't want his father to find out either. There was one better option.

Which didn't make it a good one.

I linked in to the network, trying to ignore Auden's I-told-you-so glare.

Lucky us, she was there.

Lucky, right. Good thing I was getting used to redefining that concept on a daily basis.

"Zo?" I said, hating the words as they came out of my mouth. "I need a favor."

FORGIVENESS

"She decided not to care."

Zo didn't bother asking where we'd been or how we'd ended up stranded on the side of some deserted road. She stayed linked in for the duration of the ride, her eyes closed and her lips moving silently along with the lyrics only she could hear. Auden and I didn't talk much either until we dropped him off at his place.

I kept hearing it. Tak's scream. The gunshot.

I kept seeing him fall.

I saw him fall to the concrete, as I'd seen the bodies fall into the waterfall—and then, suddenly, I got it.

It was all the same.

This night, this moment, this was the ugly truth that lay hidden behind the wild beauty of the falls, behind Jude's pretty speeches. He had called me a coward, someone who couldn't face the truth. So I forced myself to face *this*; I forced myself not to look away.

This was the core of Jude and his friends. The core of

what they did, who they were, what they wanted. A scream. A gunshot.

A gun.

Destruction and pain, in a place as broken as they were.

This is what they sought out, these people I'd thought were like me; this is what they offered, when they invited me to belong.

It wasn't romantic. Whatever Jude said, it wasn't bold, it wasn't freeing.

It was a raw, ugly need.

And it was a need I finally understood.

Or maybe Jude was right; maybe I always had.

"I'm sorry," I said as he was getting out of the car.

He shook his head once. "Don't be."

But from the way he said it, I guessed that meant I shouldn't bother apologizing—not because it wasn't necessary, but because it wasn't enough.

When we got home, Zo brushed past me into the house and went up to her room without a word, slamming the door behind her. I couldn't believe she was acting like I'd done something to her when I knew, because they'd been live-casting it on their zones, that she'd spent most of the night with Walker.

I should have just shut down for the night. And I tried. I uploaded the day's memories. I pulled off the clothes covered in city grime and slipped into my favorite pair of thermosweats. I even lay down in bed. I could have shut my eyes and been out with a thought. That's how it worked. None of that inefficient tossing and turning, trying to force your brain to slow down and your body to relax. I just decided how long I wanted to "sleep," then told myself to *shut down*, the same way I told myself to *walk* or *sit* or *scream*. It was just another command, easy to issue, instantaneously carried out. But I wasn't ready to let go of the night.

Every time I closed my eyes, I saw the neat tunnel the bullet had made in Tak's shoulder. I heard him scream; I saw him smile.

No blood. No danger.

Just the thrill of the moment. And the pain.

And I wondered.

I found a razor in a bunch of junk under the bathroom sink. Left over from the days when I had real skin that sprouted real hair. It was a little rusty, but still sharp.

It wasn't the same as what *they* did, I told myself. I wasn't seeking pain in some sick attempt to make life more interesting. I wasn't sick, not like they were. I wasn't so numb that I needed a jolt of violence to wake up my brain. I wasn't chasing a death that would forever be out of my reach.

I was just curious.

It was an experiment. Perfectly safe, perfectly normal. I just wanted to see what would hurt, and how much. I needed to see how far I could go.

The blade pierced the skin.

Although I knew better, I half expected beads of blood to bubble up along the cut. It didn't happen. Nothing happened. The razor had barely sliced through the surface layer. It was like cutting through leather, the blade leaving only a thin groove behind.

And it hurt.

But not much. My brain registered: *pain*. Like a flashing red light, a warning to stop. But I didn't *feel* it, not really.

The stronger the emotion, the more "real" it may seem.

I bore down harder.

Still nothing. Or at least, not much.

In frustration, I raked the blade from my wrist to my elbow, hard, and gasped as the pain blazed through me. Finally.

There was an echoing gasp from the doorway. I looked up to see Zo staring at me in horror.

I jumped off the bed, pressing my arm awkwardly to my side to cover up the long gash. The razor clattered to the floor.

"I wasn't doing anything," I said.

Yeah, right.

She smirked. "Whatever."

"Seriously, you can't tell," I pleaded. Our mother would freak out. Our father would . . . I didn't know. I didn't want to know.

"Why would I tell?" she said.

"I wasn't trying to . . . hurt myself, or anything, if that's what you're thinking," I said. "I was just . . . It's normal. What I was doing, it's normal, it's no big deal, so can we just—"

"I don't care," Zo said, slowly and firmly. "How many times do I have to say it before you believe me? I don't care what you do. I don't care how big a freak you want to be. I. Don't. Care."

She really didn't. She couldn't, or she wouldn't act like this. She wouldn't have stolen my friends, my boyfriend, my life. She wouldn't glare at me like she wished I would disappear. Like she wished . . .

"You wish I was dead, is that it?" I started toward her, and she backed away. "You probably think it'd be easier for everyone if I'd died in the accident, so you didn't have to deal with me like *this*."

"Shut up," she said quietly.

"Nice comeback." I couldn't take it anymore, her smug, lying face pretending that I was nothing to her. Let her hate me, fine. At least then there'd be some kind of connection, some emotion. We'd still be sisters. "Why don't you just say it? You wish I was dead."

"I don't wish anything," she insisted. "I don't care what you are or what you do. I don't care. "

"Say it. *Say it!* You wish I was dead!"

"You *are* dead!" she screamed. The mask didn't just fall off her face. It disintegrated. Her lips trembled. Her eyes spurted tears. Her cheeks blazed red as the blood drained out of the rest of her face. She swallowed hard. "My sister is dead."

"Zo . . ." I crossed the room, tried to hug her, but she slipped out of my grasp. "No, Zoie, I'm not, it's okay, I'm right here."

She turned away from me and crossed her arms, huddled into herself. "What you said before, about the accident? That it should have been me?" She paused, and when she spoke again, her voice was shaking. "It should have been me."

"No. No, I should never have said that. I didn't mean it." But I had.

"It doesn't matter. It's true. I should have been in the car. I should be dead. But now—" She choked down a sob. "Now Lia's dead, and it's my fault."

"I'm not—"

"*Lia's* dead!" she shrieked, spinning to face me. "My sister is *dead*, and I basically killed her, and then this *thing* pretending to be Lia moves into her house, into her family, into her life, and I'm supposed to pretend that's okay? It's not bad enough that I have to live with what I did, with the fact that she—" Another sob. Another hard swallow. But when she spoke again, she was steadier. "I live with that. Every day. Every minute. And that I could handle. But seeing you . . . *act* like her, try to *be* her. Watching you take her place, like you ever could?" She shook her head, and continued in a cold hiss. "I hate you."

"Zo, don't."

"You think I like it?" she asked, furious. "Wasting my time with those losers she called her friends? Joining the track team, being Daddy's perfect little girl? You think I *like* screwing my sister's boyfriend?"

I flashed on the image of the two of them, lips fused. If she wasn't enjoying it, she was a better actress than I'd thought. "Then why—"

"Because *she* would have wanted me to protect what she had." Zo looked down. "Because if someone's going to replace her, it damn well isn't going to be *you*."

"But it *is* me." I came closer again. She stiffened.

"*Don't* touch me."

"Fine." I stayed a couple feet away, hands in the air. *See? Harmless.* "I'm not dead. I'm *not*. You didn't kill me. I know I look . . . different." I wanted to laugh at the understatement, but it didn't seem like the time. "It's still me. Your sister."

Zo shook her head. "No."

"Remember when we had that food fight with the onion dip? Or when we got iced in the house for a week and filmed our own vidlife?" I asked desperately. "Or how about the time you thought I hacked your zone and posted that baby pic of you, the one in the bathtub?"

"You did," she muttered.

"Of course I did," I said, grinning. "But only because you rigged my smartjeans and I ended up bare-assed in front of the whole seventh-grade class."

She almost laughed.

"How would I know all that unless I was there?" I asked. "Every fight we ever had, every secret you ever blabbed, *everything*. I know it. Because I was there. *Me*, Zo. Lia. It's still me."

She looked like she wanted to believe it.

But she decided not to. I saw it happen. The mask fell back over her features, stiffening her lips, hardening her eyes. She decided not to care.

"No," she said. "Lia's dead. You're a machine with her memories. That doesn't make you real. It definitely doesn't make you her."

"Then why am I still here?" I asked angrily. "If I'm just some imposter, why do Mom and Dad—excuse me, *your* mother and father—want me living in *Lia's* house? In *Lia's* room."

"They don't," she murmured.

"What?" But I'd heard her.

"They don't," she said louder. "They don't want you here. They wish you'd never come."

"You're lying."

"You wish."

"They love me," I said, needing to believe it. "They know it's me."

"They *loved* their daughter. Past tense. You just make it hurt more. They thought you'd make it better. That's why they did it—made you, like you'd be some kind of replacement. But you make everything worse."

"You're lying," I said again. It was the only weapon I had.

"If I am, then why is Dad up every night, crying?"

"He doesn't cry."

"He didn't used to," Zo said. "But he does now. Thanks

to you. Every night since you came home. He waits until he thinks we're all asleep, he goes to his study, and he *cries*. Sometimes all night. Don't believe me? He's probably at it right now. See for yourself."

"Get out of my room." Nothing she said could make me believe that about my father. Nothing.

"None of us want you here," she said.

"Get out!"

Zo shook her head. "I should feel sorry for you, I guess. But I can't."

She slammed the door behind her.

I told myself she was lying. Being cruel for the sake of cruelty. And maybe I couldn't blame her, if she really thought her sister was dead, if she thought it was her fault. But that didn't mean I had to believe her about our parents.

If my mother had fallen apart, if she thought I was just an inferior copy— Well, that I could deal with. It made even more sense than Zo. Our mother was weak, always had been. It wasn't her fault; it didn't mean I didn't love her. But it meant lower expectations.

My father was different.

He was the strong one, the smart one.

And, although I knew he would never admit it—not to me, not to Zo, not to anyone—I was his favorite. He was the one who knew me the best, who *loved* me the best. No, things hadn't been the same since the accident, but they were getting better. It would take some time, but I would get him back. Because he saw me for who I was, Lia Kahn.

His daughter.

I knew Zo was lying. I was sure. But not so sure that I stayed in my room and lay down in bed and closed my eyes. Not so sure that I didn't need proof.

My parents always turned on their soundproofing before they went to bed. So they wouldn't have heard Zo and me fight, not if they were already asleep. As they should have been at three in the morning. But when I crept downstairs, I saw the light filtering through the crack between the door to the study and the marble floor. And when I pressed my ear to the heavy door, I heard something.

Gently, noiselessly, I eased open the door.

He was on his knees.

He faced away from me, his head bent. His shoulders shook.

"Please," he said, in a hoarse, anguished voice. I flinched, thinking he must be speaking to me, that he knew I was there and wanted me to leave before I hurt him even more. But it was worse than that.

"Please, God, please believe me."

My father didn't pray. My father didn't believe in God. Faith was for the weak, he had always taught us. Backward-thinking, cowering, misguided fools who preferred to imagine their destiny lay in someone else's hands.

"I'm sorry."

And worse than faith in God, my father had taught us, was the ridiculous faith in a God who listened to human prayers, who had nothing better to do than stroke egos and grant wishes. An omniscient, omnipresent, omnipotent being who troubled himself with the minor missteps of the mortal world.

"Please forgive me."

He hunched over, bringing his forehead to his knees. "I did this to her. It was *my* choice. I did this. Please. Please forgive me. If I could do it again . . ." His whole body shuddered. "I would make the right choice this time. If I had a second chance, please . . ."

I closed the door on his sobs.

The right choice.

Meaning, the choice he hadn't made.

The choice to let me die.

LETTING GO

"They would age, they would die. I would live."

There was only one place I wanted to go. And only one person I wanted with me. If he was willing. I left two messages, voice and text, both with the same apology, the same request, and the same coordinates. Then I snuck out of the house—easy enough when no one cared where you went or when—and pushed the car as fast as it would go, knowing that the longer it took to get there, the more likely I'd be to turn back. The waterfall looked even steeper than I'd remembered it.

I had forgotten how at night, you couldn't see anything of the bottom except a fuzzy mist of white far, far below. I had forgotten how loud it was.

But I had also forgotten to be afraid.

Auden wasn't there.

But then, I hadn't told him to meet me at the top. My message had been very clear, the coordinates specific. If he'd woken up—and if he'd forgiven me—he would be waiting at the bottom. I would tell him everything that had happened, what my sister had said. I might even tell him how my father had looked, trembling on his knees, bowing down to a god in whom he was, apparently, too desperate not to believe. And just telling Auden would make it better. I knew that.

But this was something I had to do without him. Just another thing he could never understand, because he was an org. He was human, and I was—it was finally time to accept this—*not*. Which is why he was waiting at the bottom, if he was waiting at all. And I was at the top, alone.

I took off my shoes. Then, on impulse, I stripped off the rest of my clothes. That felt better. Nothing between me and the night. The wind was brutal. The water, I knew, would be like ice. But my body was designed to handle that, and more. My body would be just fine.

I waded into the water, fighting to keep my balance as the current swept over my ankles, my calves, my thighs, my waist. *Wet*, my brain informed me. *Cold*. And on the riverbed, *muddy. Rocky. Sharp*. The temperatures, the textures, they didn't matter, not yet. But I knew when I got close enough to the edge, when the water swept me over, the sensations would flood me, and in the chaos the distance between me and the world would disappear.

Not that I was doing it for an adrenaline rush. Or for the fear or the pain or even the pleasure. I wasn't trying to prove something to anyone, not even myself. It wasn't about that.

It was about Zo and my father and Walker and all of them—all of them who hated what I'd become. Maybe because it had replaced the Lia they really wanted or because it was ugly and different and, just possibly, if Jude was right, better. Maybe they were scared. I didn't know. I didn't care. I just knew they hated me. I knew my sister didn't believe I existed, and wanted me gone. My father wished—*prayed*—I was dead. Maybe it would be easier for all of them if I was.

Too bad.

I was alive. In my own unique, mechanical way, maybe. But alive. And I was going to stay that way for the foreseeable future. They would age, they would die. *I* would live.

There were too many people too afraid of what I'd become. I wasn't going to be one of them. Not anymore.

I didn't take a deep breath.

I didn't close my eyes.

I stretched my arms out.

I shifted my weight forward.

I let myself fall.

The world spun around me. The wind howled, and it sounded like a voice, screaming my name. The water thundered. The spray misted my body. And then I crashed into the surface, and there was nothing but rocks and water and a whooshing roar. And the water dragged me down, gravity dragged me down, down and down and down, thumping and sliding against the rocks, water in my eyes, in my mouth, in my nose. It was too loud to hear myself scream, but I screamed, and the water flooded in and choked off the noise. There was no time, no space in my head, to think *I'm going to die* or *I can't die* or *Why am I still falling, where is the bottom, when is the end?* There was no space for anything but the thunder and the water, as if *I* was the water, pouring down the rocks, gashed and sliced and battered and slammed and still whole, still falling—and then the river rose up to meet me, and the water sucked me down and I was beneath, where it was calm. Where it was silent.

Still alive, I thought, floating in the dark, safe beneath the storm of falling water.

Still here.

I closed my eyes, opened them, but the darkness of the water was absolute. I was floating again, like I had in the beginning, a mind without a body. Eyes, a thought, maybe a soul—and nothing else. But this time I wasn't afraid.

I let myself rise to the surface. The water slammed me, like a building crumbling down on my head, and again sucked me under.

And again the silence, again up to the surface, again the storm, and again sucked down to the depths.

I wasn't afraid. I knew I could stay below, swim far enough from the base of the falls to surface in safety. When I was ready. Which I wasn't, not yet. I was content to stay in the whirlpool, limp and battered, letting the water do what it wanted, filling myself up with the knowledge that I had done it, that I had jumped, that I had fallen. I had survived. I was alive; I was invincible. I wasn't ready for it to end.

Until I surfaced and heard the wind scream my name again. Except it wasn't the wind, it was Auden, who had come for me, who was screaming. I screamed back, but the water poured into my mouth. I waved an arm, but the water sucked me down again, and when I fought back to the surface, Auden was gone.

Then I did swim, deep and swift, my mind starting to seep back into itself and with it, panic. I was still invincible; Auden wasn't. I surfaced again, a safe distance from the churning water at the base of the falls. Nothing.

"Auden!"

Nothing.

Then back down into the dark, swimming blind, my arms outstretched, so that even if I couldn't see him, I would feel him, but there was just the water, parting easily as my body sliced through, water and more water and no Auden.

Until I broke through the surface and there he was, gasping and struggling to stay afloat, his hair plastered to his face, his eyes squinty and his glasses long gone. I grabbed him, squeezed tight, kicking hard enough to keep us both afloat.

"Are you okay?" As we drifted away from the falls, the water grew shallower until we hit a point where our feet touched the bottom, midway between the base of the first waterfall and the edge of the second, smaller drop-off.

"Okay," he said, panting. The current was lighter here, easy enough to fight. "You?"

"Fine. What the hell are you doing?"

"Rescuing you." He shivered in my grasp. "You were drowning."

I shook my head.

He looked like he wanted to drop down into the water and never surface. "Stupid," he said furiously. "Of course you weren't. I just—I saw you up there, and when you fell, and you didn't come up, and I thought—"

"Thank you," I cut in, hugging him tighter. "My hero." I didn't need a hero, and I wasn't the one who'd needed rescue. But he was soaking and freezing and had nearly drowned, and I figured there was no harm in giving him a little ego stroke.

"Uh, Lia?"

"What?" I asked, hoping that he wasn't going to choose yet another horribly timed moment to start talking about the great love affair that was never going to be. An ego stroke was one thing, but there was only so far I could go.

"You're, uh, not wearing any clothes."

"Oh!" I let go, and bent my knees until I was submerged up to my neck.

"I couldn't see anything, anyway," he said. "Not without my glasses."

I grinned. "So you were looking?"

His cheeks turned red. His lips, on the other hand, were nearly blue.

"Let's get out of here," he suggested, hugging himself and jumping up and down against the cold.

I wasn't ready, not yet. "You go. I just want . . ." It was just another thing I couldn't explain to him, the way it felt to go over the falls, to know that I had absolutely no control and to just let it happen, let myself fall—and to survive. I knew I'd have to drag myself out of the water to see what damage I'd done, if any. I'd also have to deal with everything else. And I would. Just not yet. "I'm staying in. For a while."

"Then me too," he said.

"You're freezing."

He shook his head, stubborn. Stupid. "I'm fine."

"Fine. Have it your way."

So we stayed in, Auden making a valiant effort to pretend he wasn't noticing my body. While I, for the first time, *wasn't* noticing it. I wasn't ashamed, wasn't repulsed; I was just content to be where I was, what I was—and to be with him. We did backflips and somersaults and competed for who could hold a handstand longer before the current swept us over. We laughed. We didn't talk about my family or about Jude or about "us" and especially not about what had happened in the city or what was going to happen when we got back to shore. We didn't talk about much of anything, except some supposedly funny vid he'd seen of a monkey in a diaper and whether if one was in a position to eat, daily chocolate was a required element of a healthy and balanced diet. Meaningless stuff like that. Easy stuff.

I hadn't been so happy in a long time. Maybe since the accident.

"I think . . . I need . . . to get out," Auden finally said as I resurfaced from a perfect handstand. His teeth were chattering so hard he could barely form the words.

I nodded. "Race to shore?" And before he could answer I took off, digging my strokes into the water, pushing hard to win. I missed winning.

Midway to the bank I popped my head up, checking to see if he was catching up . . . but he was swimming in the wrong direction. Swimming along with the current. Away from me, away from the shore, toward the edge.

"Auden!" I shouted. "Wrong way!"

He's not wearing his glasses, I thought suddenly, horrified. *He can't see.*

"Auden! Swim toward me! Follow my voice!"

But he didn't call back. He didn't change direction. And I began to realize he wasn't swimming at all. He was drifting.

Cold, I thought as the water lapped against my body. *But how cold?* Cold enough that a person—a real, live, warm-blooded person—couldn't take it anymore? Couldn't fight back against the current? Couldn't make it to shore?

"Auden!" I screamed, and then I ducked under the water, pushing myself harder than I ever had on the track, when it didn't count, pushing the legs to kick, the arms to dig, to reach him, to grab him before the current carried him away, before the water caught him and wouldn't let go, not until it plunged over another edge, down another ripple of jagged

rock, into a storm of erupting water, and down, into the silent depths, the center of the whirlpool.

I swam fast. The current was faster. He was one arm's length away, close enough that I could see his pale face, his closed eyes, his arms floating limply and his head tipped back, bouncing along shuddering water—and then two arm's lengths, and then three, and the river carried him away from me, the river claimed him. I screamed, I lunged, one last, powerful kick forward, one desperate grasp—and his body disappeared over the edge.

I went over after him. This time there was nothing joyous about the plunge. Nothing fast or chaotic. It seemed to last forever. Enough time for me to go over it in my head, again and again, seeing him on the shore, hearing him scream my name, clinging to his body—and then letting him go. *Hold on,* I thought furiously, as if I could communicate with the past, as if the girl in the memory could make a better choice. *It's cold,* I told her. *It's too cold.*

But the girl in the memory didn't notice the cold or didn't care.

She was invincible.

I was sucked down again at the bottom, but there was no peace in the dark, quiet water. The empty stillness just meant he wasn't there. I fought my way to the surface, hoping, but I didn't see him, didn't hear him, so I dove down again, sweeping the river from one side to the other, swimming blind, arms outstretched. Telling myself that it would be like before, I would catch him, only for him to tell me that he hadn't needed rescuing, and we would laugh over the misunderstanding, and this time I wouldn't let go.

I don't know how much time passed before I realized what I had to do. Seconds, maybe. Minutes, at the most. No time at all if you didn't have breath to hold. And if you did? Too much.

Lungs filled with oxygen floated. Empty lungs sank to the bottom.

So that's where I searched next, my bare stomach scraping against the muddy riverbed. I forced myself to keep my kicks slow and steady, covering the ground methodically, hoping I would find him, hoping I wouldn't, because if he was there, a still body in the mud, if he was . . .

I didn't let myself think about it.

I swam.

And then I touched something that wasn't rock, wasn't mud, was firm and long and foot-shaped, and I wrapped my hand around it, around him. I scooped up his body and kicked toward the surface, burst out of the water. And only then did I force myself to look at what I was holding. His eyes were open, rolled back in his head. I had to turn away from the unbroken white stare. He wasn't breathing.

CPR, I thought, towing him to shore. I voiced for help, gave our coordinates, and someone would come for us, to save us—but maybe not in time.

Make him breathe. Breathe for him.

But I didn't breathe at all.

Still, there was air flowing through my throat, I thought. Hissing past my voice box, when I needed it, the stream of unfiltered air that made the artificial larynx vibrate so I could talk. I didn't know if that would work. I had to try.

The network told me what to do. I tipped his head back. I placed my lips on his. They were so cold. Blood oozed from the cuts on his face, on his arms, blood everywhere.

Breathe, I thought, forcing the air through my mouth, into his. Pumping his chest, maybe in the wrong place, maybe too light, maybe too hard, I didn't know, but pumping, once, twice, three times, thirty times, just like I was supposed to. I paused, I waited, I listened. No change.

I breathed for him again.

And again.

He coughed.

Water spurted out of his mouth, spraying me in the face.

"Auden." I cradled his face. "Auden!"

He didn't say anything. But he was breathing. I could hear him. I could see his chest rise and fall. He was breathing.

"I'm sorry," I whispered. I laid my head against his chest, listening to his heart. Night had almost ended; the sky was turning pink.

He was still breathing when help arrived. They shifted him onto a backboard, immobilized his neck and spine, gave him an oxygen feed, loaded him into an ambulance. I got in after him, because no one stopped me.

It was only when someone wrapped a blanket around me that I realized I was still naked.

No one would tell me if he was going to be okay. But I promised him he would, over and over again.

His eyes opened.

"You're okay," I told him, holding his hand. His fingers sat limply in mine. "You're going to be okay."

"I hope not," he croaked, his voice crackly.

For a second I was so happy to hear him speak that I didn't register what he said.

"They'll make me like you," he whispered. "We can be the same."

"No," I whispered back, fiercely. "You're going to be fine."

That's what I said.

That's what I wanted to believe, about him, about myself.

I didn't want to be a person who hoped he was right, that he would *not* be fine. I didn't want to hope that he was hurt so badly that there'd be no other option, that he would die, only to be reborn as a machine, just so that I wouldn't have to be alone.

I reminded myself what it would mean. I pictured him, even though it hurt—*because* it hurt—lying still on a metal slab, pale and cold, the white sheet draped over his skull, where his brain had been scooped out, carved up, replicated. I pictured him trapped in the dark, stuck in a frozen body, thinking he might be dead, then wishing he was.

I didn't want that for him.

Or at least, I didn't *want* to want that for him.

But truth? Sordid, pathetic truth? I think I did.

If Auden were a mech, if we could go through it together, everything would be different. I would no longer be alone.

"You're going to be okay," I said again, uselessly. It was better and less complicated than the truth, and maybe if I said it enough, it would come true.

"Liar." His eyes rolled back in his head.

Somewhere, an alarm sounded, and one of the men pushed me out of the way.

"Flatline," the man said, pushing on Auden's chest, fiddling with a machine, as the alarm droned on.

"What's happening?"

No one answered me.

The ambulance sped toward the hospital, and the men pounded on his chest, and the alarm beeped, and Auden's chest lay flat, his lungs empty.

Flatline.

No heartbeat.

No life.

They'll fix you, I thought, squeezing his hand, holding on, like I hadn't in the water. *They have to.*

NUMB

"Nothing hurts."

At the hospital someone gave me something to wear.
Someone else brought bandages, patched up the
gashes the rocks had torn in my skin. Even though there was
no need. Nothing was gushing or dripping. Nothing hurt.
Nothing had penetrated the hard shell around the neural cortex and—or so it seemed from the fact that I could still walk
and talk—none of the complicated wiring beneath the surface
had been shaken loose. I was fine. But I let them patch the skin.
I nodded when they told me I needed to get myself checked
out—somewhere else, of course, where they knew what to do
with things like me. I would have agreed to anything as long
as they let me stay.

Auden was gone, swept away behind a set of white double
doors, and I sat on a blue padded chair, staring at nothing,
waiting.

This isn't happening, I thought, then cut myself off. No
denial.

No rage, no bargaining, *no* acceptance. I wasn't getting sucked into any of that five stages of grieving shit, because he was still alive. Ergo, no grief. No denial.

This is *happening*.

I had wanted to feel. Now I wanted to stop. I wanted to be all those things people were afraid of. I wanted to be cold and heartless, like a computer, like a refrigerator, like a toaster. I wanted to turn myself off.

That, at least, I could do.

I didn't.

The white doors swung open, and a doctor pushed through. He sat down next to me.

Not good, I thought. If it was good news, he would stay on his feet, he would spit it out quickly, so we could all sigh and laugh and go home. But bad news, he'd want to deliver that face-to-face. He'd want to be close enough that he could pat me on the shoulder. Or catch me if I passed out. Even though, as a doctor, he would know that was an impossibility.

"Has someone contacted his parents?" the doctor asked.

I nodded. "There's just his father." It was hard to get words out. Every time I spoke—every time I sent a blast of air through my throat, past my larynx, into and then out of my mouth, I remembered doing it for him, breathing for him, and I wondered if my air had been good enough, if *I* had been good enough or—

No. I am a machine, I thought. I could control myself. I

could control my emotions. They weren't real anyway, right? Whatever happened, I could handle it. I would handle it.

"He's on his way," I said in my pathetic little voice. I didn't know that for sure, because I'd had to leave the message for him, bad enough, since how do you leave that kind of message? *Hi, your son might be dead and if he is, it's probably my fault. Have a nice day!*

The doctor sighed. He had two thin scars in front of his ears and another set framing his nose, telltale signs that he'd just finished his latest lift-tuck. It looked good. I hated myself for noticing. "I should really wait for his guardian to arrive before I go into the specifics of his situation, but—"

"You have to tell me *something*," I pleaded. "Please."

"*But*, as I was about to say, I don't think it would hurt to give you a general update." He paused, and gave me a searching look like he was trying to figure out if I was prone to noisy and embarrassing breakdowns. I wondered if there was a private little room somewhere that they used for conversations like this, a walled-in space where you could shriek and throw things without inconveniencing all those people whose lives hadn't just fallen apart.

But the waiting room was empty. We stayed where we were.

"Your boyfriend's heart stopped."

"He's not my boyfriend," I said automatically.

I have never hated myself more than I did in that silent

moment after the words were out. There was nothing I could do to take them back.

"Okay, well . . ." In that pause, I could tell. The doctor hated me too. "Your friend's heart stopped. He was technically dead for about two hours."

Was. I held tight to the verb tense.

"But we were lucky that the body temperature was already so low. . . ." The doctor shook his head. "I don't know how he managed to last as long as he did in water that cold, but it's made our job a bit easier."

The water was too cold, I thought.

My fault, I thought.

No one forced him to jump in after me, I told myself. *No one forced him to stay.*

But I knew better.

"We'll keep his temp down to slow his metabolism, and keep reperfusion as gradual as possible—resume oxygen supply too quickly and brain cells start dying, but if we do it slowly, we should be able to preserve a substantial amount of brain function."

"What does that mean?" I asked. "Substantial."

"It means we'll know more when he wakes up."

"But he *will* wake up? When?"

"That's still to be determined," the doctor said slowly. "But, yes, in cases like this, we're optimistic for a cognitive recovery."

"You mean he'll be okay," I said eagerly.

The doctor looked uncomfortable.

"You said recovery," I reminded him. "You said optimistic."

"I said *cognitive* recovery. We have every reason to hope that his brain might emerge from this intact. But his body . . . I'm told you were there, so you must know. The weight of the water crashing down on him, at the speed it was falling, and the rocks . . . There are impact injuries, crush injuries. He took quite a beating." The doctor shook his head. "The extent of the damage . . ."

"You can fix it," I said. "He has plenty of credit, enough for anything. You have to fix it."

"There are a lot of things we can fix," he agreed. "And in cases like this, there are of course"—he paused, then looked pointedly at me. No, not at me. At *the body*—"other options."

"Oh." I looked at the floor. "It's that bad?"

"It's bad," he said. "But I'm afraid I can't go into more detail until his father arrives. You're not family, so . . ."

"Of course. I understand."

I understood. I wasn't his family. I wasn't his girlfriend. I was nothing.

M. Heller arrived an hour or so later, sans wife number two. He blew past me, pushed aside the nurse who tried to stop him from going through the white double doors, and disappeared behind them. When he emerged, a few minutes later, he looked different. He looked *old*. He slumped down on the closest chair and let himself fall forward, his head toppled over his knees. He was shaking.

But when he looked up to see me standing over him, his eyes were dry.

"M. Heller, I just wanted to say, I don't know if they told you that I was with Auden when— Well, anyway, I just wanted to say I'm sorry, and I hope—"

"Get out," he said flatly.

"What?"

"I don't want you here. Get out."

"M. Heller, look, I'm not trying to upset you, but your son and I—"

"What?" he said fiercely, like he was daring me to keep going. "My son and you *what*?"

"Nothing," I said quietly. I didn't have any words.

"He's my *son*," M. Heller's voice trembled on the word. "And they're telling me he might—" His face went very still for a moment. "I can't look at you right now. Please go."

He didn't have to explain. I got it. They were telling him his son might die—or worse. Might become like me.

And didn't I know? That kind of thing could ruin a father's life.

I backed away. But I didn't leave. I just sat down on the other side of the waiting room. M. Heller didn't object. He acted like he didn't notice. So he sat on one side of the room, staring at the floor. I sat on the other side, staring at the wall. And we did what the room was meant for.

We waited.

A couple hours later they let M. Heller see him. No one said anything to me.

The day passed. I left my parents a message, the obligatory assurance I was still alive. They didn't need to know any more than that. M. Heller disappeared behind the white doors for hours. Still no one told me anything. No one on the staff would speak to me. Until finally the doctor I recognized appeared again. I grabbed him as he passed. "What's happening? Is he awake? Can I see him?"

The doctor rubbed the back of his neck. "I'm sorry, but the patient's father has insisted that he not have any visitors."

At least I knew he was still alive.

"Can you at least tell me how he's doing?"

"M. Heller has also . . ." The doctor sighed and shook his head. "I'm afraid I'm not allowed to give out any more information about the patient's status."

"Not to anyone?" I asked, already suspecting the answer. "Or . . . ?"

"Not to you."

I wanted to scream. I wanted to break something. Like M. Heller's neck. Or even the doctor's, since he was closer at hand. But instead I just sat down again, like a good little girl, following the rules.

I waited.

I waited for M. Heller to change his mind. It didn't happen. So then I changed my strategy. I waited for him to leave or fall asleep or eat. Because he would have to do one of them eventually. He had needs.

I didn't.

A day passed, and a night, and it was nearly dawn again when a nurse escorted M. Heller back into the waiting room. She stayed close, as if expecting him to stumble or to lose the ability to hold himself up. *Lean on me*, she projected, shoulders sturdy and ready to carry the burden. But he stayed upright. Separate and unruffled, like nothing could touch him. His eyes skimmed over me as if I wasn't there.

"I'll be back with his things," I heard him say, hesitating in the doorway. "You're sure it's—"

"It's okay," she assured him. "Go home and get a little sleep. Save your strength. He's going to need it."

M. Heller nodded. It took him a moment too long to raise his head again. "And you'll let me know if anything . . . changes."

"Immediately," she said. "Go."

He left. Which meant I just had to choose my moment. Wait until no one was watching. Then slip through the white doors. Find Auden's room. Find Auden. See for myself, whatever it was. Even if it was something I didn't want to see.

I waited.

• • •

He was asleep.

At least, he looked like he was asleep. His eyes were closed. That was almost all I could see of his face: his eyes. The rest was covered with bandages. It didn't look like Auden. It barely looked like a human being, not with all the tubes feeding in and out of every orifice and the regenerative shielding stretching across his torso and definitely not with the metal scaffolding encasing his head like a birdcage. Four rigid metal rods sprouted from a padded leather halter that stretched around his shoulders and collarbone. They connected to a thin metal band that circled his skull. Slim silver bits dug into his forehead at evenly spaced points, pinching the skin and holding the contraption in place. A bloody smear spread over his left eyebrow, and I tried not to imagine someone drilling the metal bit into his skull. I wondered if he'd been awake, if it had hurt; if it still hurt. I didn't want to know what it was for.

There was a metal folding chair to the left of his bed. I sat down. His right arm was in a cast. His legs were covered by a thin blue blanket. But his left arm lay exposed and, except for a few small bandages and the IV needle jabbed into his wrist, feeding some clear fluid into his bloodstream, the arm looked normal. Healthy. So, very gently, careful not to jar any of the delicately assembled machinery that surrounded his body, I rested my hand on top of his.

I wondered where his glasses were, in case he needed them.

No—*when* he needed them. Then I remembered they were probably floating downstream somewhere, miles away. Maybe they'd made it to the ocean. I didn't even know if the river hit the ocean. But everything does eventually, right?

He opened his eyes.

"Hi!" No, that was too loud, too fakely cheery. He'd see through it. "Hey," I said, softer.

Nothing.

"Auden? Can you hear me?" I leaned over him, so that he could see me, even with his head pinned in place by the metal cage. "It's me. Lia."

I wondered if he could understand what I was saying.

Substantial amount of brain function, the doctor had said without ever clarifying what "substantial" meant. Something more than none; something less than *all*.

"You're going to be okay," I said, just like I'd said on the way to the hospital, just as uselessly. I remembered, then, how much I'd hated it when people had said it to me. How ridiculous, how *unacceptable* it had sounded coming from people who were whole and healthy. *Nothing* would be okay, I'd thought after the accident. And I'd hated them for lying. "The doctor says you'll be fine."

"You must be talking to a different doctor," he said. Wheezed, more like. His words were slow and raspy, like he hadn't used his throat in a long time. And like they hurt coming out.

But still, I smiled, and my smile was real. He was back.

"I was so—" I stopped myself. He didn't need to hear how I'd been torturing myself in the waiting room, worrying. This wasn't about me, I reminded myself. It was about him. "You look like crap," I said, trying to laugh. "Does it hurt?"

"No."

It figured. They had pretty good drugs these days, and he was no doubt getting the best.

"So, I guess we've got something in common now," I said. "We've both been technically dead, and come back to life." Was it inappropriate to joke? Would it make him feel better, or would it make him think I didn't care? "Better be careful, or the Faithers will start worshipping us or something."

"Uh-huh."

Okay. Too soon to joke.

"I saw your father in the waiting room. He was really worried about you. I guess he cares more than you . . . Well. Anyway. He was worried."

"Yeah."

It probably hurt him to talk.

"Not that he has to be worried, because you're going to be fine. Doctors can do anything these days, right? Just look at me."

Wrong thing to say.

Everything I said was the wrong thing to say.

I rubbed my palm lightly across his, wishing that he would grasp my hand, squeeze my fingers, do *something* to indicate that he wanted me there. But he didn't. I held on anyway. His skin was warm, proof that he was still alive.

"You were amazing, you know that?" I said. "When you jumped in to rescue me? They said the water was so cold you shouldn't even have been able to—" I stopped. Neither of us needed the reminder. "It was really heroic. To save me."

"It was stupid."

"No, Auden. . . ."

He didn't speak again, just stared at the ceiling.

"You're tired," I said. "I should probably go, let you sleep—"

"Don't you want to know?"

"What?"

"What the doctors said." His lips turned up at the corners, but it wasn't a real smile, and not just because the bandages held most of his skin in place. "The prognosis. All the thrilling details."

"Of course I want to know." I didn't.

Especially when he started reciting it in a dry, clinical tone, words out of a medical text that didn't seem to have any connection to him, his body, his wounds. Punctured lung. Internal bleeding. Bruised kidney. Lacerations. Fractures. The heart muscle weakened by multiple arrests. A cloned liver standing by for transplant, if necessary. They would wait and see. "And the grand finale," he said, his voice like ice. He sounded like his father. "Severed spinal cord. At C5."

I didn't understand how so much damage could have been done so quickly, in thirty seconds . . . and thirty feet. *Don't forget the eighty thousand gallons of water*, I thought. And yet I was just fine.

"Auden, I'm so . . . I'm so sorry." I threaded my hand through the metal cage and brushed my fingers against his cheek.

"Don't touch me," he said. *"Don't."*

I yanked my hand away. But my left hand still rested on his. Out of his sight line, I realized. I squeezed his fingers, tight, waiting for him to tell me to let go.

He didn't.

"What?" he asked, sounding irritated.

I stared at his fingers, the fingers that hadn't moved since I came into the room. The fingers that he was letting me touch, even though he didn't want me touching him.

"Does it hurt?" I asked again, for a different reason this time.

"Nothing hurts." He sounded like a robot. He sounded like I sounded before I got control of my voice again, when I had to communicate through an electronic box.

"What does it mean? What's going to happen?"

"C5. That's *C* for cervical, five for the fifth vertebra down," he said. "They've got it all mapped out. C5 means I keep head and neck motion. Shoulders, too. Eventually. It means right now I can't feel anything beneath my neck. It means I'm fucked for life."

"Not anymore," I protested. "They can fix that now. Can't they?"

"They fuse the cord back together. Yeah. And then nerve regeneration. You get some feeling back. You get some motion. They call it 'limited mobility.' It means you can walk, like, a little. A couple hours a day. And apparently if I practice, I might be able to piss for myself again."

"So that sounds . . ." It sounded like a life sentence to hell. "Hopeful."

"Yeah. As in, they hope it won't hurt so much I spend the rest of my life doped up, but they're not sure. As in, they hope they can put me back together enough that I don't die in ten years, but they're not sure. Fucking high hopes, right?"

There had always been something sweet to Auden, something carefully hidden beneath the cynicism and the conspiracy theories and the family baggage, as if he was afraid to reveal his secret reservoir of hope. But that was gone now. There was nothing beneath the bitter but more bitter. *It's temporary,* I told myself.

Things change.

"If it's that bad, why don't you . . . take the other option?" I asked.

"And exactly what might you be referring to?"

I hesitated. "Nothing." So that was it. He didn't want to be like me, no matter what he may have said. He'd rather be miserable, debilitated, in pain, than be like me. Maybe I couldn't blame him.

"Say it."

"Nothing."

"Say it!" Something beeped, and he took a deep, gasping breath. "Better listen to me," he said, panting. "I'm not supposed to get agitated."

"Why don't you download?" I said quickly, remembering something else I'd hated when I was the one trapped in a bed. The way everyone suddenly got so scared of nouns, as if vague mentions of "what happened" and "your circumstances" would make me forget what was actually going on. As if by not saying it out loud, they were helping anyone but themselves.

"Brain scans."

"I'm sorry, I don't— What?"

"They took brains scans," he said, haltingly. "And there was an anomaly."

I still didn't understand.

"I'm disqualified," he said. "Structural abnormalities. Predisposition for mental disorder and/or decay. Unlikely but possible. So just in case—automatic disqualification. They don't want me living forever if I'm going to go crazy, right?" He laughed. "It's funny, isn't it?"

I pressed my lips together.

"Yeah, no one else seems to think so either," he said. "Maybe I'm crazy already."

"They can't fix it?" I asked softly. "Whatever it is?"

"They could have. Before I was born. If they'd known

about it, if my mother had let them screen for that kind of thing. But she thought it was superfluous. She only wanted the basics." He laughed again. It was a weirdly tinny, mechanical sound, since his body was immobilized and his lungs were barely pumping any air. "Thanks, Mom."

"There's got to be something you can do, if you paid enough, some way to change their minds?"

"Nothing. No brand-new body for me. I'm stuck with this one. For life." He paused. "As long as that lasts."

I squeezed his hand again. Not that he felt it.

"Funny, isn't it?" he said. "They can make a fake body from scratch, but they can't fix a real one. Guess there's only so much you can do when you're stuck with damaged goods." He didn't laugh. "No, I guess that's not very funny either."

"I can help," I told him. "I know how it feels, lying there, thinking your life is over. I understand."

"You understand *nothing*," he spat out. "That's what you always used to tell me, right? 'You can't understand, not unless you've been there.' You've never been here."

"You're alive," I said, aware that I was sounding like call-me-Ben, like Sascha, like every medical cheerleader I'd ever wanted to strangle. And now I finally got why they'd said all that. They needed to believe it. You couldn't look at someone so broken and *not* believe they could, somehow, be fixed. "That's something."

"Something I don't want. Not like this."

So I said what all those cheerleaders never had. The truth. "Neither would I. And . . . it's never going to be like it was before. *Never*. That will never be okay. But *you* will."

He snorted.

"I know you don't believe it," I said desperately. "I know it all sounds like greeting-card bullshit that doesn't apply to you, but it does. Maybe I can't understand everything, but I understand that. The way you feel? I honestly don't know if that goes away. But people—*you*—can get used to things, even if it seems impossible now. You can make it work."

"Oh really?" he said, bitterness chewing the edges of the false cheer. "Thanks *so* much for the insight. So I can get used to a machine telling me when it's time to pee, and when it's time to shit, and then helping me do it—and that's *after* all the regeneration surgery's done. Until then, I just get a diaper. You think you could get used to changing it for me? I can get used to internal electrodes that spark my muscles into action and let me walk around and pretend I'm normal until it hurts so much that I fall down and have to get someone to cart me away? They tell me that part's the medical miracle. Twenty years ago I might have been a lump in this fucking bed for the rest of my life, with people feeding me and turning me and wiping my ass. So you think I can get used to people telling me how fucking grateful I should be? And I can get used to my lungs working at half capacity, if I'm *lucky*, and feeling like I've got an elephant stomping on my chest—at least until the fluid builds up, and while I wait around for them to come suck it out, it just feels like I'm drowning? Not that you would know anything about that."

"It sucks," I said. "I know that. But you're not alone. You don't have to do this alone. I'm here, just like you were there for me." I remembered the day I froze in the quad, the way he knew exactly what to say and what to do, even though he didn't know me at all. And now no one knew me except for him. "We'll do this together."

"Together." He snorted. "Right. And maybe you'll finally fall deeply in love with me and make all my dreams come true. We'll live happily ever after. As long as they can rig me up with some kind of hydraulic system. Not like I ever got to do it the normal way, so I guess I won't even notice the difference."

"Auden, don't—"

"Don't what? Tell you all about how my penis may get 'moderate sensation' back, and if I respond well to the electrical-impulse therapy—which, let me tell you, my penis and I are really looking forward to—I might, *might* be able to get the fucking thing up, up for some fucking, I mean, but—"

"Please don't."

"Oh, I'm sorry, am I grossing you out with all the medical details? Or is it the thought of having *sex* with me that disgusts you?"

He wanted me to fight with him. I wasn't going to do it. Not now. Not here. "I thought my life was over when I woke up like this," I said. "But you're the one who told me that I could handle it. That I could start fresh."

"This is different."

"I know, but—"

"No!" The beeping started again. "You *don't* know. This isn't what you went through. This isn't what you understand. This is *me*, my life. This is the way it's going to be forever: shit." He closed his eyes, sucking in heavy gulps of air.

"I'm sorry," I whispered, silently pleading with him to stay calm. "Just tell me what you want from me. What can I do?"

"You can get out."

I stood up. "You're right. You should try to sleep. I'll come back later."

"No. You should get out and not come back. Ever."

"What are you talking about?"

"This is your fault," he said in a low voice. "What happened . . . It's your fault."

"It was an accident. You were just trying to . . . save me." When I didn't need saving.

"Seems like I've been doing that a lot," he said. "You do something stupid, you do something reckless, and I fix it. You treat me like crap, and I save you again. Because I'm stupid. Was stupid."

I closed my eyes. "You're my best friend."

He went on like he hadn't heard. Or didn't want to. "You're probably happy, aren't you? Why should anyone else get to be healthy and normal if you've got to walk around like some kind of mechanical freak, right?"

He's just trying to hurt me, I told myself. And I had to let him do it if that's what he needed. I had to do whatever he needed.

This is not my fault.

"Maybe this was the plan all along. Is that it? Is that why you kept dragging me along with you, making me take all those stupid risks? You were trying to get me killed— Excuse me, I mean, get me *broken*?"

"Of course not! This was an *accident*."

"This was inevitable. And if you didn't see that, you're as stupid as I was."

"Auden, come on. I . . . I love you."

"But not in *that* way, right?"

I would have happily lied if I'd thought there was even a chance he would believe me. "No. But—"

"But I'm supposed to grovel at your feet, thankful for whatever I can get from you, right? Sorry, not in the mood today. I'm not feeling too well."

"Tell me how to make this better. Please."

"I already did: Get out. The only reason I'm talking to you now is that I wanted you to hear it from me. What you did. Now you know. So we're done."

I didn't move.

"Obviously I can't force you," he said. "I'm just going to

close my eyes and pretend you're not here. And hopefully when I open them, you won't be. You want to do something for me? Do that. Help me pretend I still have some fucking control over *something*."

He closed his eyes.

I left.

But I didn't leave the hospital. Because he was right: He didn't have control over anything anymore. Including me.

I went back to the waiting room. I watched his father return. I watched the doctors and nurses pass through on the way from one crisis to another.

I waited.

I waited until late that night, after his father had fallen asleep and the few remaining doctors and nurses were too busy watching the clock to watch me. And once outside his doorway, I waited again, watching, making sure Auden was asleep.

Then I crept inside. I lifted the chair and placed it at the foot of his bed where, even if he woke up, he wouldn't be able to see me. He obviously wouldn't hear me breathing. And he wouldn't feel my hands resting on the lumpy blanket, cradling his useless feet.

BETTER OFF

"None of us are volunteers."

He's not dead, I told myself, standing outside the hospital, wondering what to do next. *That's what counts. He won't die, not for a long time—and not because of this.*

It should have felt like good news.

He doesn't want to die, I told myself. He may have said it. But only because he didn't yet understand that some things are bearable, even when you're sure that they're not.

I understand, I told myself. *I can help him.*

But the second part of that was a lie. And maybe he was right, and the first part was too.

I told myself: *This is not your fault.*

I told myself the anger would pass, and he would forgive.

Denial bleeds into anger, I told myself. Then would come bargaining and depression, and then, finally, always, acceptance. He would grieve the loss of the life he had wanted. He would accept my help.

I told myself I would find a way to get by without his.

I lied.

It was a cold day. It was always a cold day. And, as always, it didn't matter to me.

Who was I supposed to go to with this? *Auden* was the person I went to. Auden was the one who understood. He was supposed to be the solution, not the problem. So who was I supposed to talk to about losing the only person I could talk to? Who was supposed to cure my loneliness if I was alone?

I was alone.

And maybe it was my fault.

Or maybe not, I thought suddenly. Auden would never have been hurt if I hadn't gone to the waterfall, but I would never have gone to the waterfall if Jude hadn't shown me the way. If he hadn't practically *dared* me to jump, turned it into some huge symbolic statement of my identity instead of what it was: a dumb stunt. Crazy, like Auden had said. Not that I had bothered to listen.

I need to see you, now, I texted Jude, and he sent me an address without asking why. Maybe he just assumed I'd always needed him and was only now realizing it. He was just enough of an ass to think that way.

This is not my fault, I told myself again, and there was more force behind it this time. *It's his.*

It was a different house than before. More of an estate, really; almost a feudal village, complete with outlying buildings dotting the grounds and, atop the highest hill, a turreted Gothic monstrosity that looked like a fairy-tale castle if the fairy tale was *Sleeping Beauty*, where the princess's home was decrepit, covered with thorns and forgotten. Jude met me outside.

"You live *here*?"

"It's Quinn's," Jude said. "She's invited some of us to stay . . . for a while."

"She barely knows you."

His lips curled up. "I guess she knows enough." He guided us down an overgrown path, headed toward a giant greenhouse. There was nothing inside but a thicket of dead plants. Most of the windowpanes were empty; the ground crunched with shattered glass. "So, you come here to chat about real estate?"

"It's Auden," I said, suddenly sorry I had come. It felt wrong to say his name out loud, here. To Jude. "He's hurt."

Jude nodded. "He's an org. I hear it happens from time to time."

I couldn't believe him. "You don't even care? You're not even going to ask how bad?"

"He's not my friend, as he's always been so quick to point out. Why should I care?"

"Bad," I informed him, whether he cared or not. "Thanks to *you*."

Jude raised an eyebrow. Nothing touched him. *Nothing*.

"You pushed me," I said. "You wouldn't accept that I wasn't like you. And you just had to keep pushing and pushing, all that crap about losing control and letting go and I finally did, and *he's* the one who has to pay? Congratulations, Jude," I said bitterly. "It all worked out according to your plan. He hates me, and I've got nothing, just like you wanted. Just like you predicted, right? I'm fucking alone. Thanks for your help. Thanks a lot."

Jude leaned against the door frame of the greenhouse, ignoring the protruding shards of glass. "Deciphering incoherent rants isn't really a specialty of mine," he said, still perfectly calm. Detached. "But if I've got this right, you did something, your org got hurt, and this is somehow my fault because I told you to do it in the first place? You always do everything you're told?"

I let myself sink to the ground. It sounded even stupider out loud than it had in my head. The grass was still wet from a morning rain, and the cold water seeped into my filthy, borrowed clothes.

"I hate you," I said.

"Not much of an apology. But I'll take it. Want to tell me what happened?"

I told him. All of it, from the fight with Zo straight through to the moment in the hospital room, the sound of Auden's voice—the *tone* of Auden's voice, cold and mechanical—when he told me to leave.

And when I was done, Jude nodded. "Tragic," he said. As emotionless as ever. I wondered if he'd discovered the secret to shutting down his emotions for good. And if he would teach it to me.

"Feel free to do your little happy dance," I said. "I know you hated him."

"I never hated him. I hated the idea of you pretending that he could matter to you or that he could ever understand you. That the two of you were anything but a disaster."

"Disaster's right. *I* was the disaster," I said. "I ruined his life."

Jude didn't say anything. I looked up. "Aren't you going to tell me it wasn't my fault? That I shouldn't blame myself?"

Jude shrugged. "I don't lie."

"*He* decided to jump in after me. I didn't force him. I didn't need saving."

"*I* know," Jude said. "Because of who I am. He didn't— because of who he is."

"Why is it so important to you to believe that we're different, mechs and orgs?" I said. "Why do you need me to hate them?"

He shook his head slowly. "We don't hate them, Lia. They hate us."

Auden didn't hate me.

At least, he didn't used to.

"We're machines," Jude said. "Unchanging. Perfect—and that perfection is our only flaw. They age, they get sick, injured, always something. They *decay*. We stay the same. We drift in time; they drown in it. They've got a deadline; we don't. And it's the one thing they can't forgive."

"It doesn't have to make us inhuman."

"It *does!*" he shouted, raising his voice for the first time. "Humans are mortals. Mortals die. Living creatures *die*. The whole concept of *living* is meaningless without its opposite. Light is defined by dark. Life is defined by death. Death makes them what they are. Absence of death makes us what *we* are. That's the difference. It's absolute. You don't get to just wish it away." Jude slammed his fist against the door frame, splintering the rotted wood. "You never understood. You never even bothered to try. It didn't occur to you that *that's* why we go to the waterfall, why we take risks, why we push ourselves past the brink? It's a reminder—that for us, death is not an option. It's a reminder of everything that makes us different. You can blame yourself for Auden all you want—because *you* didn't want to remember. So you let yourself forget."

"But—"

"No," he said fiercely. "*You* came to *me* this time. So you can either go or you can listen. You want to hear this or not?"

And maybe that was the real reason I'd come. To hear what I already knew but couldn't believe. Not unless I heard it from someone else. I nodded.

"You got careless," Jude said. "You let yourself believe that you and Auden were the same. You got emotionally tied to an org and refused to accept the reality of who you are—and the fact that it's *not* who you were. You ignored the truth, and that put everyone around you in danger. Especially him."

"It was an accident," I argued. "Bad luck."

"What would it have been if *he'd* gotten shot last night, in the city?" Jude asked. "Or if some thug had jumped him while we were up on the roof? Could've happened."

"I didn't think—I don't know."

"You do know," Jude said. "You knew then, too. You did what you wanted to do anyway. Like you should have. But he didn't belong there in the first place. You knew that, too. You just didn't care enough to stop."

"I care about him more than someone like *you* could understand," I spat out.

"You care about yourself," Jude said, smiling. "Something I understand entirely too well."

I stood up. "I don't have to stay here and listen to this."

"No." Jude stretched himself along the door frame like a cat. "Run away. It's what you're best at."

I stayed.

"You brought him to that waterfall," Jude said. "You brought him to the city. You would have dragged him somewhere else tomorrow. Or the next day. He's probably lucky this happened. The next stupid decision might have gotten him killed."

"I would never—"

"And that would have been your fault too."

"So what do you want me to do?" I asked. "Lock myself in a closet and shut down, to keep the world safe from the horror that is me?"

"None of my business," Jude said. "There's no one I care about in the world. The org world, at least. But if I were you, and I still had someone, someone important . . ."

Auden, I thought, in his metal cage. My father, on his knees. Zo, hiding behind a locked door, guilt tearing her apart. We had more in common now, I thought suddenly. Just imagine the sisterly bonding possibilities: *So, who did you almost kill today?*

"I would think about what I was doing to them by denying reality," Jude said. "By pretending. I'd think about who I was hurting and who I would hurt next."

And again, I saw him. My father. On his knees. Wishing me dead.

"You've got options," Jude said.

"You?" I asked in disgust.

"Us. You're one of us. Under the right conditions, you could thrive. Or . . ." He glanced behind him, into the yellowish brown forest of dead plants. "You know what they say. Live like an org . . ."

"Die like an org?" I guessed sourly.

Jude frowned. "Except that *you'll* never be the one to die."

"I'm not like you," I said. "I don't want to be like you."

Jude stared at me, and when he spoke, his voice was low

and intense, filled with a new emotion. Anger, maybe. Or regret. "*None* of us are volunteers."

I left a message for my parents that I would meet them at BioMax, that I needed all of them, Zo included. That I was in trouble. And after not hearing from me in a couple days, I knew they would come.

Which meant I would be free to go home. Slip into the empty house, pack up the few things I couldn't live without, and disappear again without any messy good-byes. Without anyone crying and pleading with me to stay, which I didn't think I could handle. Or without anyone smiling and waving me out the door.

Which I *knew* I couldn't handle.

My parents fell for it. But when I opened the door to my bedroom, Zo was sitting inside. Waiting for me.

"You're not allowed in here when I'm not home," I said automatically.

"This is my sister's room. I'm allowed in here whenever I want."

I decided to ignore her. She couldn't stop me from leaving. Maybe it would even be easier with her there. The perfect reminder of why I couldn't stay. Why everyone would be better off if I left.

"Whatever you are, I know how you think," Zo said. "Because you think like Lia. Which means you can't fool me."

I stuffed some clothes into a bag. Not my favorites, just whatever was lying on top of the pile. I was supposed to be starting a new life, creating a new identity. Which meant my old favorites were irrelevant.

"You're running away," Zo said.

"What clued you in?" I muttered, even though I'd promised myself I wouldn't engage. Also not needed in the bag or in the new life: My track trophies. The dried petals from the rose Walker gave me after our first breakup and makeup. The stuffed tiger that had belonged to my mother and my grandmother when they were children, that I had never actually slept with myself because it smelled. The book, an actual paper book, Auden had found in his attic and given to me, because he liked that kind of thing and so I pretended to, something called *Galapagos*. I hadn't read it, partly because I was afraid of breaking it and partly because it looked boring. Still, it had meant something to me, because it had meant something to him. Not anymore. I didn't need any of it, I realized. Or at least, I shouldn't. I shouldn't have come home at all.

"This is going to kill Mom and Dad," Zo said. "Did you think about that?"

I dropped the bag, kicked it under the bed. I could get new clothes. Wasn't that the point? New everything. "You're the one who said I should disappear. That everyone would be happier that way."

Zo shifted her weight and started rubbing her thumb back

SKINNED

and forth across the knuckles of her other hand. The way she did when she was uncomfortable. Or embarrassed. "If this is about all that stuff I said . . . Look, I'm sorry, okay? I didn't mean to make you—you know. Leave."

"Not everything's about you."

Zo gave me a weak smile. "Isn't that usually my line?"

It was tempting to believe that was the beginning of something, that the smile was some sign of weakness—or forgiveness. An indication that maybe we could be sisters again, like we used to be.

Nothing is like it used to be, I reminded myself. I wasn't going to forget that again.

"I have to go."

"Don't," Zo said. She hopped off the bed, but stayed where she was, safely across the room from me.

"Mom and Dad will get over it. They have you."

Zo shook her head, rubbed at her eye with the back of her hand, like a little kid, furious that her body would betray her. "Like that's ever been good enough."

I shrugged. "It'll have to be."

"Where will you even go?" she asked, being very careful not to sound like she cared.

"Somewhere." And I made it clear that I didn't care either.

"You're being an idiot," she said. "This is stupid."

"Because *you* want me to stay?" I asked, surprised. On guard. I'd made a decision—I was going to stick to it. I had to.

Zo stared at the floor.

"Tell me to stay," I said.

But Zo didn't say anything.

"Better yet, tell me I'm your sister. Lia. And you want me here." I waited in the doorway, waited for her to speak, waited to be ready to leave behind the room I had lived in since I was three years old. "Tell me all that, and maybe I can stay."

Zo finally looked up.

"Tell me I'm your sister," I said again, aware that I was begging. I didn't care anymore. I needed her to say it. I needed to hear it.

Maybe it would even be enough to make me stay.

"I'm sorry," she said.

The doorway was wide enough that when she walked out of the room, we didn't even touch.

It's not that I bought into Jude's bullshit.

Not all of it, at least.

And it's not that I was so eager to move into Quinn's creepy castle and start painting my face silver and dangling off the side of buildings just because I could. It's not that I wanted more face time with Jude, who obviously didn't care about anyone or anything.

Unlike me, who did.

That's what hurt.

I didn't leave because I was brave, ready to face the world

on my own. I didn't leave as some great sacrifice, eager to cast off my happiness—not that there'd been much of that lately—for the greater good. I didn't leave because I was a coward, afraid to face what I'd done to Auden or what I could do next. I wasn't a coward.

I was tired.

Tired of being trapped in limbo, living as half one thing, half another, not quite anything at all. Not quite dead, not quite alive. Not an original, not a copy. Not human, not machine. Not myself—but who else was there?

I was tired of pretending that nothing had changed. That even with an artificial body and a computer for a brain, I was still the same person I'd been before.

Denial was exhausting. As was anger. Bargaining was useless. Depression was bottomless. I was tired of it all.

Which meant I was ready to accept it. The new reality of nonlife after nondeath. *My* new reality.

Lia Kahn is dead.

I am Lia Kahn.

Except, I finally realized, here's the thing.

Maybe I'm not.

Lia's story continues in...

CRASHED

W hen I was alive, I dreamed of flying.

Or maybe I should say: When I was alive, I dreamed.

Sometimes it was flying; more often it was falling. Or burning—trying to scream, trying to run, but frozen and silent and consumed by flames. I dreamed of being alone. Of my face melting or my teeth falling out.

I dreamed of Walker, his body tangled up in mine. Sometimes I dreamed I *was* Walker, that my hands were his hands, my fingers the ones massaging soft, smooth skin, getting caught in long strands of blond hair. Awake, people talk about becoming one—but in dreams it can really happen. His lips, my lips. Our lips. Our bodies. Our need.

In dreams you can become everything you're not. You can

reverse the most fundamental truths of your life. You can taste death, the ultimate opposite.

I can't. Not anymore. Machines can't die, can't dream.

But we can fly.

From inside the plane, jumps don't look like jumps. One second there's a figure in the jump hatch, fingers gripping the edge, hair whipping in the wind, wingsuit rippling. Then the wind snatches another victim, an invisible hand yanking its prey out of the plane. Leaving nothing behind but an empty patch of murky gray sky.

Quinn and Ani jumped first, hand in hand. The first few times, I'd watched them fall, linked together and spiraling around an invisible axis, two whirling dots red against the snow.

But the novelty had worn off. These days I kept my seat.

Riley went next, and I was glad. Never speaking, never changing expression, eyes drilling through the floor. Until he thought I wasn't looking, and then he'd fix me with that stony, unblinking stare. I wasn't impressed: None of us blinked.

In another life I would have thought he was going for the dark, tortured thing, that whole moody, broody, aren't-I-deep-and-soulful trip. I might even have fallen for it. But the new Lia, version 2.0, knew better. Riley could sulk and skulk all he wanted, but whatever his problem was, he could deal with it himself.

It was like Jude said: *Orgs are weak and need each other. Mechs only need themselves.*

And then Riley jumped and I was left alone with the mech I needed least. Jude stood at the hatch with his back to the clouds and his amber eyes on me. The sun glinted off the silvery whorls etched into his skin. I traced my fingers along the metallic streaks staining my face and neck.

I'd been convinced by Jude's reasoning. We needed to puncture the illusion that we were human, that beneath the self-healing synflesh, hearts pumped, lungs breathed, organs throbbed and cleansed and churned.

I believed in the honesty. I wanted my outsides to match what lay within, the circuits and the energy converters and the twining networks of wires carrying artificial nerve impulses to an artificial brain. But that didn't mean I wanted to look like *him*.

He reached out a hand, as he always did. His lips curled into a smirk, like he knew I would yet again say no—but that eventually I would say yes.

His lips moved, and—thanks to my latest upgrade—the word bubbled inside my head. **"Coming?"**

I waved him away. He shrugged and let himself drop into the sky.

I edged toward the hatch.

The first time I jumped, the fear almost drowned me. That was the point. To let go of the steel frame separating us from a five-mile drop, let go of the rigid, rational, *controlled* mode separating us from the blood-and-gut orgs. Absolute control yielded to absolute release. The artificial sensation of fear released artificial endorphins, stimulated artificial nerve endings, unleashed a flood of artificial panic. And in the rush of wind and speed and terror, it all felt real.

But the danger was an illusion, which meant the fear was a lie, and my body was beginning to figure out the truth.

Pausing in the threshold, I raised my arms, and the woven aeronylon of the wingsuit stretched beneath them, silvery filaments shimmering. Then I stepped into the empty.

Buffeted by the wind, I maneuvered myself flat, face-down, limbs outstretched. The suit's webbed wings acted as an airfoil, harnessing the updraft to slow my free fall. Beneath me, snowcapped mountains drifted by at a leisurely hundred miles per hour; above me, nothing but soupy sky.

Here's the thing about flying: It gets old.

I processed the sensations—*processed*, not felt. The temperature, fifteen degrees below freezing, frosting the few patches of exposed artificial skin. The thunder of the wind. The silver sky, the blinding white below, the specks of red, violet, and black, circling and swooping in the distance.

The air had no taste, no smell. Orgs had five senses; mechs had three.

The suit's instruments recorded a speed of 105 mph horizontal, 67 vertical, but this far from the ground, there was no fast and no slow. Despite the rushing wind, I felt like I was floating down a river, ambling and aimless.

There was no fear.

I let my body drift horizontal to the ground, and the wind sucked me into a flat spin, swinging me around at a dizzying speed. For orgs a flat spin was death. The body whirled like a centrifuge, a crushing 20g force sending rivers of blood gushing toward the head, the hands, the feet, starving the heart until it gave up beating. But for mechs, flat spins were just another perk, a way to turn the world into an incomprehensible smear. Without a puddle of fluid jostling in the inner ear, dizzying speed wasn't even dizzying. For mechs, "dizzy" was just a meaningless expression. Like "thirsty," or "nerve wracked." Or "bored to death."

I pulled abruptly out of the spin. Quinn and Ani swooped up, flanking me.

"Looking good. As always," Quinn VM'd, her digitized voice clear, her meaning more so.

I shifted my body weight and let a gust of air blast me off to the right, buzzing past Quinn with enough force to spin her upside down. "Obviously I'm a natural." Natural: the joke that never got old.

"Naturally annoying," Quinn shot back, regaining her balance. She dipped down, dive-bombing Ani, who squealed as she wriggled away, flipping in midair. Quinn grabbed her wrist and pulled her into a vertical drop. "Catch us if you can!" she called back to me.

I could; I didn't. I activated the lifting jets, let my legs drop and began to climb, past fourteen thousand feet, past twenty thousand. Higher.

"Going somewhere?" There was something metallic about Jude's voice, sharp and brittle as his features. It was strange the way the digitized VM voices took on some character of their owners.

"Away from you." But even ten thousand feet below, he was in my head.

"GOOD LUCK WITH THAT."

I climbed higher, leveling out at twenty-eight thousand feet. *I could stay up forever,* I thought, letting my body carve lazy circles through the clouds. No more struggle to feel—or not to—nothing but a body and mind in motion, simple and pure. Jude would approve.

"You're too high, Lia." Jude again, a violet dot against the snow. Always telling me what to do. As he spoke, the jets sputtered out in the thin air and my webwings lurched, losing their lift.

"I can take care of myself." I tilted forward into a dive, arms pressed against my sides to streamline the suit. I was done flying.

I was a bullet streaking toward the ground. Critical velocity came fast as gravity took over, sucking me down. The mountains rose below me, snowy peaks exploded from the earth, and *now* came the flood of fear. The others blew past, smears of color. Screaming.

"Pull up, you're coming in too fast!" Ani.

"What the hell are you trying to do!" Quinn.

"Again?" Jude.

Riley, a black shadow against the snow, said nothing.

The ground came up fast, too fast, and I barely had time to level out before I was skimming powder, slicing down the slope, a white cloud billowing in my wake. Something was wrong. The slope too steep, the angle too sharp, the snow too shallow, and I heard the impact before I felt it, the sharp crack of my head crashing into rocky ground, my neck nearly snapping free of my spine.

And then I was rolling down the side of the mountain, blinded by snow.

And then I felt alive.

And then all motion jerked to a stop, a wave of white crashed over me, and the snow filled my mouth, my nose, my ears, and the world went very still and very silent.

And very dark.

I couldn't see; I couldn't move. I was a statue under the snow.

"We're coming for you." That was Riley in my ear, puncturing the silence. He felt so near, like we were alone together in the dark.

I didn't answer.

They began to argue about how to reach me, and I cut the link, retreating into the quiet. The GPS would pinpoint my location, and my fellow fliers would eventually show up with snowfusers to dig me out. It didn't matter how long it took; I could bide my time for centuries, arise icy but intact to a brave new world. It wasn't so different from flying, I decided. Substitute dark for light and still for speed, but in the end, it was the same. Empty.

Once, I was afraid of the dark. Not the bedtime kind of dark, with dim moonlight filtering through the shades and shadows playing at the corners of the room, but absolute dark. The black night behind your lids.

I'd been trapped there for weeks after the accident, dark, still, and alone. A prisoner in my own body. And then I opened my eyes to discover that my body was gone. That I—whatever part of "I" they'd managed to extricate from my flesh-and-blood brain and input into their quantum cerebral matrix— was trapped after all in a body that wasn't a body. There was no escape from that. Not into my own body, which had been mangled by the accident, flayed by the doctors, then burned as medical waste. Not into death; death was off the table.

After that, darkness seemed irrelevant. Temporary, like everything else.

With snow packing my eyes and ears, there was no warning. Just pressure, then a jolt. Fingers gripping me, hauling me upward. I dropped back flat against the fresh powder. System diagnostics lit up behind my lids: The network was intact, already repairing itself. Synflesh knitting together, ceramic bones and tendons snapping back into place.

A hand brushed the snow from my eyes. Riley knelt over me, his fingertips light on my cheek. Behind him, Ani, worried. The sky had faded to a purplish gray. "You okay?" Riley asked.

"She's fine," Jude said. "Just a drama queen in search of an audience."

"Shut up." Riley took my shoulders and propped me up into a sitting position. "Everything still working?" The mountains loomed over us, white and silent. Years before, this had been a vacation spot, a haven for insane orgs who enjoyed hurtling down slopes at breakneck speeds even though their necks, once broken, stayed that way. But when the temperature plummeted along with the air quality, mountain gliding and its attendant risks were cancelled for good. Leaving the snow free and clear for those of us who needed neither warmth nor unfettered oxygen; those of us who just wanted to be left alone.

I knocked the snow from my shoulders and shook it out of my hair. The rush had faded as soon as I slammed into the ground—I was back in mech mode now, cool and hollow.

I pulled my lips into a half grin. It had been hard, relearning emotional expression in the new body, twitching artificial cheek and eye muscles in search of something approximating a human smile. But by now I had total control in a way that orgs never did. Orgs smiled when they were happy, the motion automatic, a seamless reflex of muscle reacting to mind, neural and physiological systems so intertwined that forcing a smile was often enough to boost a mood. Like a natural b-mod, its behavior-modifying effects were brief but instantaneous. My smiles were deliberate, like everything else, and no amount of curled lips and bared teeth would mod my mood.

I let the grin widen. "Who wants to go again?"

Abruptly, Riley dropped his arms, dumping me into the snow. It was Jude who hauled me to my feet and Jude who bundled me up and strapped me into the waiting plane, while Quinn and Ani cuddled in the next seat and Riley sulked in a far corner.

"Have a nice fall?" Jude asked, as the plane lifted off and carried us back toward the estate. The thunder of the engines wrapped us in a soundproof cocoon.

I leaned back, pointing and flexing my toes. Everything was in working order. "I've had better."

Jude arched an eyebrow. "You know, you continue to surprise me."

"Because?"

"I didn't expect someone like you to be such a quick study."

I didn't have to ask what he meant by "someone like me." Rich bitch Lia Kahn, spoiled and selfish and so sure she's better than everyone else. "Someone like the person I *used* to be," I reminded him. "That person's gone. You showed me that."

"And I'm still waiting for an appropriate demonstration of gratitude."

"You expecting me to buy you flowers?"

"Why would I need flowers when I have your sunny disposition to brighten my day?"

"What can I say?" I simpered at him. "You bring out the best in me."

Jude stripped out of his suit, balled it up, and tossed it across the plane. "Funny how I tend to have that effect on people."

"Oh, please." I stabbed a finger down my throat. "Do *not* start lumping me in with your groupies."

"They're not groupies."

But I could tell he enjoyed the designation. "What would you call them?"

"They're lost, searching for answers—can I help it if they come to me?" Jude crossed his arms, pleased with himself. "I suppose I'd call them wisdom seekers."

"And they're seeking it in your pants?"

"So vulgar." Jude tsked. "When the problem is your body, it's not so difficult to imagine that the body is where the solution lies." He reached for my hand, but I snatched it away.

"Save it for the groupies."

"What?" he asked, amber eyes wide with innocence.

I turned my back on him, watching the clouds stream by the windows. Even now there was something disconcerting about being up in the air without a pilot. Self-navigating cars were the norm—these days, only control freaks drove themselves—but the self-piloting planes were fresh on the market, powered by some new smarttech that, according to the pop-ups, was the world's first true artificial intelligence. Unlike the smartcars, smartfridges, smarttoilets, smarteverything we were used to, the new tech could respond to unforeseen circumstances, could experiment, could *learn*. It could, theoretically, shuttle passengers at seven hundred miles an hour from point A to point B without breaking a sweat. It just couldn't smile and reassure you that if a bird accidentally flew into the engine, it would know what to do.

Not that there were many birds anymore.

Especially where most of the AI planes were destined to fly, the poison air of the eastern war zones. This was military tech; action at distance was the only way to win without having to fight. Thinking planes, thinking tanks, thinking landcrawlers equipped with baby nukes saved orgs from having to think for themselves. Saved them from having to die for themselves. Not many had credit to spare to snatch up a smartplane of their own for peacetime purposes—but as far as Quinn was concerned, no luxury was too luxurious, especially when Jude was the one placing the request.

The ground was hidden beneath a thick layer of fog, and it was tempting to imagine it had disappeared. "Flying's getting old," I said, keeping my back to Jude.

"For you maybe."

"We need to find something better." More dangerous, I meant. Wilder, faster, steeper. *Bigger*.

"You want better?" He slipped a small, hard cube into my palm. "For later."

"You know I don't do that crap." But I closed my fingers around it.

"For later," he said again. So smug.

I just kept staring out the window, wondering what it would feel like if the plane crashed. How long would we stay conscious, our mangled bodies melting into the burnt fuselage? Would we be aware as fuel leaked from the wreckage, lit by a stray spark? What would it feel like at the moment of explosion, our brains and bodies blasted into a million pieces?

I would never know. The moment this brain burst into fire, someone at BioMax would set to work retrieving my stored memories, downloading them into a newly made body, waking me up to yet another new life. That "me" would remember everything up to my last backup and nothing more. No flying, no crashing, no explosion.

For the best, I decided. Maybe when it came to dying, once was enough.

ROBIN WASSERMAN is the author of *Hacking Harvard*, the Seven Deadly Sins series, and the Chasing Yesterday trilogy. She lives in Brooklyn, New York.

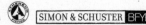

Pulse It

Did you love this book?

Want to get access to
the hottest books for free?

Log on to simonandschuster.com/pulseit
to find out how to join,

get access to cool sweepstakes,

and hear about your favorite authors!

Become part of Pulse IT and tell us what you think!